Also by A. J. Mahler

Power – The Betty Chronicles, Volume II

MONEY

A Novel

THE BETTY CHRONICLES

Volume I

BY **A. J. MAHLER**

For information about special discounts for bulk purchases please contact sales@whitebradford.com.

For additional information — http://www.whitebradford.com

Betty Thursten has a Facebook page — friend her at https://www.facebook.com/betty.thursten

Cover photo © Jeff Thrower/Shutterstock

For My Children

Luke, Evan, Zoe, and Fiona —
Your patience will be rewarded.

Sprung from my heart true
Life, a sentence, clarity
Meaning with purpose

PREFACE

THE ENDNOTE PROVIDES historical perspective to Betty's world. While most of these 'facts' are based on real life events and people, some creative license is observed. It is not necessary to read the Endnote to enjoy *Money*, but it may give you a broader and deeper perspective of the story. This information was presented as a Prologue in the first edition. An excerpt of *Power, Volume II of The Betty Chronicles,* is included at the end of *Money*.

ONE

THE SCAR

THE NOON SUN GLINTED off the worn, shiny spots of the corrugated tin roof; the spots that rubbed against each other on the windy days. Light splashing in through the rusty gaps washed across Betty's face as she swung in her hammock. Brushing her raven black hair away from her forehead, Betty felt the scar, causing her to contemplate the past week of whirlwind clandestine activity.

Betty's family thought she was in Denver for another week-long continuing education conference with seminars including: *An In Depth Look at Cancellation of Removal, Immigration Consequences of Criminal Entanglement for the Business Immigration Lawyer, Picking the Right Training Visa,* and *Traversing the New Prevailing Wage Determination Process.* Instead, she studied the material on the flights to and from South America: Columbia, Venezuela, Peru, Chile, Honduras, and Panama. Being a brilliant lawyer and quick learner allowed her to just skim the material instead of sitting all day drinking bad coffee in a stuffy hotel banquet room with fifty bored lawyers. Betty usually called her parents back in Rochester, New York, from a quiet spot to drone on in a monotone about the seminars until her listener was bored enough to change the subject. This was an excellent way to prevent questions about her covert trips lest she start anew on the seminars.

The light dancing on her forehead reminded her of how different her life was now. Ten years ago, she finished her law degree at Georgetown. Six years ago, Betty was promised to Lieutenant Tom Howell and waiting his return from Iraq to begin the next chapter of their idyllic life together. That relationship fell apart. Two years ago, her new fiancé José was murdered in his Georgetown apartment just as Betty was about to become the wife of a rising star in Brazilian politics. Instead, Betty Thursten became a covert agent who also happens to be a high-powered immigration lawyer catering to the rich and powerful from her Washington D.C. office.

Now, here in the jungles on the Colombian-Venezuelan border, Betty was contemplating how to explain the scar on her forehead. She had not covered it in her phone calls home. There would be questions she could not answer if she did not get her thoughts straight.

It was so random, the other night. She had heard a noise; it was one of those stupid guards. They were always so easy to fool and if one did get too curious, Betty would either play the drunk girl or the flirty girl. In seconds flat, the guard would forget his perimeter and instead be thinking about the sex kitten in front of him, but it did not work this time. The guard was the bad boy jihadist pretending to be a fundamentalist. He had slapped her across her face and his ring had cut deep.

The stitches were out now, and the bandage off. *My beauty mark,* thought Betty.

She liked that idea. She chewed on it, rolling the idea around on her tongue like a bit of sweet meat off a skewer. She liked the tangy taste of that. A visible reminder of the things she had done that would mean nothing to anyone else. A tattoo would be the guy thing, but she could not go to the pool with a snake crawling up her arm or heaven forbid her leg.

Yes, this scar, in hindsight was the perfect token of her valor. Now, she had to concoct a story. *The best lie is the truth with some details left out and some rearranged. Harder to get caught that way.* She could not claim the usual careless accident because there would be insurance records and an emergency room visit for stitches to explain.

Gil slapped the tin siding, making a loud bang, to snap Betty out of her daydream. "Betty, get your ass out of the hammock. We're out of here in ten minutes, you'll have all the time you need to rest on the flight back. Get your kit together girl."

Betty glared at her fellow agent, Gil Richardson. *Arrogant bastard!* Gil had been an Army Ranger Medic before joining the Special Forces. Now he was a black operations specialist. The black operations performed by the duo left no trail back to the United States or more importantly to the president. Betty, besides being an immigration lawyer and a black belt in jujitsu, specialized in the more subtle aspects of espionage. Betty's good looks, fluent Spanish and Portuguese, and quick mind were all that she usually needed. Her five foot eight inch frame looked lean, but she was packing some potent muscle.

Looking back now, Betty realized the guard had caught her as she was looking away, checking to see if Gil was in position. *If Gil had been in his position the guard would never have laid a hand on me!* Betty returned to that moment visualizing the scene.

With blood trickling down her face, her glare was enough to make the guard cower. By pulling his left arm with her left combined with a quick sweep of her right leg, she placed the hapless guard in a submission hold on the ground faster than a cobra strike. A wet, salty, metallic taste entered her gritted teeth; she twisted his arm harder, making him pay for the cut to her forehead. The pain mixed with a triangular chokehold rendered him unconscious. Gil came up from his hiding place just in time for Betty to hiss at him.

"What were you doing? Why were you out of position?" hissed Betty.

"I was busy. Grab his arms, we'll put him over in those bushes," Gil pointed with his head while getting a grip on the guard's body.

Gil and Betty dragged the limp guard to the underbrush. No need to gag or bind the guard, a shot of horse tranquilizer was quicker and left almost no trace. The guard would likely be chastised later for sleeping while on duty. Gil bandaged her wound and stitched it up later back at camp.

Betty started to pack her kit and get moving, shaking the long thoughts and memories from her consciousness when it hit her, the explanation for the scar. *I was in a bar to wind down after my last class and got in the middle of a fight between two locals as I was headed to the bathroom. A piece of a smashed glass came flying at me and cut my forehead. Thank God an off duty paramedic was there. I didn't want to make a big deal about it and the paramedic agreed to stitch me up. He came to the hotel later to check on me and remove the stitches. Crap, that would make it seem like I was having a fling with the medic! I'll have to work on the details during the flight home, after I catch up on my damn continuing education, of course.*

Two

The Squall

THE SQUALL OFF THE COAST of Caracas, Venezuela was not in the weather report nor was it part of the plan for tonight's activities. Betty planned to give the idiot who predicted a peaceful moonless night a swift kick, but right now she had to figure out how to get the guard away from the gate. Normally there were two guards at the main entrance to Ernesto Montoya's compound. The other guard had left five minutes before with what appeared to be food poisoning and a need for a change of clothing; meanwhile, his replacement had not arrived yet. Earlier in the day, a new food vendor, planted by Control, had stopped by to visit the guard shack at the usual time. Normally both guards bought an early evening snack to tide them over for their shifts. Tonight, only one guard was hungry.

The one remaining guard between the gate and Betty had decided earlier in the day to begin a diet due to his advancing gut and the rejection of his advances by a lover. He did not make enough to buy her affection and his once proud physique was not doing the job any longer. He was a man with needs. He did not need the enchilada tonight as badly as he needed his mistress. Even if this new vendor offered it for free, hoping to gain the guard's business. The new vendor was a Control agent permanently embedded into the Caracas concrete jungle, searching for crumbs of information to send back up the chain.

The cloudless midday sky had passed to a gathering storm at night. The heavy, fat, lumbering, behemoth clouds let loose a thunderstorm of epic proportions for Caracas. The rain came in sheets. First no rain, then a heavy drenching leading to a light sprinkle only to drench again.

The squall line of rain came in waves: giant sheets of water on God's clothesline.

The air was rich with ozone from the lightning arcing through the air. As the rain passed, the smell of clean air filled Betty's nostrils. The original plan of walking up to the guard shack and flirting with the occupant just did not seem practical or logical. Being the lone person on the street in this weather would draw the wrong conclusions. She wanted to get the guard's attention, not his suspicion.

Say, that isn't a bad idea, thought Betty. *Instead of seducing the guard, I'll be the helpless woman.* The streets of Caracas were normally busy, even at 2a.m., but the storm had pushed the denizens of this barrio deep into their homes for protection from the heavy rain. This was not the night for a peaceful walk, but it was the perfect night for a damsel in distress. Checking the back seat of the Toyota Hilux Quad, she found the jumper cables. Betty parked the Hilux and found an old beat-up Dodge Avenger parked on a quiet side street. *Not that anyone is going to notice me jacking a car in this weather.* The door was unlocked. *Who would steal this piece of shit anyway?*

The Avenger was perfect for her plan; it would be a miracle for this car to make it to the guard shack. The windshield wipers sucked. A couple of times she had to stick her head out the window just to keep from hitting parked cars, the headlights flickering on and off like some possessed flashlight. Betty pulled up slowly, checked the guard out, and stalled the motor. The string she tied to the choke plate kept the car from restarting as planned and in no time, the battery was dead.

The guard tried to ignore her, but when she got out of the car her bra-less, x-small rain soaked shirt grabbed the guard's attention and would not let it go. Betty was the only participant in this wet t-shirt contest and the judge liked what he saw. The moth staggered toward Betty, drawn to the bright neon flashing light reflecting off her damp curvaceous body. Betty leaned into the open cavity of the engine compartment causing her breasts to nearly spill out of her shirt, hanging like hand grenades ready to explode. Her supple, wet body slid along the metal of the car, her leg lifted up into the air to maintain her balance as she desperately tried to figure out what was wrong. Signaling for Betty to get the heap out of the way, the guard moved closer to inspect the drenched beauty in front of him, while the swelling feeling below goaded him into deciding that this damsel was certainly in distress and definitely needed his immediate assistance. Betty grabbed the jumper cables and pointed to the jeep in the shadow of the front gate. "¿Arrancar utilizando pinzas de batería?" Betty asked sweetly.

The guard hesitated, but Betty's pout and pleading eyes were too much for the poor bastard. He ran to his jeep, not to stay dry, that is for sure, he was already soaked. The noise of the guard's vintage military heap would normally be a worry, but with this storm, no one would notice. Another sheet of water had started coming down from the squall right on cue. Gil would be watching from nearby and ready to move on her signal.

Betty had been briefed about the compound by Howell; her former lover, near fiancé, and now spymaster. It belonged to a middleman named Ernesto Montoya. Ernesto moved money for the elite Cabal of the ultra wealthy who controlled two thirds of the world's money supply. He did not appear to be under their thumb. Ernesto's independence from the world dominating aristocracy was his most intriguing asset. This was atypical of the known worker bees. A man with loose ties might talk if the persuasion was right. Ernesto did not have anything to lose except for a client if he cooperated; unlike others, under direct control of the Cabal, who had much to lose if they talked. Henchmen were controlled by their desire for wealth and their fear of retribution; the Cabal reminded them, when necessary, that their families, wealth, and status would be erased if the Cabal were ever crossed.

Control, the organization Betty and Gil worked for, had very little intelligence on Ernesto Montoya. He seemed to be a banker who controlled large investments, but these transactions were cloudy, the vapor trails of his work barely decipherable. The mission was to breach his security, find weaknesses, and document the layout of the compound. They were to be ghosts. The first priority was to learn how to shut down the surveillance cameras. In the briefing room ideas were floated such as a lightning strike, an incendiary charge, or mechanical failure. Tonight's mission was to identify the best angle for success without obvious sabotage as the cause of the system failure.

Entry into the compound was needed. Strangely, there were no records available on the property. Though construction had been ongoing: no permits, no information, and no plans were available. Even the Venezuelan government left Ernesto Montoya alone. His compound and guards kept him safe. He rarely ventured out of the confines of his palatial estate.

If the papacy had a secular equivalent, Ernesto Montoya was it and international banking was his religion. Just as the Pope has palaces surrounding the countryside, Ernesto has bank branches throughout South America and the world. The branches allowed the middle class and the wealthy to deposit their money knowing it would go off shore, safe from the sticky fingers of governments and revolutions. A safe haven meant healthy profits and knowledge of secret incomes. Ernesto knew where the skeletons were buried. Even government officials deposited their illicit gains in his bank: the Americas International Bank.

The wealth controlled by Ernesto represented a third of all the wealth in the world. Just as the Pope was a pauper, so was Ernesto. Power or money: that was his choice. A truly powerful man has endless wealth at his disposal. Ernesto protected the wealth of the Cabal. Its families trusted him, but they did not trust each other. No one family in the Cabal controlled Ernesto Montoya. Ernesto had no family. Ernesto had no heir. Ernesto did not own a house or even a car. Just the same, Ernesto always had a car of the finest quality available with a driver of his choosing and guards representing each family to protect him. Should any guard fail his job, the others would know who was to blame. At sixty-two his career would seem to be at its zenith; his predecessor lived to be sixty-six after serving twenty-four years. Ernesto rose to power at forty-one and desired to be in power until he died. The Cabal preferred stability in their financial planning and had a tendency to end careers when stability faltered. Ernesto's predecessor was assassinated when he refused to step aside after the collapse of the world stock markets on Black Monday, October 19, 1987, when the Cabal's portfolios took a twenty-percent decline on the programmed trades he had devised. Ernesto had survived the financial downturns in 2001 and 2008 by deftly managing his clients portfolios and predicting the downturns correctly, thus maintaining his clients wealth and his own well being. Ernesto resisted training a successor to better protect his status and job; however, the Cabal had insisted he consider several candidates for his replacement, even if it was to be far off. Betty's José was being groomed by the Cabal for Ernesto's position prior to his untimely death. Betty did not know about this connection to the World Order. The Cabal would rue the day they did not take care of Betty when they could have.

Betty got the jumper cables ready, handing one end to the guard and holding the other end in wait. The guard carefully, but quickly, got his end hooked up. Betty called out, "Aquí" in a singsong sexy voice and motioned the guard closer. The guard was unprepared for what came next; it was like shooting fish in a barrel. Betty jammed the negative clamp on his family jewels and the positive to his neck. The poor bastard shook in pain alternatively grabbing for his crotch then his neck as Betty kept jamming both into his flesh as she summoned a mental picture of the prick weatherman who made this stunt necessary. It did not take long for the white searing pain to put the guard out. He was going to have a very bad memory in the morning, but he would live; the weatherman on the other hand, might not.

Gil appeared at her side out of nowhere. "Damn it, Gil, I about shiv'd you when you tapped my shoulder," hissed Betty.

Betty sheathed her black SOG (special operations gear) fixed blade knife as Gil got the jeep back where it belonged with the unconscious guard in back. A quick shot of a Ketamine Xylazine Butorphanol cocktail would keep him out for at least an hour; long enough for what they needed to do, though, the guard might be looking for a new job and a new girlfriend in the morning.

Betty took the emergency brake off the Avenger and glided it out of sight. Someone would find it the next day and assume it was a broken down piece of shit that did not make it all the way home the night before, which was true if you ignore the jacking part. Control agents always try to leave as little trace behind as possible. Admittedly, the guard was going to know what hit him, but who would believe him and why would he tell the truth? His boss would think that he tried to put a move on the owner of the car and got kicked in the nuts for his stupidity. He was not supposed to leave his post no matter what. Betty and Gil split up to make quick work of the evening's agenda. In an hour, they would be back on the boat in warm dry clothes sipping a cold cerveza. Betty mused; *A beer would be nice after playing in the cold rain.*

In twelve hours, she would be on her way back home from her latest adventure; a four day weekend "shopping trip" in Chicago. Major Howell would arrange all usual cover story items: ticket stubs, hotel

A. J. M a h l e r

bills, and gifts. *God,* thought Betty, *I sure hope Howell doesn't get the usual schlock trinkets from Water Tower Place. It would be nice to have something decent to take back to my parents.*

Three

Gundpowder

THE ACRID SMELL OF SMOKE permeated the room. Smoke from gunfire, that is. That sweet, yet acrid smell of gunpowder. *You either love it or hate it,* thought Betty *nothing in between.* Betty took a deep breath and savored the aroma of a good gun battle. She could not linger or there would be trouble; despite the thumping music and mating dance of the Garoto Cafe' patrons, eventually the Caracas police would notice the muffled sound of gunfire and bodies falling to the hard wooden floor. The floors of the second story apartment above the bar had a shiny polyurethane finish, hand polished bamboo, which must have replaced the original floor. *The molding around the perimeter doesn't match the rest of the molding exactly, but it is tasteful just the same. I wouldn't have picked those avocado drapes, though.* Interrupting her thoughts, a rude terrorist poked his head around the corner giving Betty a perfect target for the next round. *Phhhfffft...tink ...tink...tink...ting* of the round firing and the shell bouncing on the bamboo followed by the jumbled thud of the dead terrorist's body crumpling. Betty's night vision goggles gave her an unfair advantage, but she did not mind.

Love that sound, thought Betty. *The best thing about the Matrix, the original one, is the sound of brass hitting marble* pondered Betty as she visualized how she would look in patent leather clothing like Trinity's. *Phhhfffft...tink ...tink...tink...ting,* another terrorist down for the count. *Crap. Time to reload and get the hell out of here. It won't matter how many more I take out,* Betty thought as she imagined what Trinity would do, *if I don't get my ass moving before the outside world comes crashing in. Where the hell is Gil? He was supposed to be right outside with the car.* Without a getaway car, her escape would be nearly impossible. Betty, in her current attire, would stick out on the streets of Caracas and she would be an easy target even with a crowd to get lost in.

A siren was headed her way. Betty could hear the wail of a siren coming closer and closer. Was it for her or was it just some heart attack in the middle of the night. Betty knew by the high pitch of the siren that it was coming closer. She held still to better hear and determine if it was time to bail, ride or no ride. The siren came closer and then, to Betty's relief, the pitch of the siren lowered indicating it had passed without stopping.

Betty was not going to lie to herself. *As successful as I've been tonight taking out this cell of terrorists, it's not a silent job.* Betty was leaving calling cards all over the place. The original plan had been to get the terrorists to shoot each other with the lights out and lots of yelling. *No plan survives first contact with the enemy. Instead of starting a fight, I'm just getting target practice. Can I take each terrorist out one bullet at a time instead?* Self-preservation won out over lack of evidence.

Phhhfffft...tink...tink...tink...ting. Betty moved to the window facing the alley. *How many more can there be? Who knows? At least tonight, there are a lot less.* Betty fired at the last terrorist brave enough to show his face, scoring a headshot as she went out the window and down the fire escape. "Damn it, Gil! Where are you?" whispered Betty into the warm night air.

The Cabal had many ways of controlling governments. One was the use of terrorists. The Colombian-Venezuelan border had become a breeding ground and safe haven for militias, terrorists, and mobsters. Pick your name, they all had the same goal: money. Some sold drugs, guns, or people; guards took bribes to cross the border while officials sold their offices to the highest bidder. Money buys power. Power gives control. Control generates money. By keeping governments off balance, always worrying about an insurgent group or illicit activity, the Cabal controlled the direction and focus of the people in power. Often, merely selling even more equipment and information to a government worried about its flank would suffice. If the government was dependent on their products or information the Cabal had control. Tonight, Betty's job was to stop a cell of terrorists from using their money to buy a cache of weapons. Right now, all the money in the world could not protect her without Gil to extract her as planned.

Gil should have been here by now—late as always! The squeal of tires and lurching metal came around the corner. Her reflexes said dive under the dumpster, but her nerves of steel said stand her ground. Only Gil would be driving like a complete idiot through the narrow alleys. With a last minute touch of bravado, Gil fishtailed the Dodge Challenger within twelve inches of Betty's thigh. She stood her ground without flinching. The door popped open and she jumped in cool as a cucumber. Betty waited thirty seconds to lay into Gil as he roared out of the alley.

"Where the hell were you?" Betty asked trying to hold back telling him how she really felt—turned on, wanting to grab Gil and kiss him right there, but that would not be professional. Betty would have really sworn a blue streak had she been truly worried, but instead she gave him the June Cleaver version of swearing. *God, Gil is sexy,* thought Betty, *even if he only pulled up at the last second to get me out of there. He's so calm and cool despite being barely in control;* Gil's driving gave him a sex appeal Betty could not deny. *He wouldn't have done it that way if everything had gone as planned, but damn he looks good doing it. I can't wait to debrief him to find out what kept him.* She needed all her strength to keep her cool. *I'm a professional and I'm going to keep my emotions in check here!*

"Damn it, Gil, what the hell happened back there?" grilled Betty.

Gil gave her his bad-boy devilish grin and shrugged his shoulders as he turned the wheel hard to cut through another alley as they lost their last tail.

In thirty minutes, they were back to port and hidden in a shipping container. In a few hours, they would board a private Gulfstream G650 jet for their unscheduled flight back to the States, no one the wiser. *The container must have been used for rotten cabbage on the last trip.* Betty tried to breathe through her mouth. *What a smell! Is this Major Howell's way of putting me in my place? Does he know about my secret desire for Gil?* During their workouts in the gym, it was easy to steal long looks. Especially at the weight bench as she spotted his bench press; Gil always wore a white t-shirt that was probably a size too small, and as the sweat built up the shirt clung to his form showing off his powerful muscles. He was not some big gorilla—that would not do for fieldwork. He was sculpted out of marble and bronzed by the sun.

Major Howell had warned Betty that Gil was a lady's man and to stay away from him. More than one agent had been moved because of tangled relationships. Betty was determined to not be one of those casualties. Yet, each day they were together it became harder and harder to resist.

Two months before, Gil caught her in his arms when she jumped into the rubber boat from a freighter. She felt no fear in those arms. The world seemed to stop for a moment. Time expanded into an eternity. Silence. Despite the roar of the sea, the crashing of the waves against the hull of the ship, and the whine of the motor: during that moment, their eyes locked and Betty thought she saw Gil's soul. Their lips were inches apart until Gil cleared his throat bringing reality back and he gently put Betty down.

"We better get going." Gil fired at the terrorists on the boat above with the assault rifle strapped around his neck to make them dive for cover.

Betty nodded slowly, "I suppose we should." Betty covered their exit with a burst of gunfire as Gil gunned the motor of the NSW Rigid-hull Inflatable Boat (RHIB) and cast the line that had kept them tethered.

Time and adrenaline surged. The crew above began to fire into the water around them. The pitch-black night, black clothing, and black rubber boat blending into the sea to protect them was better than any armored plating.

†

The ripe aroma complimented the dark and dingy steel of the container. This is not where Betty had dreamed of being at this point in her life: the standard issue middle class dream, the life she almost had, now was only a misty memory. Her engagement to Lieutenant Howell; well, there had not been an engagement ring, but there was a promise. They had planned for two children, a house and all that. She was going to stay home for each child, then go back to practicing law when they were old enough for preschool. Planning for two children, a year apart would only cause a three-year gap in her career.

She was going to work from home to keep her fingers and her mind busy. Continuing education every year and a two week vacation alone with her husband to keep things fresh. Then he disappeared, April 13, 2003. The night he left, just when Betty's world seemed to be all planned out, he had said it was important, but he would be back. He came back a year later and shoved her out of his life. He wanted to meet in another year to see if they were still meant for each other, but he did not show.

She had moved on after another year of waiting: no contact, no hope, and little to hang onto. There was some light dating, but nothing as serious as the lieutenant. By the summer of 2006, she was still without word from Lieutenant Howell, and she let her last vestige of hope let go. It was easy to fall for the striking, foreign-born José.

Betty was an immigration lawyer who specialized in the high end. She helped important people get through the government red tape to work or live in America. José Eduardo Santos Almeida Melo Silva was from Brazil and had grown up near São Paulo. His family had vast tracts of land in the countryside; they were powerful elites in the Brazilian hierarchy. Mr. Silva hired Betty to assist José's transition to America for graduate school. When Betty met José for the first time, on her business trip to Uruguay in 2000, he played soccer for the Brazilian national fútbol team and was finishing his undergraduate degree. Now, he was finished with his MBA and on his way to a doctorate in economics. It would not be long before he was running the family business and running the country's economy. Either way, she needed to learn Portuguese and she now had a fluent instructor.

José would tease her incessantly about her pronunciation, but with every waking hour of the summer to work on it, she was able to perfect her accent to José's satisfaction. Then, darkness came to her life. No one could tell her why or even make sense of the killing. She came home to their apartment to find it in shambles and José dead on their bed with a single bullet wound to the forehead. The police were of no use. No leads, no suspects and no chance of closure.

It took a year and a half for her to find her way out of that hell. She threw herself into her jujitsu and mixed martial arts classes imagining she was killing the assassin with every blow. Many of her sparing partners complained that she seemed intent on actually killing them. Then, on the night she was awarded her black belt in jujitsu, he showed up. He was Major Howell now according to the change in hardware on his uniform.

They did not talk, but she spotted him in the back row. He walked toward her, but stopped short to congratulate a friend, a fellow army officer in a tight crew cut, on his ascension to black belt. Betty remembered knocking the snot out of the guy on more than one occasion. Howell looked up briefly, but pretended to not see Betty.

Six years after he disappeared into the hell of Iraq, Major Howell did come back. Back with an offer she could not refuse. He knew her weaknesses and said just the right things.

"We will be working together to find José's murderer," said Howell to a disbelieving Betty.

"What? We're going to be in the field together?" asked Betty incredulously.

"No, you'll go undercover—using your legal work as cover. I'll guide you from Control," corrected Howell.

"Great, I'll be getting shot at while you stare at a monitor. Sounds like a fair deal," mocked Betty.

"We'll be working together, going after the bad guys who caused you so much pain. You get revenge and I get an agent who can get into places others can't go."

"You never did play fair. If you ever fuck with me," Betty leaned in pointing her finger into Howell's chest, causing him to take a step back.

"We have work to do. As a team," Howell attempted to reassure her.

That was two years ago. They had both moved on emotionally. Howell worked long hours and never took a date. He was called the "Monk" at the office for his ascetic lifestyle. No one believed he actually had more than one pair of pajamas and a toothbrush at his efficiency apartment.

Betty did not date; only chance encounters to satisfy the need for closeness with another human being. Someone without a gun in their waistband and totally lacking an agenda other than what was to be had during that moment together. She never gave her number or address. She did not want a commitment. She wanted intimacy without strings attached. People she got close to died, disappeared, or got injured. She was a woman with needs even if the solution was ephemeral. They were two mayflies, efimera, meeting for a moment, living for only a few hours while they were together, with the sole purpose of mating. There would be no offspring from these dalliances, but that was fine with these lovers. No entanglements. No phone numbers. No second dates. Only seeking la petite mort, the little death, an orgasm. Surely, all the male's future conquests were compared to that brief yet all consuming paring with the efímera—Betty.

Betty sank into the leather of the car seat. The stench of the rotting cabbage refocused her attention to the here and now. The Challenger fit easily into the forty-foot long ten-foot wide steel shipping container common on ocean freighters. The car was destined for the cleaners. Betty had no idea where the car would end up nor did she care. That was not her job. The cleaners made things disappear. Betty's tools of the trade: unspent munitions, guns, costumes, and other paraphernalia; no trace was left behind. She tried to pretend someone besides Gil was next to her in the dark. Betty tried to "clean" her sexual desire for Gil. To make it disappear. The six inches between them might as well be a mile. Deep yoga breaths. Betty centered herself by slowing down her heart. Time to move on, for the moment. This job had no time for an office romance, a sure way to get killed or transferred.

Four

Alone

THE ACHE IN HER BELLY was like a ball of fire eating her intestines. Betty's last solid meal was three days before in Cucuta, Columbia. Nothing to eat but what she carried into the mountains between Columbia and Venezuela. Good thing too, because the stench in the ditch was unbearable having been stuck here for the past twenty-four hours. She could barely breathe and only move every couple of hours to keep up her circulation. An ill-timed noise could give her position away. Armed guards surrounded the property and frequently walked the perimeter. Betty was hiding in the drainage ditch along the main entrance just outside the walking path surrounding the property. Close enough for an accurate shot, but too close to relax.

Getting into the mountainous region between Columbia and Venezuela was easy. Getting out of Cucuta was going to be harder. Once the primary mission objective was accomplished, security forces would be alerted and watching. Being a woman was to Betty's advantage. They would be looking for a military man, a special operations soldier. Not Betty Thursten, she was just an immigration lawyer in the region on business with enough time for a private excursion to the country. An influential man accused of drug cartel connections wanted entry into the U.S. and it was Betty's job to clear the way. Not very difficult and it certainly did not warrant a trip to Columbia, but Betty required a personal visit prior to taking cases near points of interest. The clients were rich and could afford her travel expenses. She had connections no one else had to offer. Usually Gil would come in separately using a tourist visa or fly covertly via special operations helicopters if the location was too remote or time was of the essence.

That bastard! How dare he not be available for this mission! I wouldn't be stuck in this hole if I had some Goddamn back up to make some noise. This, of course, was being said inside Betty's head. Even muttering under her breath was a bad idea. *How long must this go on? Why hasn't that SOB terrorist returned from a fifteen minute chat with his boss and why hasn't the boss come back with him as he insisted he would?*

She only needed visual contact for thirty seconds to put a M110 7.62mm round in the foreheads of the terrorist and his boss. Then she could get out of this damn hole to stretch her legs and everything else attached.

This is really all Howell's fault, thought Betty. Major Howell claimed Gil had asked for some personal time. Betty did not buy it and her aching gut believed Howell had gotten a sniff of Betty's desires for Gil. Was this the major's way of cooling her off? The job in front of her was not particularly dangerous nor did it require backup, but she truly detested waiting like this. She was a woman of action, not patience: especially not for Howell.

I waited for that man for three years, for God's sake and he wants me to wait here for him as well? thought Betty as she scanned the main building of the compound through her sniper scope.

That noise, focus Betty, focus...in the hall outside the main room. Motion. A blur. *Just the house-boy bringing breakfast.* Betty's stomach gurgled. *Damn, breakfast would be good right now.* Betty silently told it to piss off, that she did not want to be found out because her stomach was growling. *Imagine the scene at my parents. Mom would answer the door to find a somber looking Major Howell. "Mrs. Thursten, I regret to inform you that your daughter died in action, of which I can tell you no details, other than that she was found and killed because her stomach had growled after not eating for three days. The smell of bacon, apparently, had been too much for her." Mom and Dad would shriek at Howell that he had killed their baby; they had trusted him like the son in law he was supposed to have been.* Betty almost hoped to be found out just to make Howell have to go through with her imagined penance.

My almost fucking fiancé! Her friends had ribbed her about hyphenating her name so she could be Thursten-Howell and that their first born son should be named Gilligan or Skipper and the girls could be

Mary Anne or Ginger if she was a redhead. Oh, they laughed at that one especially. Well, they never got their satisfaction, did they? No chance for children now, no marriage, no little house on the corner.

"Betty! Snap out of it." She could almost hear Gil yelling at her in her head.

The question now on Betty's mind was *what did that prick Howell make Gil do for penance? He wouldn't have done this to just me, no, the major is much too thorough for that. Wouldn't sitting in court listening to some judge drone on about procedure have been enough punishment? Certainly, he could have arranged a day in court with that bore Judge Landaue. God he loved to hear himself talk.* Her mind was wandering again. *I haven't slept in, what, two, maybe three days?* Betty's thoughts were blurring into a jumbled mess. She had caught tiny naps here and there, but never more than fifteen minutes. *Something has to give soon; with daylight coming, either I get my target or get out. In a few hours, I'll be snoring or dead in this God forsaken ditch!*

Betty's mind snapped to attention. *A car door? I didn't hear it drive up!* "Oh, a Prius." Betty muttered out loud to herself; she mentally cringed at her mistake, continuing the line of thought silently, *Damn things are too quiet if you ask me. I should have heard the tires rolling; fresh asphalt just doesn't generate the same noise as a good old fashioned gravel driveway.*

There he is, the terrorist and his boss. She did not care for any kind of terrorist, but an eco-terrorist was the worst in her book. The shot was blocked.

Come this way, keep coming, why are they arguing in the front lawn? Betty commented to herself. *Don't they know the world's best terrorist killer is in a Gillie suit in the ditch across the way?*

With the twigs, grass and leaves attached to the portable camouflage mesh of the Gillie suit she could not be seen even if you walked within a few feet of her. You would have to step on her to find her. Betty wanted a clean shot of both, but they were waving their arms around and bouncing about as they argued.

Damn it. Sit still so I can cap the both of you, Betty thought. The air was calm, so no adjustments for windage. The temperature was a cool sixty-four degrees. The target was three hundred meters out, well within the effective range of the M110.

Snap...Snap. Snap. Snap...Snap. The first shot was clean, a perfect headshot, the second shot was just to be sure as the boss crumpled. Three into the junior terrorist was a little excessive—or was it because she was visualizing Major Howell's head on the junior terrorist's body? *They have about the same hair color and in this lighting, who could tell, maybe I got lucky? No such luck,* Betty knew Howell would be tucked away in Control, monitoring the hit. *Hell, he probably already knows the mission was a success, whatever that means.* Betty felt uncertain about the job at hand and many questions ran through her mind. *Why assassinations by sniper fire? Why both guys? Why am I doing this by myself? Howell has some questions to answer!*

Betty started her escape. This was going to be tricky, the sun was coming up, but what do you do? As she crossed the hill, she dumped her Gillie suit and dropped the M110 semi-automatic rifle into the hole she had prepared. The cleaners would stop by in a few days and pick this little gem up. Hell, it might even happen in a few hours from now. She never could tell how close they were. She just never wanted to be part of their mission. "I never did mind the little things," she said to herself with a wry smile.

As she topped the hill, she found the bike hidden in the tall grass where she had left it three days before. Just like Betty in her Gillie suit, the bike was camouflaged with grass, sticks, and leaves. *Thank God the goo pack and endurance bar are still in their sanitary packing,* thought Betty, *though I probably would have eaten them anyway. Now I'm an eco-tourist riding her triathlon bike through the mountains of Colombia on a scenic training ride. No deadly sniper here. Keep moving citizens, nothing to see.*

FIVE

MINUTIA

THE LITTLE THINGS ARE what matter, Betty told herself time and again. *The little courtesies we give each other. The thought is what counts.* And at this moment she was thinking of giving Howell the courtesy of a 9mm to the skull for the little things he had done to her the past few weeks and the past decade for that matter. *Sending me out without Gil and bad intelligence on three separate jobs! How does he expect me to leave no trace with such bad intel?*

"Gil! Where the hell have you been?" she almost screamed as he came through the door. "I had to sit in a damn ditch ankle deep in sheep shit waiting for three days for my last shot." So, she was exaggerating the sheep shit, sue her. Besides, how would he know differently?

"Sheep shit? Where the hell have you been is what I want to know? I was neck deep in terrorists trying to get to the center without losing my head. I needed you to be on the lookout for me so I could keep moving forward instead of taking two steps back for every step forward. God, damn it Betty, what was up with your request for 'personal time?'"

Betty gave him that look, the one where men suddenly feel the need to protect both their knees and their groin, but they do not have enough hands. Her focus shifted from Gil to the door, and then Howell as he entered. Gil relaxed a little bit, but still was ready for anything. *I may not be a terrorist, but Betty is painting my forehead with a bull's-eye,* thought Gil.

Major Howell about did a U-turn upon seeing the looks in the eyes of his two best operatives the moment he crossed into the conference room, but he knew it was too late. He was going to have to smooth some ruffled feathers and quick. *I wouldn't be in this predicament if I hadn't been summoned double time to D.C.* He had only just gotten back on the red eye to Control. Shaving in flight using a left over razor blade and cold water combined with sudden turbulence and the aerobatic maneuvers of the small plane left him with toilet paper stuck to his chin to prove it. He could still feel the welt on the top of his head from bouncing off the ceiling.

"Now you two stow it," commanded Major Howell.

Betty closed her left eye while tilting her head to the right. Her index finger pointed at Howell's head, she flexed her thumb as if taking a shot.

"Put the guns down before one of you two kids kill somebody," said Howell.

Betty and Gil were not amused. They crossed their arms and glared at Major Howell.

"I would have been here to explain in person, but General Getner ordered me to report at eighteen hundred hours last night in D.C., the White House to be exact," continued Howell.

Howell paused to gauge what affect that statement had on their mood. Tensions were still high, but lessening.

"Before your last missions I was ordered to spread my operative assets, especially you two, to take advantage of the Mideast Summit today. The objectives were vulnerable and the media's attention elsewhere," informed Howell.

Howell tossed a couple of small boxes onto the conference table and said with a sarcastic smirk, "I'd make a big deal about these Bronze Stars, but I know you just do this for the paycheck."

Betty and Gil did not look like they were going to kill him anymore, but they did look confused. "Mind telling us what the hell is going on?" Gil insisted as he and Betty took their seats.

The major sat down and started to verbally draw out the big picture. "The mole hasn't been identified, but the list is getting shorter. We have several rich targets to go after. Your target is a floating armory—a smorgasbord of weapons for terrorists to come pick and choose. I want this target taken out, but it has to look like the cache exploded on its own," said Howell as he pulled briefing papers out of a folder for Betty and Gil to review.

Betty's mood began to lift as a plan of action gelled. She reached over and pick up her Bronze Star. She paused, looked at the medal and then at Howell's chin. "You're going to get a Purple Heart for that nick aren't you?"

Howell chuckled and replied, "Only if it turns out the pilot is a spy. Damn turbulence bounced me around while I was shaving in that tin can. I have a goose egg to prove it too."

Did Betty still feel something for her former lover, her former near-fiancé? Was she really caring that he nicked himself with a cheap razor? That was out of the question. Or was it? Betty put her left hand on her chin to re-center herself. Betty reached out with her right and mildly patted Howell's hand pretending to be condescending to avoid the appearance of caring too much. "There, there, Major Howell, we'll take good care of you. Gil, get some paper and a purple marker, we'll make our own 'Purple Heart' for our dear leader."

Gil chuckled and eased up himself. What was the point of getting all worked up for? They succeeded in their missions, neither one got hurt and it looked like Howell got the worse end of the deal between the nasty flight and having to deal with General Getner. Maybe being a field op was not so bad.

"Now that we have gotten through the pleasantries, can we get down to business? We have terrorists to kill and plans to foil," intoned Major Howell.

He began to outline the particulars of their next mission, "This one is for the both of you. You are going to have to watch each other's back to get out alive." Betty and Gil visibly relaxed and began focusing on memorizing the details of the operation. This was big. The objective was a fat, juicy one, but the risks were equally large. For two adrenaline junkies, however, this was just their kind of fun.

Six

The Mundane

SOMETIMES THE REAL WORLD, the one that seemed so far away most of the time for Betty, intruded in unexpected ways. In her life as an operative, the life that seemed most real, she was forever twenty-eight in her mind. Perhaps that age rang true because it was the last truly happy time for Betty, before Tom went away. Her thirty-third birthday was only weeks after the brutal killing of her fiancé José. Her life before his untimely death was surreal in that she was going to be married to the son of one of the richest families in Brazil. Anything she wanted she would be able to have, within reason and prudence, that is. Trips to Lake Victoria just to see the falls on a whim would be within her reach. Now a trip to Lake Victoria would be just as random or arbitrary, but it would involve the death of an international arms dealer, drug lord, terrorist, or other unsavory character. Preferably, the death would appear to be caused by an occupational hazard: a drug overdose, a warehouse explosion, or a training accident. Being untraceable back to Control was more important than how the kill took place. No one was to suspect an outside hand or a cat's paw.

Today's brush with her true reality lay in the mundane. She had to renew her State of Virginia driver's license. Not only did she have to confirm her date of birth, proving undeniably that she was going to be thirty-five in a few short days, but the unholy light they used to sharpen every feature seemed to age her another ten or fifteen years, at least on the digital display the clerk showed her to approve the photo. She had never seen gray in her hair before, let alone felt the urgent need for a dye job. She was a specimen of fitness, but the five extra pounds she had put on resting up from the last mission seemed to add twenty in the photo. The harsh light of reality lit up her past in a way she could not brush aside or ignore.

She felt very old and very tired at that moment. On the wall behind the clerk was a poster promoting seatbelts. It depicted the death of a teenage driver. His crumbled, bloodied body resting on the pavement in front of the overturned car, the windshield broken and the driver's window missing. *He looks like José did, life interrupted.* It gave her pause to think back to that night; the night she found José sprawled on their bed with a hole in his forehead. She had never told anyone about the pictures and letters strewn about the corpse. *God, how can I use the word 'corpse' for José's broken body? His fingers broken, even a few toes. His nose bloody and broken. These details were left out of the fraudulent autopsy report making his death look like a suicide. A cover up to protect a wealthy family. Don't know of any suicides involving breaking one's own fingers and toes.*

The harsh light of day showed the toll on José. With her professional training, she now believed she had interrupted or had just missed the perpetrators of this heinous crime. It may have been only seconds between their exit from the room and her entrance. Betty remembered a drape moving more than the wind would have caused let alone why was the twelfth floor balcony door open in the first place? The curtains parted and the late evening sun splashed across his fractured face accentuating the bruises and contusions. Even his left kneecap had been broken. She knew he was strong headed, but she never guessed that he was tough enough of a character to take that much damage without giving in. She did not believe that it was torture for torture's sake. The doctored photos depicting him in compromising positions were meant to break him, but they did not. *At least Howell had the decency to let me know José stayed true to the end,* thought Betty as she turned away from the poster and put her hand to her eyes to wipe away pesky tears.

José knew his past and his future. He would have never admitted to doing something he had not done, good or bad. Betty took a deep breath, trying to calm the disturbance within her. Betty thought back to when Howell told her about José's death.

"No one knows for sure how long the torture lasted. The surveillance camera only covers the front door, but by the complexity of his injuries it must have been prolonged," Howell looked up from the report and noted Betty's white complexion. *José's family is very strong on protecting the family's reputation: apparently a little too strong for her taste,* thought Major Howell.

Betty had left early that morning to stop in her office before making the final arrangements for their engagement party. The caterer required the finalized guest list, which included friends, family, and the usual B list D.C. career bureaucrats that Betty depended on to make the impossible possible. These bureaucrats were the reason José was still in the United States.

Long before their dating and engagement, Betty pulled some strings to keep José in the country when his youthful ways had embarrassed the wrong people and bruised the egos of powerful players. Somehow, she had gotten everyone to calm down and treat it as one of those boys will be boys moments, but even she did not buy that. This bad boy got her attention. After their professional relationship ended, a new personal one started.

"...license ma'am," Betty heard in the distance. "Ma'am, your license, it's finished," repeated the uniformed woman as she held out the newly minted license.

The warmth of the clerk's accent pulled Betty from the dark recesses of her memory. Just the same, her rich southern drawl did not make it any easier being called "ma'am." Maybe it was the way the picture on the license made Betty look a hundred and five or maybe it was just that the clerk called every woman over the age of twenty-one ma'am. Betty was hoping for the later.

SEVEN

MR. SLIM TO NUN

"**B**ETTY, THIS IS MR. SLIM," said McFluffy in his barely decipherable Scottish brogue to Betty as she entered the tech room.

Mr. Slim was not so much skinny as incredibly tall. He had to duck under the door frame to get into the room. With his high-heeled cowboy boots and the black ten gallon hat, Slim was a light brushing seven foot four inches. Mr. Slim removed his hat to greet Betty and did what seemed an impossible feat of bending down at the waist to take her hand and air kiss it like a European nobleman.

"I sure am pleased to meet you, Ms. Betty," said the giant as his Vandyke tickled the back of her hand even though his lips never touched.

"The pleasure is all mine," demurred Betty.

Betty was five foot eight inches but seemed to be half this giant's size and weight. McFluffy and Howell's lack of forewarning that Mr. Slim would be present caused her to pause a few seconds to regain her composure. Betty gave Mr. Slim a long slow glance from his silver tipped boots to the massive Resistol 4X Beaver Western hat that looked proportional to the giant mitt holding it. By the label and the newness of the hat, Betty figured Mr. Slim had recently been to Court's Saddlery & Western Wear in Bryant, Texas. She did not know what to think, but was giving him extra points for turning his height into a statement instead of a liability. His shiny shaved head only added to the mystery of this man. Slim could not possibly be this giant's real last name, but in this business you did not ask too many personal questions.

McFluffy was a rotund man who was almost wider than he was tall. A snarl of a beard riddled with white, gray, black, red, and who knows what for lunch sat on his chin like a pet. The thick glasses made his eyes seem as large as half dollars. He looked like a cross between a beach ball and a thistle, if that genetic combination were even possible. His Scottish brogue could be incomprehensible. Betty usually had to ask him to say something two or three times. Did he just say haggis or have this?

McFluffy was not his real name and no one knew what it was for sure. He had said his name to her and it sounded like he was hacking up a loogie. She gave up on even trying to pronounce it the second she heard that bramble of consonants and vowels. She had been warned by Howell not to even try. McFluffy was partially deaf anyway, so he did not seem to mind everyone calling him McFluffy. Junior members called him Mr. McFluffy, which always seemed to cause snickering. This caused consternation and confusion for the big old puffball.

McFluffy cleared his throat to get their attention and said something unintelligible, but his intention of moving forward was obvious as he fiddled with the controls in front of him.

Betty blushed and awkwardly, almost reluctantly, removed her hand from that massive meat grinder that had so tenderly held her hand.

Betty had been scheduled for a fitting of her new form-fitting undergarment that allowed for the plethora of concealed weapons and tools she relied on to stay alive in tight situations. This required several body scans. Of course, these had to be performed in the nude, which made for a rather awkward situation given the presence of Mr. Slim. Mr. Slim attempted to fit his body into an office chair set for McFluffy's diminutive height, putting his knees into his chest. There was no way to perform this test and preserve your modesty. The tester had to be able to look in to make sure the lasers were lined up correctly for the person's height and width. McFluffy was always discrete: though she suspected her appointment was the highlight of his day by his pensiveness. She just was not sure about Mr. Slim.

"Is Mr. Slim's presence necessary for this procedure?" Betty asked with a sharpness in her voice she had not intended.

"I assure you, young lass, Mister Slim's presence is required," McFluffy replied with his thick and impenetrable brogue.

She did not know which to fight, understanding the meatball of a man or the presence of *Mr. OMG you're tall*. Betty began to darkly wonder if McFluffy owed Mr. Slim a personal debt or had he lost a bet and was paying up? This was very awkward, even more so than being air kissed by a giant imitating an accordion as he gathered himself. She would just have to make the best of it. She felt her personal space was being violated, which seemed ridiculous considering the form-fitting clothing she tended to wear and her pride in her perfectly sculpted body.

McFluffy handed her a form requesting personal information such as height, weight, name (first only), and serial number. Why did he want this? He already knew who she was; he had setup her appointment by secure encrypted email. Thank God, he at least typed the Kings English. Betty was not a prude by any means, but having to state for the record what she thought her measurements were against laser accuracy seemed absurd and downright childish.

She filled out the form and shoved it back into McFluffy's hand with a sharp look as if to say, *"Stop f'ing with me and get this over with."*

Maybe I should change cover stories? A nun's habit would be perfect for hiding weapons. Who would ever suspect a peaceful nun of poisoning your drink or sniping you from one hundred meters? H-E double toothpicks, I could even hide a rifle in the habit let alone a samurai sword for backup. Then again, she thought, *nuns just aren't wearing the penguin suit like they used to.*

"I suppose I would stick out like a sore thumb," Betty said to herself under her breath.

"What?" Mr. Slim intoned with his deep bass voice. "I'm sorry, do I make you uncomfortable? I can wait outside for this part."

He graciously rose to leave, almost knocking a florescent bulb out of the light fixture with his hat and sudden rise to full stature.

Betty wryly replied, "You can stay, but only if I get to stay for your scan."

Slightly startled yet cockily sure of himself, Mr. Slim replied, "We'll darling, that's what I'm here for and if it would please you to 'observe' my fitting, I would be plum happy to oblige you the same courtesy."

The gauntlet had been thrown down. Betty had been called to the mat. *How can I turn down an offer like that? What the hell, I'm no nun.*

Eight

Peek-a-boo, I See You

BETTY HAD OFFERED TO LET Slim go first, secretly hoping to get the big brute out of the room by the time it was her turn. Ever the "gentleman", he insisted "ladies first." McFluffy was not going to wait for them to figure this out, so he ordered her to strip and enter the chamber "on the pronto." Well, that was kind of what it sounded like.

Slim made a show of averting his eyes while Betty stripped, but he was all hands on deck as she climbed in for the peep show. Betty's only consolation was that she would be seeing Slim in the same predicament.

The scanning rig was a clear Plexiglas cube eight feet deep by eight feet wide and eight feet tall. Even a giant like Slim could hold his arms out with fingertips extended. Lasers on six axes roamed and reflected off the surface of the body to the sensors surrounding the box. This provided a 3-D image and the ability to produce a photo realistic hologram of the subject. On the floor of the box was a clear turntable that rotated the subject to insure a smooth scan from all sides. Observers could see the subject, but the sensors tended to partially block the view of the observer at strategic points.

The scan goggles fit snugly over her face to prevent the UV radiation from causing damage to the cornea and premature cataracts. *That's the least of my worries if we don't find the mole soon,* thought Betty. From the outside, it was like watching a copier scan a piece of paper from all directions at once, but with a cool blue laser. Agents joked that a side benefit of the scan was hair removal, which was slightly believable as the eyebrows were covered by the goggles and your hair was in a UV protective cap. The men in this elite group were well groomed, which may have started the rumor in the first place.

I suppose, thought Betty, *today is the day we put that rumor to rest.*

Betty assumed her pose imagining herself on a carousel. All she needed now was some stripper music and a pole to hang onto. Her feminine figure bathed in a stripe of blue laser light that accentuated each part of her body during the scan. The first pass you raised your arms up high. Wryly, Betty considered the flattering affect that would have on her bosom, lifting and firming her already attractive breasts for the pleasure of Mr. Slim. Betty was a natural B cup with a 34" chest, 24" waist and 34" hips. Her form was so stunningly fit that Slim was mesmerized as the laser scanned up her legs. Though he was wearing the same goggles as Betty and could see well enough through the colored lenses, the view was obstructed by the rigs structure and equipment. Slim tried to peek around the sensors as Betty spun slowly. Annoyed by the dark tinting of the goggles and the blocking of the sensors, Slim peeked over the protective goggles and stood on tiptoes. The laser's reflection found his retinas. Slim covered his eyes from the sting of the laser just as Betty's vivacious form finished rotating, giving a full frontal view to her audience. By the time he regained his vision it was too late for him to find out the veracity of the rumor on shaving vs. laser epidermal hair removal. Not only that but he missed the 'best' part of the show. McFluffy was chortling, perhaps at the expense of Mr. Slim losing the advantage he had so craftily gained.

Betty heard the commotion and Slim's cries and understood immediately what had happened. The show was over almost as soon as it had begun. Slim was sitting in McFluffy's chair once more with his head in his knees, this time in pain and suffering for his loss, rather than just because the seat was two feet too low for his form. Betty quickly dressed and rejoined the men.

"McFluffy, I'm gonna change my name to Slim Pickens, 'cause that's all I got out of this arrangement," sighed a dejected man.

McFluffy began to hum the mad scientist anthem *She Blinded Me With Science.*

Slim was not amused.

Betty came up to the redwood of a man, grabbed his shirtfront with a single finger pulling him closer. With a husky, breathless voice and a wry smile she said, "Your turn big boy."

Slim rose to his full stature, straightened his shoulders, threw out his chest and strutted to the changing area like a soldier to the gallows. "Got a light for a dying man?" Slim asked rakishly as he began to disrobe. He purposely pretended to be modest, but was not really trying to hide anything. The scan went as before, but the giant's height strained the technological marvel of McFluffy's twisted mind. Slim was a man of proportions, as if an average six foot man had visited Alice's *Wonderland* for the "Grow Me" pill. Betty liked what she saw, but was attempting to appear indifferent, not that McFluffy or Slim were looking her way. His abs and buttocks reminded her of the Spartans in the movie *300*. Slim could not put his arms straight up in the air like Betty, so he crossed them behind his head and held his elbows.

As the carousel turned Slim around Betty got a good view of Slim. *Yes, Slim does shave and oh la la! No disappointment down there and if he knows how to use that "thing" any women is going to be interested.*

As if to say his presentation was not to its fullest, Slim protested to McFluffy "Partner, it's a little cold in here...could y'all turn up the heat?" Betty was already feeling the heat, letting slip a smile.

The scan finished, Slim emerged from the chamber holding a small hand towel to his front once again pretending modesty. He quickly dressed and the two agents looked each other over, both fully dressed. Betty focused her memory on his sculpted body while Slim attempted to recreate the missed view of her curvaceous body before turning and walking out purposefully. McFluffy dismissed Betty with a wave of his hand. Betty had been dismissed this way before by Howell, at the Capital Grille. She did not like it then and she did not like it now. Betty gave McFluffy a scowl and menacing glare. The puffball retreated to his equipment and began muttering to himself in a manner unintelligible to Betty.

I need some rest. Her watch read 11:45am. *Time enough to take a nap if I skip lunch.* Betty strode past the commissary and headed for her quarters; a stern look in her eye gave her all the privacy she needed in the crowded hallway.

NINE

BLOW BACK

MAJOR HOWELL RARELY RAISED his voice let alone yelled at anyone. He ran such a tight ship that there was rarely a reason to do so. The coffee dripping down the other side of the conference room wall and the tray of donuts lying on the floor indicated otherwise. Gil and Betty walked gingerly into the room, not sure which was more of a concern, stepping on a brutalized donut or being brutalized by a normally imperturbable Major Howell. The previous meeting had been with the stoop shouldered, nearsighted, longhair wiz kids of the Intel team; they gathered and analyzed information for Control missions from afar. Of course, there were agents on the ground doing the grunt work, but these geeks took the raw intelligence and attempted to make a meaningful synthesis out of it. The reports they generated were what kept Betty and Gil alive and effective in the field. When they screwed up, it forced Betty and Gil to improvise. When agents improvised, traces tended to be left behind that could lead to conclusions other than what had been planned; when things went wrong—terribly wrong—an agent could end up dead.

A perfect mission meant that a drug lord was killed by an underling in a shootout instead of assassinated for bankrolling a terrorist. Gil's personal favorite was getting the jealous husband to kill the banker in a fit of rage over an affair. These types of deaths only made the local news. That was the true power of this team. If there is no trace there is no blowback. Anyone could walk up and kill the third prince of some patch of sand, but to make it look like an inside job made the hit invisible and people who knew better nervous. It took security teams off balance leading to much bigger results down the road than a straight up take down. Major Howell had drilled his team for years about this strength.

Lately, things had been going wrong. Very wrong. That meant either his team was incompetent or there was a mole in Control. It probably was not an agent. A star quarterback throwing twenty interceptions in a game? Not likely. One or two? It happens. Three or four? A bad night. More than that and the coach is likely to bench his star. This was more insidious.

Guards were out of position the night of a mission, maps showing inaccurate positions of rooms, insiders who acted the opposite of what was expected. There was a job in particular in Caracas, a terrorist cell; the team had concocted a plan to cause one faction to start shooting at the other over a slight. A young buck thought he would make a better leader and felt it was his duty to wrest control from an ineffectual panty-waist unwilling to make the tough calls like killing women and children for the good of the cause. A new leader who would not accept second-guessing, even from the nephew of his boss. Setting these two up for a dual to the death should have been easy using disinformation, mistresses and faked documents. Instead, Betty ended up taking them out one by one in the dark with great risk to herself and the team. Had she been found out any sooner or in a more compromising position she could have been killed and the team dismantled. Hell, Gil was chased half way across the city and only made it at the last second to pick up Betty and make their getaway. Were they allowed to get away or was the mission only partially compromised?

This mole had to be found out and quickly. Major Howell did not seem to think it was more than one person on the team, but that was always a possibility. Traps had been set to sniff out the mole, but no internal wires had been tripped as of yet. The major was frustrated with the lack of progress. He had been able to trust his staff without question for so long, he was not used to triple and quadruple checking.

The mission to the base of the Andes had been a straight up assassination. Not the typical job for his team. It was specifically set up to identify the mole. One set of intelligence was fed to the junior leader through a priest named José, in reality a foreign agent, while another similar set was sent through the normal channels. The bait was set. Betty waited two extra days in the scrub to be sure. She did not know why she had to do what she did, but being the professional, she did what she was asked to do. Either the mole was not one of the suspects or he ignored the false information and did not warn the terrorist leader. Either way, a bad guy was dead and the field of suspects was narrowing.

You can't tell a soldier to do something against her training too many times before she starts to ask why, even if it is an order, Betty stewed as she listened to Howell go on and on.

"That job wasn't even necessary," said Betty accusingly. "Sure the target deserved to die and won't be missed. Hell, ten more were ready to step into his shoes five seconds after the body was disposed of over the side of the mountain."

"The job was ordered because it was designed to trip up a possible mole. The leader showing up means either the mole saw this coming or the mole was higher up than I had anticipated," Howell retorted.

The mission was making more sense now, but Betty was not about to let Howell off the hook. *He needs to squirm a little. He needs to pay for making me sit in a hole without food or sleep for nearly two days. He needs to give a little blood for the past, for that matter,* thought Betty.

Howell reported directly to General Getner. There was not anyone in between. That would mean it was either one of Getner's staff or the mole in Control was smart enough to lay low for the previous mission. McFluffy, Stein (a well placed foreign government informant), and Miguel were on the short list of suspects. Stein worked in D.C. with limited supervision and Miguel was a landowner and a secret member of the rebels attempting to overthrow the Venezuelan government. There were other possibilities, but so remote they did not deserve special consideration. It would be like suspecting your family. You had to trust someone.

Howell had not slept properly in weeks. It had been three days since he slept through the night. He did not even bother going back to his efficiency apartment in Georgetown. Control was approximately an hour by air. Rather than commute, Howell spent the weeknights in the barracks with the other staff of Control. On the occasional free weekend or if he was in town for a meeting at the White House, he would seclude himself in his apartment to think; four painted walls and a grimy view of a brick building. These days he needed it even more than ever, his monk's cell, to deal with the tension of Washington, General Getner, the president, and the mole.

"Sit down Betty—Gil, can I get you a cup of..." Major Howell looked in the direction of what had been coffee and donuts. "...no sense having this meeting standing up."

Gil graciously chimed in "No thanks Major. I had a cup of coffee in the mess hall while we were waiting."

"Speak for yourself, Mr. I stopped at Starbucks on the way over." Betty thought about giving Gil a swift kick to the shin, but he was inconveniently out of reach.

"Well, let me get to the heart of the matter. We have a mole. I don't believe it is either of you two or one of you would be dead by now. The Cabal isn't likely to let either of you live if they have half a chance," said Howell.

Somehow, that did not seem very reassuring. Betty glanced at Gil and then back at Howell, her eyes narrowed to slits as she thought about it for a nanosecond then moved on. Neither one of these two were the mole. Call it a woman's intuition or just blind trust. She was sure that either of these men would die for her.

Major Howell took out of his breast pocket a sealed envelope, slitting it open with a small penknife. For what seemed to be exaggerated theatrics, he stabbed the knife into the top of the conference table. "Here is how we are going to catch the bastard."

Ten

Oh, Yes, Faster, Faster

GENERAL GETNER HAD AGREED, after hearing Howell's side of the story during his last trip to D.C., that they had one chance to bring this to a positive conclusion or the team would be shut down to prevent blowback reaching the president. The origins of Control had been established during prior administrations, but any problems now were owned by whoever was currently in power. Teams came and went. Everyone on the outside was focused on the CIA and NSA. This group had no known name, building, or bureaucracy in the capital area making it difficult to pin anything on anybody. Offices were spread all over in many different organizations. Control was the spy for the president in the CIA, NSA, military, and even the U.S. Congress. The organization was cellular as if they were an overseas operation. In a way, they were now the eyes and ears of the president; above the fray of normal capital politics; for example, there was no budget to be approved or congressional oversight of missions. Administrative assistant A did not know agent B or agent G let alone ever meet them and did not need to for the purpose of issuing a new passport or two. Everything was compartmentalized except for Control headquarters.

Control headquarters was a problem. Here was a group of people, no more than thirty, almost all contained in a situation room within a military style base. The teams outside of headquarters worked undercover for government departments or the military. Military resources, such as helicopters, appeared to be paid for by some other spy agency while their operational income primarily came from patents on medical devices.

There was nothing to trace. Control was spying on its own government as well as the rest of the world. They solved the president's problems or prevented them by getting around the real moles and traitors of the U.S. Government. This was a slippery slope and the members of Control were drilled with the knowledge that discretion and honor were the only things keeping them from going too far. General Getner had given Major Howell some slack, but the rope was not very long and the fuse was short. He would expose the mole or his team was to be scratched.

Howell had gotten this plum job back when Getner was a colonel, both were rising stars; Getner because he had the right connections, Howell because he had been asked to perform the impossible and succeeded. This was another one of those impossible missions and the only option was success.

The story of Howell and Getner's rise to prominence, as told by those not actually present, went that Getner had a special vehicle designed for patrolling roads for improvised explosive devices (IEDs). The vehicle had performed brilliantly up until the final test run the night before the demonstration for the defense department staff. A sample IED went off unexpectedly during a dry run in a way that would have killed any soldier sitting behind the driver due to the angle of deflection or the compression wave of the blast.

What happened next is what mattered to both their careers. The modified Humvee had a gaping hole in its side from the IED. There was no obvious way to present this to the assembled generals the next day that would justify the project for further funding. Getner told Lieutenant Howell to fix the problem. Howell, not knowing any better, succeeded. Normally there would have been extra material and equipment to fix anything on the rig, but because they had already moved to a remote testing ground, they only had dirt and rocks.

Howell somehow came up with a huge piece of stainless steel and the means to attach it, all by 3 in the morning. At the time, Getner did not ask too many questions. Later, he discovered that Howell had raced to the four star hotel where the generals were staying. Bursting into the kitchen, he commandeered a prep table and two of the cleaning crew to carry it out.

"Oh, yes!" Howell chortled with delight when he saw a stainless steel table about the right size for the job.

The two commandeered helpers were unsure of their task. They did not know who to fear more, this crazed military officer or their boss in the morning. Neither choice was good being poorly documented for their stay in the U.S. It seemed the best course was to do as they were told, no matter who was doing the ordering.

"Faster, faster. ¡Asegurado, asegurado!" Howell prodded as time was of the essence.

Once he roped them into the job, they were hell bent for leather to get this table to wherever he wanted it just so they could get away from this crazy gringo. Howell hotwired a beat-up old wrecker that had a welder and torch on board and drove like a madman, pushing the old horse to its limits to get back to the testing grounds in time. The torching and welding were the easiest part of the job. The freshly repaired and reinforced tub of the Humvee now looked like a ship's hull once again. In the morning test run, the modified Humvee took a direct IED hit and kept on humming.

"Colonel Getner—that was an interesting demonstration. Though from the look of the wet paint and that non-military issued equipment over there I would say you had a FUBAR situation last night. Care to tell me about it?" asked General Stark, one of the observers of the test run.

Colonel Getner began to hem and haw until he looked over at Howell and said, "General, I can't take credit for Lieutenant Howell's extraordinary work last night. You're right. Had he not gone the extra mile and taken unusual actions, our presentation would have been...how to say it? Less than stellar."

General Stark chuckled slightly, "We knew something was up this morning because the kitchen was a mess at the hotel. Staff were going on and on in Spanish about some crazy soldier gringo." The general paused for a moment. "You may have not done the work, but you sure knew how to pick the right man for the mission. I think I see a new slot in your future, Colonel. Report to me in three days at my office in the Pentagon."

Getner was promoted to general and put in charge of using spies like Howell to ferret out equipment and personnel problems in the field. The operation was intended to get real intelligence on equipment failures in the field, not the ones spoon-fed up the chain of command. Howell was his first operative. The jobs were more about insertion and remediation than the usual destruction. Howell was a natural, but this gift carried a heavy price: he would have to leave Betty. Getner promised the world and any assignment Howell wanted in a year; however, for that year he was going to have to spend most of his time in Afghanistan and Iraq, far from his beloved Betty and civilization. This was the type of career move Howell could only make when he was unencumbered by civilized society.

Howell told Betty he would be back, this was important, that it would lead to a huge advancement in his career without much risk. He would be gone for a year, but then he would be at the DOD and a train ride for a commute; however, it did not work out that way.

All of this history came crashing back to Howell as he struck the knife into the conference room table. "Here is how we are going to catch the bastard."

There was more to that gesture than meets the eye, thought Betty. As the threesome left the conference room, Mr. Slim rounded the corner looking impossibly tall.

Howell winked, "Betty, I don't think you two have met yet, I'd like you to meet Mr. Slim. He will be your partner for the Panama Canal train ride; you two will get to know each other—very well."

"Well, Major Howell, I have already had the pleasure," said Mr. Slim as he removed a cigar from his breast pocket and began to wet the end as if he was going to smoke it.

Betty did not even think twice as she swung her toe into what should have been soft flesh and bone where Howell's shin meets his calf. The "ting" of her toe hitting something metal and plastic shook her very soul. Howell barely budged, but suddenly he had the look of a ghost on his face. Suddenly the hallway was awkward in every direction for fifty meters. Each set off in a different direction and tried to not say anything more.

Betty's mind raced as buried emotions bubbled up from the depths of her soul. *This could only mean one thing. Howell lost part of his leg somehow during that year we were apart.* "Why didn't the bastard tell me?" Betty mumbled under her breath. *His gait is so natural, that prosthetic must be the latest generation. Is his leg why he didn't come back to me?* All these thoughts raced through Betty's mind in a jumbled mess.

As Betty stormed away from Major "Prick" Howell and Mr. Slim, she tried to regain control of her emotions. *Calm down. Deep breaths.* She was not quite sure why she had reacted so extremely to Howell's wink and nod toward Slim. *He probably heard about our "his and her" showing in McFluffy's lair. I didn't think that one through,* Betty came to a full stop, *Shit! The cameras!* The security cameras pan even into the clear Plexiglas scanning chamber, though procedure dictated that all surveillance records be wiped within twenty-four hours to ensure personal privacy. Control needed to take security precautions to catch infiltrators or turncoats, but it also did not need that kind of paparazzi photo spreading around the world. *Did Howell see me naked?*

ELEVEN

BANG BANG, YOU'RE DEAD

W HILE IN IRAQ, HOWELL was assigned by General Getner to protect the civilian materials engineer Barbara "Babs" McGillicutty. They were inspecting the new turret shields for the Humvee gunners; shields that were designed to give the gunners a fifty percent better chance of surviving the focused energy blast of the new IEDs coming from Iran—designed to act like a cannon shot instead of a bomb. This potent innovation was deadly to the previously exposed gunners. Babs was a brilliant and beautiful doctor of mechanical engineering. Her specialty was material science or the way metals reacted to heat, energy, impact, and such. Her job was to evaluate how the new shields were working in the real world rather than basing their value on the number of body bags saved.

Howell's job was to do whatever Babs needed done when she was in the combat zone, get her whatever tools she needed and get her out alive. This put them in close quarters. Babs was single, beautiful, and available. She made sure he knew the last part one day as they were riding together in a Humvee that took a hit. As the blast struck their vehicle, Babs grabbed a hold of Howell's leg and then some. She was not in a hurry to let him go after the excitement had died down. She even went so far as to give him a smooch, a squeeze and yelled, "Yes, it worked!" when it became obvious, no one had been scratched.

It got rather awkward for a while as Howell tried to decide, was he Betty's man-in-waiting or was Babs an adventure worth having? It took all of a second to remember that Betty was the only one for him and Babs, a dessert he did not need and could be refused.

Not long after this episode, there were other attempts by Babs to entice Howell. Because of Babs's contractor status and gender combined with Howell's rank and operational status, private quarters were arranged in one of the many confiscated palaces of the previous regime. The simple cots afforded for sleeping appeared as plain as the rooms were grand. While visiting this "base camp" for showers and sleep, Babs "mistakenly" entered Howell's private room wearing only a wet towel. She pretended to be startled and dropped the towel. There was no mistaking Babs's intent or her femininity.

This is one of those tests, thought Howell, *that God likes to give those who he knows are strong enough to resist.*

Babs insisted this was her room and what was that scamp Howell doing there. She climbed on top of the practically naked Howell, clothed only in his boxer shorts. With her hands pinning his arms down she leaned forward, her ample bosom now inches from his face. Howell was staring at a false paradise, a paradise that would cost him his true love, Betty. Howell turned his head and closed his eyes as Babs rubbed her body against his. His involuntary arousal, the rush of blood and rise: this temptress knew what she wanted and was not going to play fair. Howell summoned all of his resolve as Babs reached down into his boxers and he shoved her off roughly.

"I can't guard you if we do this," he lied.

Babs grabbed her towel and left in a huff. "Bastard!"

†

They were in the field soon after inspecting a failed turret shield. "Babs— hold up! The site hasn't been checked out yet," Howell reached for Babs' arm to stop her, but she shrugged him off.

"For the past week you've given me the silent treatment. Grow up or you'll get us both killed!" Howell scanned for possible danger in the area.

Babs charged ahead to the inspection site, only turning to stick her tongue out at her protector.

"Babs, what the hell are you doing? Get back, we haven't checked that out with the bomb unit yet," yelled Howell, but it was too late.

An explosion that would have easily been stopped by a Humvee or the new turret shield was too much for the flak jacket Babs was wearing. It ripped into her body shredding that beautiful face and figure. Howell, ignoring the sharp sting of pain in his right arm, hustled over to the Humvee. He drove it next to Babs and grabbed the medic kit with his left hand. Returning to Babs's side, he did what he could to stop the worst of the bleeding. He lifted Babs up into the vehicle with one motion, jumped into the driver's seat, and roared off to base. He had a nagging feeling something was wrong with his right arm, the red stain on his sleeve seemed to be getting larger, but the adrenaline of the moment and the mangled body of Babs focused his attention on the road. *This is not how this was supposed to work. My job was to protect her. I've failed. Maybe if I had succumbed to Babs's temptation, would this have happened?* His mind was tortured with what was best for Babs, for Betty, and for Tom Howell.

Howell radioed in his status and Babs's condition. The ETA for a helicopter was thirty minutes. If he headed that way now he could cut it down to fifteen. He put the pedal to the metal and roared off.

Babs was calling out to him from the back of the Humvee. "I'm dying!" she cried. "I need you," faded into a bloody hacking cough, then nothing.

Howell pulled over to the side of the road, *Why am I bothering? The road is closed until it can be cleared!* "You're not dying! Help is on its way!" Howell said with authority he did not feel.

He went to Babs and brushed her hair out of her face. Removing what was left of her flak jacket seemed to help her breathe. "You're going to be fine—it's just superficial." Tom lied to comfort her. She smiled a bloody smile as if to say thanks. He took water from his camelback to wet his handkerchief. He washed the blood from her once beautiful face.

She was whispering to him in a very tired voice, "...kiss me...kiss me...before I die."

Howell bent over close and kissed her on the cheek. "The medic will be here in a few minutes. Hang on!"

"...kiss me like you love me...," Babs pleaded, momentarily regaining her strength.

Howell tenderly placed his lips on hers. He mustered up all his love for Betty and the passion he had ignored for Babs and kissed her goodbye. She was not dead yet, but did not have long to live. He jumped out of the back of the Hummer to get to the driver's seat. Just as he realized he still had Babs's flak jacket in his hands—*Blam!* His world stopped. He suddenly was an observer of his own demise. Tom could virtually rotate his world on a three hundred sixty degree axis and view what had just happened from any angle in his mind. He looked back at Babs through the door window. Tom had somehow missed the land mine now exploding at his feet while getting out of the Humvee the first time. Far in the distance he imagined the helicopters racing his way, suddenly suspended in air, rotors still. The shrapnel was hurtling toward him, yet strangely paused in mid air. If only he could reach out and brush the offending metal aside—he would be on his way to save Babs. There was still time to save her. His mission now was to save her. He had failed once, how could he fail twice in the same day. This time he was failing himself, Betty, and Babs. He could not die. This was not his time.

Whhhooooshhh. The air that had expanded with the heat of the explosion compressed with a sucking sound. Time accelerated now as if to make up for the gift he had received of that moment when time had stood still. His world turned blood red as the burning shrapnel struck his body tearing apart his right leg. Shrapnel penetrated Babs's flak jacket in his hands only to bounce harmlessly off his own. Other than his once strong, purposeful leg looking like hamburger, it seemed he had no other serious injuries. He took his handkerchief, wet with Babs's blood, and tied a tourniquet as quickly as he could. He had to move fast. If he released the tourniquet he would lose too much blood. If he did not loosen it every fifteen minutes, he could lose his leg. He had four hours to get help or the leg would be lost for sure. With super human strength, the desire to see Betty again, and the will to complete his mission he dragged himself to the driver's door and pulled himself into the Humvee.

His right foot would not obey his orders, so he did the best he could with his left. Faint from loss of blood, he tried to visualize all that truly mattered to him just to keep going. The pain was searing in his mind. He could not use the morphine in the kit without compromising his ability to drive them back to base. He got on the radio again and updated his position and status. As the helicopter heading his way grew near, he pulled the Humvee over and fell out as he tried to get down. The rotor wash was the last thing he remembered.

TWELVE

IF YOU STILL LOVE ME

BETTY WAS ON HER WAY to meet Tom for the first time since he had returned to the states. He had refused her visits to the rehabilitation center where he was staying for his physical therapy. He would not take her calls except to briefly ask how she was and to tell her he had just taken a pain pill and would be asleep any moment. Betty was both dismayed and stunned by Tom's standoffishness. *Is this the same man I planned on spending the rest of my life with? Didn't we talk into the night about children, the home we would buy, his career, my career, what it would be like to have a fiftieth wedding anniversary? Is this the same man or a doppelganger: looks almost the same but so unlike the man I love?*

Betty finally got Tom to come to the phone.

"I'm leaving the rehab clinic today to report tomorrow for duty at the Pentagon." This was the cold and heartless Howell talking, not the loving warm Tom she knew.

"Do you have time for a walk or dinner tonight? Catch up?" pleaded Betty.

"I'm not as mobile as I would like—the shrapnel did some nerve damage to my leg. I don't think a walk is a good idea."

"Dinner, then? Somewhere convenient for you?" Betty needed to see him, touch him, and believe that this was not some stranger in Tom's clothes.

"I'll meet you at the Capital Grille. Seven sharp. That will give me enough time to—to rest, get a nap in." There was hesitancy in his voice.

"Great! I'll see you then. Get some rest. Love you!" Betty hung on the phone waiting for Tom to say he loved her back.

"OK, I'll see you at seven sharp," was all Howell said before hanging up the phone without giving a proper goodbye.

He's just tired, that's all. Nothing to worry about. He's had a hard time. Seven! What am I going to wear? These and many more thoughts raced through Betty's mind. "Margaret! I'm leaving early. Is there anything important I need to do in the next hour?" Betty shouted to her legal assistant who should have been at her own desk.

"Well, is he going to meet you for dinner then?" Margaret was standing at the door to Betty's office.

"Oh, Margaret, I didn't see you there. Yes. The Capital Grille at seven. I need to go home and get ready. Seriously, is there anything I have to take care of right now?" demanded Betty.

"Everything will hold till the day after tomorrow. Sam will take any calls that come in for you that can't wait. He is just preparing a brief for Judge Landaue." Margaret rolled her eyes at the mention of the judge.

Betty could barely stand the wait. She counted down the hours before walking from the metro station near the White House at G Street and 12th to the Capital Grille. The view of the Capitol Building was amazing in the evening light. This was a walk Tom used to love, before he went away. *How bad is the nerve damage? Will he still want to go on walks?* Betty pondered what the future might hold, what limitations Tom would have post recovery. He and Betty often walked the Capitol area in the evenings before he went away. The Jefferson Memorial was a favorite, but the waterfalls of the FDR Memorial held a special fascination. The sound of the water cascading down was so calming during the hectic time that was their life: Betty always on her way to meet some far away client dying to get into the U.S. and Tom meeting with colonels and sometimes generals to discuss new war technology.

Walking these special places the past year had calmed her nerves as she worried about his safety. She would usually take a girlfriend along for these walks, but sometimes family would be in town for a visit. She would play tour guide. They would be suitably impressed that she knew so much and that such a rising star of D.C. would take the time to walk them around the monuments.

During the lonely times spent waiting for Tom to return, she would often jog the mall: starting at their Georgetown loft, and working her way around Arlington National Cemetery, or along the Vietnam Memorial, past the Korean Memorial looping around the White House and back past the Reflecting Pool, her pace slowing slightly by the Washington Monument as she remembered her commitment to living with him—a dry run at marriage. Running along the Reflecting Pool she often dreamed that her reflection was Tom running beside her, the pace quickening as the mirage led her, urging her to their future together. As she reached the flight of steps leading to the somber Lincoln sitting in judgment, her suitor, the mirage, waiting just out of sight in the brackish water gave her cause to look back and slow her pace. *Is it the stairs or Abe's serious gaze that slows me down?* The doubt raised by the mirage's parting bothered her, so she looked for other explanations for her reduced pace at the foot of the colossus statue of Abraham Lincoln.

Running through the war memorials, she fantasized about the heroics that he must be performing overseas. Her focus on Tom outside of work had been all encompassing. The wait between calls was agonizing. He had told her of Babs's advances but assured her he was fully committed to their relationship and would be proposing when he got back. Betty did not concern herself with Babs nearly as much as she had about the danger surrounding the IEDs he was working with. The bomb squad would be checking the sites out before Tom got there, but you never could be sure that all the IEDs had been disarmed.

A near miss with a cab refocused Betty's attention as she worked her way to the Capital Grille. *I'm early; I must have had a faster tempo than I thought!* Her excitement had been translated into a quick pace on the way over. *I don't see Tom. He is always early, but with my pace I am way early. I guess I'll have to wait fifteen or twenty minutes for him.* The maître d' came directly to her and said, "Ms. Thursten? Captain Howell is waiting for you in the private room." *He must have described me to Samuel, though we are here enough, he might recognize me without Tom on my arm.*

Captain? Why didn't Tom tell me he was promoted to captain? This was news she would have expected to hear in a letter or a phone call, not by noticing the shiny new bars on his shoulders. *He looks smart in his uniform, but why is he sitting at a table for two in a room for twenty? Why isn't he making any move to get up to seat me?* The maître d' did the honors for Howell, as if he knew in advance this would be his role to seat Betty.

The doppelganger Howell immediately apologized for his lack of social graces. "As I mentioned on the phone, I was injured in Iraq; nothing for you to worry about, but I hope you won't mind if I stay seated. The shrapnel removed from my leg caused some nerve damage and it is still difficult getting around."

Crutches were leaning against the wall, too far for him to get on his own without hobbling, but the staff at the Capital Grille was known for their attentiveness. The waiter and busboy standing nearby surely were prepared to bring him his crutches.

They had never dined in private before, though they had been to the Capital Grille on several occasions: the dinner with friends, to celebrate Betty's raise, new office, and Margaret becoming her legal assistant. Each time Tom would pilfer a bottle from his father's private wine locker and the cheeky boy would leave Tom Sr. notes grading the wine.

The table was set and Howell had ordered for Betty, which put her off a bit. He seemed all bravado, but it was a thin coat he wore. He would stare off in the distance during their conversation, often changing the subject for what seemed like no particular reason. Betty kept trying to get information from him without seeming to pry by occasionally referring to a relative's recent medical treatment or talking about her runs and walks. They had much to catch up on, but she was the one doing the talking. He seemed attentive, but distant; his responses stilted. During dessert, he gave the waiter a look that apparently meant bring the envelope and the box, because that is what he did.

Howell said, "I thought you should have the pendant back and please read the card later."

"What the hell does that mean?" demanded Betty.

Howell ignored her request for clarification and kept going. "In the envelope is the money I owe you for my share of the loft and expenses, while I was gone. I am sorry it took me so long to take care of this matter."

"Take care of the matter? Do you think I care about the money? I'm just glad to have you home!" Betty could not believe her ears. This was not a welcome home party or a celebration of his advancement in rank. This was a goodbye.

"Betty," a glimmer of Tom showed before the doppelganger Howell shoved him back down.

"I don't need your money. I need you!" Betty protested, "Business is good. My practice is growing—" Howell waved her objections away. She opened the box. Inside was an inexpensive, broken heart pendant that lovers give each other. Betty had given Tom his half before Tom left for Iraq; a time that now seemed so very far away. She started to tear up and could not bear this much longer. The waiter came over with a handkerchief to soak up her tears and blow her nose. Betty could not believe this. This was not the man she had grown to love.

"What does this mean?" asked Betty as she began to shake noticeably.

"We are done," stated Howell flatly.

"Why are you doing this? I...I love you! You love me," stammered Betty.

"I don't love you," Howell said as he looked away.

"I don't believe you!" said Betty as she started to shove her chair back for more room, her arms trying to convey the meaning of her words that Tom seemed to be oblivious to.

"I'm sorry if I misled you," Tom's words cut deeply into Betty's heart.

"We are to be together the rest of our lives. If you need more time, that is fine, I understand, war does hard things to strong men." Betty was grasping for straws; nothing made sense anymore. Her world was imploding. "Why?"

Howell would not look her in the eye. He said nothing. A slight wave of his hand and the waiter came over to take Betty's chair out for her signaling it was time to go. Betty gave him a look that could melt steel or freeze antifreeze. The waiter wisely removed his hand before it was handed to him. Betty got up from the table, walked around to face Howell eye to eye. There was a distant, sad look in his eyes. Betty slapped Howell as hard as she could across his face. Howell turned his cheek as if to say he deserved another and Betty gave it to him. Howell took the blows with no emotion.

Crying uncontrollably she ran out of the private dining room into the arms of the waiting maître d'.

"Ms. Thursten, I have a private car waiting for you outside," said Samuel gently as he led her out the front door and opened the waiting limo's door.

Thirteen

Early Dismissal

THE STRESS OF BECOMING a spy had been mounting. McFluffy's cavalier dismissal of Betty from the scanning session really meant nothing, but it was the straw that broke the camel's back. The stern look on her face belied the emotions tumbling inside her head and heart as she walked back to her quarters to rest for an hour before her next training session with Gil and Howell. Lying in bed, eyes closed, she dwelt on her failed relationships, especially Tom and Jil: abandonment without explanation. Tears began to form in Betty's eyes as she thought about the night Tom was taken over by the doppelganger Howell. *No one can see or hear me—just for this hour, I'll let myself wallow in self pity. Just for a bit.*

Dismissed by Howell. That was the only way she could read what had happened at the Capital Grille so many years before. Howell gave back the pendant, paid off his debts, and sent her on her way with the minor courtesy of arranging a car and her former best friend, Jil, to calm her down. *It wasn't right! Tom wouldn't have done this to me, only Howell would.*

Unbelievably, Jil had been waiting in the limo with no sure idea of what had happened but hoped she had been summoned for a happy occasion. Only a month before, Jil had slapped Betty for calling her a whore. Howell could not possibly have known about their fight; Jil would have lied or not said anything and Betty had not mentioned it to Tom. She did not care at that point; if Jil was willing to pretend nothing had happened, then so was Betty. She needed comfort and Howell was not going to give it to her. Her former best friend would have to do for the sake of dealing with what Tom—no—Howell had just said and done; she was willing to let bygones be bygones for the sake of her sanity.

"Jil! What are you…" stammered Betty at the sight of Jil.

"Where's Tom? I thought he was proposing?" Jil's tone changed as Betty's tear filled eyes turned to her and told the story.

"I don't know that man in there," said Betty as she dried her tears.

"What man? Who are you talking about?

"Did Howell tell you what he was going to do?"

"Weren't you having dinner with Tom?" Jil was confused by the quickly changing situation.

"That Howell has stolen my Tom. He's a doppelganger in Tom's body," said Betty as she turned the card repeatedly in her hands.

"I still don't know what went on inside there—will you please tell me?"

"Tom dumped me!" Betty began to shake as fresh tears poured forth.

"I'm so sorry." Jil reached over and gave her friend a deep hug. "I came because Tom asked me to and I wanted to be here for you."

"What, so you could gloat over Tom dumping me?" chided Betty as she looked down her nose at Jil.

"No, like you've been there for me," softly retorted Jil.

"That's just it..."

"What?" Jil was confused.

"I've always been there for you."

"I Know. You have."

"But you haven't been around lately when I've needed you!" Betty felt a rush of emotion, a longing for the simpler times with Jil.

"But I thought this was going to be a happy occasion!" Jil protested.

"Not this time, that doppelganger Howell has stolen Tom from me!" Betty felt the tears creeping out of her eyes.

"I'm sorry. I'm sorry for not being a better friend." Jil was looking down at her shoes. The ones she had picked out for a happy occasion.

"I forgive you. Just don't ever do it again," Betty was searching her clutch for a tissue, but could not see through her tears.

"Here, I at least came prepared for happy tears," Jil passed a handkerchief to her best and possibly only friend.

52   A. J. M a h l e r

After a few minutes of deep sobs, Betty used her finger to pull the flap open on the envelope. She read the note several times before handing it to Jil.

If you still love me a year from now, I will be waiting at the FDR Memorial near his statue at 4 p.m. on April 12th. I would not blame you for not showing, but I will be there.

Betty could not believe her eyes. "I want to both kill this man and run to him at the same time," stated Betty as she hit her fists against her thighs.

"I don't understand," said Jil as she put the note down.

"He was obviously hurting more, much more, than he was letting on. What could possibly have driven him so far away from me?" Betty wiped away her tears, put away the handkerchief and took Jil's hands in hers turning sideways to look Jil in the eye. "Don't be sorry for me. He hasn't told me everything. I just know he is hurting but won't tell me what it is."

"Why?"

Betty tried to put on a brave face, "You know guys, always trying to be tough."

Jil had heard about Babs on their walks through the monuments, but thought the situation was under control by both Betty and Tom. *The situation has changed,* Jil thought. "Are you sure it isn't that engineer, Babs? The one who went to Iraq with Tom?"

"It must be that Babs. Why didn't I see this sooner? He warned me that she was making moves on him, trying to lure him into her clutches." Betty was losing herself to the thought of the other woman.

"Men, they are so easily distracted!" said Jil as she stared out the window of the limo as traffic came to a halt. The flashing lights of police cars and motorcycles illuminated the night as the massive presidential motorcade drove past. Traffic would be stopped for at least fifteen minutes.

"Well, if that is what he wants, he can have her. I deserve better," said a distraught Betty.

Betty threw herself into the rich black leather of the limo and cried fresh tears. *How can I think that Tom would have weakened under Babs's advances? Don't I know him better? He is a strong man and wouldn't have willingly gone there. Oh, my mind is going in a thousand places.*

All of our...no...my plans for our future are thrown out the window like so much trash; thrown out by Howell. Betty grabbed her chest as if in pain, pain she felt because she loved him so deeply. "If I didn't love him so much, this wouldn't hurt so bad and I could walk away!" softly moaned Betty to no one in particular.

"Driver, stay put. I'm going to run in here while we're stuck and get a couple quarts of ice cream. Double chocolate and cookie dough?"

Betty nodded her head slowly and forced a small smile.

"When the motorcade clears we'll go to my place. You can borrow some pajamas. Tomorrow is Saturday and we'll walk the Mall. It will be good to get out and exercise in the morning. You don't want to go back to that loft tonight, do you?"

Betty nodded her head in agreement and started staring off at the commotion of the capital through wet and tired eyes. *So much history here. So much that has been done and yet to be accomplished. I'm still young. There is still time.*

Jil left the limo and was back before the fifteen minutes of motorcade passed by, ice cream in hand. "Men, they push you away when they really want to pull you close!" Jil exclaimed, trying to make sense of the strange events of the evening.

Another year will be an eternity, thought Betty. "I'm not going be the one to call or write. If Tom wants me, he'll have to be the one to call...or show up."

"You're going to meet him next year?" asked Jil incredulously.

"I don't know. My heart says yes," said Betty. *A thousand times, yes.* Betty began to cry once more.

As they entered the penthouse, Betty could see packing boxes and little left in the apartment of a personal nature. *It feels like yesterday that Jil threw me out or did I let myself out?*

After changing into warm pajamas and lighting a fire, Betty and Jil sat down on the living room couch to eat their ice cream.

"What are all the boxes for?" Betty took a large scoop of her double chocolate and cookie dough ice cream and licked the cold concoction off the spoon.

"I'm leaving him, the senator, that is. I am to get a place for myself and wait to be told what to do," Jil dug into her own large sample of ice cream.

"Who and what are you going to do for work?" Betty's tone became more critical. *Can I trust anything she tells me?*

"I won't be a call girl anymore!" Jil sounded hurt, but quickly moved on. "They are setting me up as a lobbyist, getting my own firm, can you believe it?" Jil chuckled slightly as she got busy with her dessert.

Betty was neither shocked nor pleased to hear the news. *It's an improvement, but not much. Jil is still selling herself; it's just more formal now.* "Whose setting you up?" pressed Betty.

"Oh, the company that helped Daddy get out of his mess—the white knight."

Betty started to form a sentence on her lips to press Jil harder for the facts but thought better of it. *More like an arranged marriage. Now isn't the time to get into it, though.* "Where are you going to live?" Betty stared at her spoon as she tried to focus on her ice cream to distract herself from her self-pity.

"I'm still looking, but they gave me some suggestions. I'll let you know, this time." Jil acknowledged her lack of forthrightness to Betty in that simple statement.

"Oh, crap!" Betty stabbed the ice cream back into the quart container and began crying all over again. Jil reached for Betty and caressed her; rubbing her hand on Betty's back with her chin on Betty's shoulder. *I don't know which one of us is worse off at the moment,* opined Betty. That judgment was going to have to wait until the light of another day and perhaps a little more distance between now and then.

FOURTEEN

DOING THE "RIGHT THING"

HOWELL HELD FIRM until Betty had left the private dining room of the Capital Grille. As soon as the maître d' had whisked her out, he collapsed. The pain was too much. The pain he felt at this moment was greater than any of the physical therapy pain in the past month and even, yes, even greater than the pain of having his right leg shattered by a landmine. This was gut wrenching and cruel. Cruel to Betty and cruel to himself. The near death experience he had in the desert was eye opening. He did not want to ever cause Betty the heartache of losing a loved one in combat. He had promised her he would return in one piece, that nothing would happen. A lot had happened. Babs had happened. Though he had remained faithful to Betty the whole time he was there, that kiss of compassion, the failure of doing his job to protect Babs, his failure to protect himself and by extension Betty, took a tremendous toll on his soul.

"You did the right thing," said Colonel Getner as he came in from the side door and put his hands on Howell's shoulders. Getner squeezed Tom's shoulders gently "Son, you did what you had to do and I am proud of you. That is one beautiful woman who loves you deeply. You get through this next year and I guarantee you that little lady will be there at FDR's statue if I have to put her there myself."

Howell brushed aside the colonel's hand from his left shoulder. "Betty has to be there because she wants to, not because you or I made her. Don't you see? I've given her the excuse, the reason to pass on meeting next year."

"You know how important our work is. We can't have any distractions, either of us. It's only for a year until things are settled down." Getner picked an olive off the plate and popped it into his mouth. "She loves you and will wait. You have nothing to worry about!"

"She's off the hook. Any little reason she has is now good enough." Howell straightened his shoulders and motioned to the busboy for his crutches. Getner pulled the chair out as Howell rose to his full height, keeping his right foot slightly off the ground as if it was tender. In reality, it was not the stump of his leg that was tender; it was his heart, shredded by his own words—shredded like his leg by the landmine. *I gave my leg for Babs and now I'm cutting out my own heart for Betty. I'm not sure which one hurts worse.*

Fifteen

Bouncing Betty

"**L**IEUTENANT. LIEUTENANT. I NEED YOU to stay with me," yelled the medic.

Howell's eyes fluttered, the Iraqi sand kicked up by the prop wash was too much, but by squinting he could see the medic's name. Richardson was shielding Howell's face from the wash of the chopper with his body, while trying to keep the damaged leg from getting any more contaminant than it already had. Howell grabbed the medic by the shirt collar and pulled him close.

"You take care of Babs first, do you hear me? That's an order," screamed Howell over the rotor wash.

Richardson looked at him like he was crazy and yelled into his ear, "Sir, you are in my world now. You don't out rank me in my world. We can't save her, but we can save your leg if we take care of you first. She isn't going to make it, Sir. Let me save your leg."

Howell griped tighter on Richardson's flight suit, pulled his .45 caliber M1911 from its holster and pointed it at Richardson's chest. "Take care of Babs first or so help me God you will be the next one to die."

Richardson thought Howell must be one crazy son of a bitch. This Babs must be something special to the lieutenant. He had not seen that kind of loyalty for a contractor before.

Babs was a mess. She had lost a lot of blood. Her face looked like it had gone three rounds with a cheese grater. Her chest was a mess of superficial shrapnel wounds; the flak jacket had done the best it could, but that close to the IED, a focused one, was too much for her upper torso. Her legs had been spared by the debris of the Humvee turret sitting between her and the second IED. They had come to inspect the tossed and tumbled shell of a Humvee taken out by the first IED. The explosive force caused the Humvee to tip over at high speed, tossing the turret fifty feet, rolling to a stop in front of the second IED. If it had not been for the turret, Babs would have died ten seconds after the explosion by bleeding out. As it was, she had a twenty-five percent chance of making it if you were a glass half full kind of guy. Richardson was the kind of guy that thought the glass had been the wrong size; contractors like Babs, women in general, should not be in the line of fire.

Richardson did the best he could to stabilize Babs, it was going to be close and he was not promising anything. She had lost a lot of blood from a lot of little wounds. She needed two units right away just to make it to base. After getting Babs on board, the medic returned to Howell. Richardson covered Howell with his torso while the chopper roared off. He released the tourniquet, but saw that the circulation was already compromised by the damage, time, and tourniquet.

The OZM-4 mine was of Russian origin; a knock off of the Nazi original S-mine. The mine bounds into the air with a solid cast-iron body that fragments: spraying shrapnel in all directions waist high, was lethal up to twenty meters and could inflict casualties up to one hundred meters away. Had Howell not been holding Babs's flak jacket and fallen to his back as the mine detonated, he surely would have died on the spot.

"Your leg looks pretty rough—I've seen worse," sugarcoated the medic. "Maybe save the knee, probably not," mumbled Richardson, drowned out by the noise of the approaching helicopter. The patella was dangling by the ACL. Richardson stabbed Howell with a shot of morphine. Howell relaxed some. He could still feel the pain, but the morphine kept him from caring.

The second chopper landed not far away. The marines loaded the lieutenant gingerly and took off for base.

"You're going home Lieutenant," shouted Gil Richardson over the roar of the rotor driven wind. "You're one lucky son of a bitch. I don't know how you survived that Bouncing Betty."

SIXTEEN

THE NIGHTMARE

THE RHYTHMIC SOUND OF BEEPS and whirs was slowly drawing Tom Howell out of his deep sleep. He really was not sure where he was. The sounds faintly reminded him of when he was a boy in the hospital, sleeping on the couch as his mother lay all wired up to machines. He was using his father's coat as a pillow. It had been snowing that day. The flakes were coming down slowly, big fat flakes that were piling up quickly outside. Normally, he would be building a snowman or a snow fort. Or playing soldier with his buddies using snowballs as hand grenades or running around with their mouths open to catch snowflakes on their tongues, drinking the fresh water that melted so quickly.

Tom was thirsty. A snowflake or two would be quite nice at the moment. Sounds surrounded Tom. Beeps, whistles, and a PA system calling for help stirred Tom from his slumber. He tried to open his eyes and rise up on his elbows, but a huge weight seemed to keep him down, like someone was sitting on his chest. Was it a ghost? No, it was that "Old Hag," the one from the Johahn Henrich Fuseli painting *The Nightmare*. Tom could remember from his college psychology class about sleep paralysis, when the brain awakes from a REM state, but body paralysis persists. Tom was fully conscious, but unable to move. Tom started to panic. He started to remember the mine leaping into the air as he tried to duck under the Humvee and cover himself with Babs's flak jacket. Had he been paralyzed? The panic grew until he suddenly was able to move his left arm. His right arm seemed to be tied down, but he was able to move his legs now, though his right leg seemed light...strange. He rubbed his eyes with his left hand as the beeps and whistles became more focused in his brain. He could hear someone talking in the distance, her voice slowly coming into focus. At first, he thought it was Betty coming to wake him from a bad dream.

"He's waking up," said a voice.

"Try to remain still. You are in the Landstuhl Regional Medical Center. You are coming out of sedation. Can you understand me?" A doctor was trying to calm Tom down, to make him realize where he was.

"What...what happened...Babs, did Babs make it?" stammered Tom.

Doctor Gilpin touched Tom's shoulder saying, "I don't know of any Babs. You came in by yourself. You were airlifted out of Iraq to Germany."

"Germany? What the hell?" asked a shaky Tom.

"You have suffered a serious concussion from a mine and apparently an IED as well." Doctor Gilpin slowly revealed the extent of Tom's injuries.

"Is that why my right leg feels funny?" pressed Tom.

Ignoring the question, Doctor Gilpin continued, "The rest of your wounds were mostly superficial and only required bandages or small stitches. Other than your leg you will be one hundred percent."

"Except for my leg? What does that mean? How can I be one hundred percent if there is something wrong with my leg?" Tom's agitation caught the attention of the nurse who increased the morphine drip.

"I am sorry, but we had to amputate your right leg above the knee."

"What...wait...am I going to be in a wheelchair?" asked a confused Tom.

"How you recover from here is up to you. You are going to be on some heavy pain meds for a few more days. We need you to rest. You'll be fitted with a prosthetic leg and start physical therapy in a couple of weeks, as soon as your skin has healed. You'll be transferred back state side when you are up to traveling. You're very lucky."

"Lucky? I'm missing my leg!" Tom pointed to the missing limb with his free left hand.

"Most of my patients who have experienced this type of trauma have suffered severe brain injuries. Get some rest, soldier, that's an order." The doctor turned and left as abruptly as he had come. He had many more patients to check on before his shift would be over.

The nurse pushed a button to release still more morphine into the IV drip stuck into his right arm and Tom's eyelids suddenly became very heavy, as well as his heart. He had so many questions to ask, but his mind was going back to the deep sleep. As the light faded, he knew his career with the army was over. His life was over. *What is Betty going to say when she sees me like this? Will I....*

SEVENTEEN

ANGLING FOR PRESTIGE

JIL HARPER HAD ALWAYS MOVED in the right circles, even as a child. Ballet classes led to a role in the annual *Nutcracker Suite*. Swim lessons led to the New York State title in the hundred-meter breaststroke and an athletic scholarship for college (even though her family did not need the money). Horseback riding, polo, beauty pageants, and talent contests; Jil was in them all. The one thing she did not seem to have as a child was time to be a child. Perhaps that is why she was not as serious about college as Betty. She did well, but just did not have the burning desire of an up and comer.

Betty had a very different upbringing. Her father was in middle management for IBM, stuck half way because he spent too much time with his family instead of going the extra mile for the company. Her mom was a schoolteacher before having children and returned to work when they were of school age. Betty was the middle child, between Rob and Bill. Beth Thursten made sure the children excelled at school while Robert Sr. coached the children in sports and made sure they enjoyed the outdoors. The family would frequently go off camping, mainly so the "men" could go fishing while the "women" took care of the campsite. Well, that was the theory. Betty rarely let the boys go with their father without her. On more than one occasion, a fistfight broke out between Betty and whichever brother was telling her she could not go fishing.

Betty often got the biggest or best fish and her mission was to do twice as well as her brothers to ensure she kept her spot in the boat. She learned to fight, cuss, and brag with the "men." When back in camp, she frequently had to do an about face: cleaning up her language as well as her looks to keep in her mother's good graces. Often, Beth insisted Betty stay behind to help with the chores. Betty complained it was not fair, but Mom was in charge.

Jil and Betty first met on one of these outings. Beth had made Betty stay behind. She was bored to tears when Jil walked up to say "hi." Jil's older sister Ruth was back from boarding school and wanted all of their mother Janice's attention, so Jil was pushed out of the Harper's camp. Betty was more than happy to socialize with Jil rather than do one more chore. Jil's father Larry became fast fishing buddies with Robert Sr. and adopted the two boys as his own.

The two girls became inseparable on the camping trip. Jil pulled Betty into her circle of friends and activities during their freshman year at Our Lady of Mercy High School. Betty enjoyed the rarefied air of Jil's life: the rich boys at the polo matches, the yacht club set, and the preparations for a pageant. She became Jil's lady-in-waiting and a big fish in a small pond.

When it came time to pick colleges there was no question that the two would find a way to be together. Jil had prestigious offers from Ivy League schools like Princeton, Harvard and lower status schools like Columbia, but she knew the limitations of the Thursten family. Betty applied for academic scholarships and won the usual little scholarships from the Rotary Club, Kiwanis Club, and partial scholarships to the big schools like Princeton. No single or combination of scholarships was enough to cover the tuition at a school that cost as much each year as her father's take home pay. Besides, Betty's brothers needed to go to school as well.

The good news came in the mail. Betty won a full ride academic scholarship to Syracuse University from IBM. Betty could work toward any degree as long as she also studied computational logic and mathematics. She called Jil to tell her she had news, important news. They needed to get together right away.

"Why can't you tell me over the phone?" Jil opined, "Besides, maybe I have something important to tell you."

"Fine, I guess you don't need to know where I'm going to college after all," pretend pouted Betty.

Jil knew this could only mean that Betty had gotten a full ride.

When they met at the Greece Ridge Mall, Betty could hardly

contain herself. Syracuse University had come through with a full ride scholarship sponsored by IBM, Robert Sr.'s employer. Jil was excited for Betty, but became serious when it was time to tell Betty her news. Jil had been accepted to both Princeton and Columbia. Those snobs at Harvard and Yale had snubbed her, but who cared about them. Sure, she was a fourth generation Princeton legacy on her Mom's side and anybody who was anybody could get into Columbia, but two out of the top five was not bad. Betty did not tell Jil that she had been accepted to all of those and more. What was the point? Betty's parents could not possibly afford an Ivy League school.

Jil could see that Betty was apprehensive. Rochester, Syracuse University, and Princeton University were hours apart. Neither girl liked to be away from their families let alone each other. Jil would talk to her parents. Something had to be worked out—something.

A week later, Jil called Betty to tell her she had exciting news and once again they found themselves at the Greece Ridge Mall. "I pushed and prodded my parents. I asked them to help you with your tuition or pull some strings for a scholarship."

"You did that for me?" gushed Betty.

"Why can't they do something? My parents told me that every family needs to make their own way through life. That your parents and you shouldn't be beholden or owe my family for you getting into a school."

"Well, they are right, I need to make my own way," said Betty.

"My dad was so mean, he said 'Besides, you girls can see each other on breaks.'" decried Jil.

"Well, he's just a stinker!" affirmed Betty.

"Nothing seemed to be working until Mom reminded Dad how he had gotten into school, that and how he had met Mom," Jil's self-righteous tone dripping as she began to describe the scene with her father.

"Dad looked down at his shoes for a moment before talking. His Topsiders are an emblem," Jil paused as she thought about all her designer clothes.

"An emblem?" queried Betty.

"Marking how far our family has come rather than where we're from. Dad got all sanctimonious and said," Jil began talking in a deeper voice to mimic her father's baritone, "'Your Great-Grandfather

Burt worked in the steel mill.' And I said as a manager, right? 'Not as a manager, but as a laborer, moving the steel from one process to the next.'"

Jil's imitation of her father amused Betty. "You do such a good imitation of your dad!" guffawed Betty, causing Jil to giggle with her.

"As a young man, my Grandpa Randall was encouraged to work in the fine restaurants as a busboy instead of the mill." Jil inspected her recently manicured hands for any dirt under the nails.

"Why? He wasn't going to make a fortune as a busboy!" Betty scrunched her nose up slightly imagining Jil's grandpa as a busboy.

"No, silly, by listening carefully to what the old men were saying at the club he was able to learn how to invest in stocks and bonds to make money," Jil explained.

"How was he going to invest on a busboy's wages?" Betty thought of the expensive technology stocks like IBM, Microsoft, and Intel that her dad had mentioned in passing.

"Grandpa Randall went to what's called a bucket shop. A parlor where you could buy part of a share," Jil gestured with her hands as if she was carrying a bucket.

"Oh, fractional shares?" Betty started to understand.

"Grandpa was a stock speculator." Jil looked down as she said, "Our fortune is made off of the backs of people like my Great-Grandfather Burt, the mill worker."

Betty looked into the distance as she searched her memory, "I don't remember ever hearing about your great-grandparents."

"They don't get talked about much." Jil paused to think of a way to explain. "Haven't you noticed that there aren't any really old photographs on our walls?"

"I guess I never noticed."

"Grandpa Randall was the kind of investor that would bet against a company and cause its stock to crash, making money on their failure."

Betty was shocked to hear this. "Was he stealing?"

"Oh, no, not stealing." Jil nervously giggled, "It's still legal to do this kind of investing, but it is harder to do."

"Harder?"

"Well, I don't know, Dad says it is. Anyway, Grandpa was a millionaire by his twenty-first birthday!"

"How did he do it so quickly?" asked Betty.

"He got hot tips from the big boys who felt comfortable bragging to the busboy. They didn't think he would actually do anything with the tips." Jil gave a knowing wink. "He worked during the day as a runner at the investment firm and at the restaurant at night. After the first million, he began spending all of his time just trading his own stock. He even had an office with a ticker tape machine installed," Jil explained.

So, the truth came out. Jil's grandpa had been a social climber. "He had wiped the coal dust off the family tree and refused to look back. Great-Grandfather Burt told Grandpa Randall he was a crook and wanted nothing to do with his money. Grandpa Randall wanted to buy his parents a house closer to New York City where he lived and worked. Soon, they weren't speaking to each other and not long after that Great-Grandfather Burt had a heart attack and died at age sixty-two."

"That is so sad! No wonder there aren't any pictures," sighed Betty. "What happened to your great-grandmother?"

"Great-Grandma Ruvie moved to New Jersey to be with her sister and after that there was no contact," Jil rubbed her arm gently as if soothing herself. "Grandpa never seemed to forgive himself nor could he ever make enough money."

"But, how did your parents meet?"

"Grandpa sent Dad to Princeton to marry well!" Jil exclaimed.

"No! Your parents love each other so much!" Betty protested.

"Mom and Dad found each other out of love, not social climbing, but it was the type of union grandpa wanted. Mom's family is old money and Dad's is nouveau riche."

"Oh, well, I see," Betty felt a little better about Janice and Larry.

"When I was little, Grandpa Randall had a heart attack and died at sixty-two, just like his dad," Jil looked sad as she described the family trait of a weak heart. "Grandma Sophia had already died the year before of breast cancer. Mom says Grandpa Randall died of a broken heart."

"That is such a sweet way to think of it," agreed Betty.

"Dad became obsessed with fear that he was next. Your dad eventually convinced him on one of their fishing trips that worrying about it was the last thing he should be doing," Jil touched Betty's arm as a thank you gesture.

"I remember when your family first started meeting up with ours at the camping spot. Now it's such a great annual event! Just think, we wouldn't be best friends otherwise," Betty gave Jil a big hug. "But what about college?"

"Dad relented, we're going to Syracuse together!" exclaimed Jil, who then gave Betty a big hug back.

Eighteen

The Cancer Within

THE LONG WINDING ROAD to Control was filled with sharp switchbacks. Traffic to the remote former mineshaft was limited to approved trucks and cars by a network of guard posts. The road was dangerous for a reason—narrowing sometimes to barely one lane without a guardrail—and the only way in by ground. A short stretch of road covered with pine trees served as the landing strip. A small opening in the treetops barely allowed for the landing and takeoff of small jets and helicopters. The staff that worked at Control did not actually know where it was and neither did the drivers or pilots. Special equipment was installed and with training, pilots were able to navigate with IFR (instrument flight rules) that worked like a video game. The vehicles used by Control on this road had blacked out windows. The drivers navigated by a GPS that only indicated if they should steer left or right, speed up, slow down, or stop. This 'video game' was pretty simple, but you only got one life. Their only job was to keep the aircraft or truck in the middle of the "lines" that represented the road or airspace they were in. The job was deadly if you did not pay attention. Very effective for preventing anybody from knowing where Control was located. People were expendable, but Control was sacred.

If a driver ever did try to find his or her way without the shades blocking their view, they would find that the road, besides being incredibly dangerous to drive on, had so many forks, switchbacks, and dead ends that it would take a miracle to find the way without the GPS software. Pilots who did fly this route equated it to evasive maneuvers of combat. Trying to straighten out that flight path would take a genius and ten years. In reality, Control was only thirty minutes as the crow flies from the capital, but one mile underground. There were twenty checkpoints between leaving D.C. and arriving at your destination. The guards were instructed to shoot to kill and occasionally they did, though the rumor mill claimed these were staged to keep everyone on their toes.

Someone once knew everything about this place in order to design and build the facility. They are now either dead or in a mental institution enjoying a frontal lobotomy. Even Howell and Getner were only given partial knowledge; compartmentalization was the key to protecting Control. You were only told as much as you needed to know and no more. No one knew for sure when Control was built. It was at least thirty years old, but it might as well be a hundred years old.

There were very powerful states, organizations and, more to the point, influential powers that did not want Control to exist. These forces could gain control of the United States and then the world if Control were eliminated. Whenever one of the powers got too close, an accident would set them back. The trail led to a black hole and always went cold. The void of information indicated something was there, even if it could not be seen. Someone or something was stopping the takeover. Accidents just did not happen this consistently. The continued existence of the United States of America hinged on Control being more secret than the codes to the nuclear weapons the president of the United States had at his disposal.

Less than a hundred souls were lost creating and protecting Control. Less than the number of lives lost creating the Hoover Dam. To date, at least two million lives have already been saved by Control. People who will never know the danger they were threatened with. Control was threatened now; not by some huge red army or even a lone pilot with a plane full of TNT. Control was threatened from within by a single mole. This cancer had to be cut out—before Control died.

NINETEEN

A ROSE IS A ROSE IS A ROSE

THE GLINT OF THE KNIFE was all that could be seen in the moonless night. A distant yard light had come on via a motion detector triggered by a barking dog sounding the alarm: intruder amongst us! A black form paused to gauge the danger, by *the sound of it, a German shepherd behind a fence.* The drowsy pet owner aroused from a nap in front of a television long enough to step out into the chill of the autumn evening to yell at the dog to be quiet. *The fools. If they only knew what the dog knows*, thought the intruder as he moved silently through the back yards of this suburban dream bent on one thing only with no concern for a dog's alarm.

Tha-tink, tha-tink went the knife as it cut. *A little more,* thought the black form, *just a little bit more. Tha-tink, tha-tink. There. That's enough.* The prize was carefully wrapped in a wet paper towel, followed by saran wrap. Tin foil or newspaper would make noise; the saran wrap was almost silent but a bitch to control once off the roll. As quickly and quietly as he could, Tom retreated to his black Nissan 280z. He drove the short distance to Betty's apartment in Georgetown as quickly as he could without drawing attention to himself.

During and now after law school, Betty shared an apartment with Jil on the first floor of an old Georgetown brick townhouse that had been cut up into four apartments. A foreign student, with a name only Betty could pronounce, occupied the basement apartment. The back entrance served the basement, second, and third floors. The doorbell on the front door was an old-fashioned mechanical brass bell with the turn on the outside of the massive bright red wooden door. Ivy clung to the brick portal giving it a mantel of green that seemed to simultaneously welcome you and warn you that you would soon be ensnared and swallowed by the building once you crossed its threshold. Ivy lips, giant red tongue, and limestone teeth.

Tom turned the flat kidney shaped brass handle causing the bell's clapper to strike the dome with a distinctive and startling *drrriiiinng*. He always twisted the handle quickly at first and let off at the end to make the biggest, sharpest ring he could. Betty frequently complained that he needed to use the modern doorbell, the push button type with the round metal housing and glowing pale yellow plastic button. The more archaic bell gave Tom a sense of control and ensured Betty knew that it was him at the door.

"Tom, what a surprise! When are you going to learn to use the doorbell? You about gave me a heart attack with that thing. I've asked Mr. Martin to remove it, but he just won't do it." She was wagging her finger at Tom until her eyes got wide and her attitude changed as Tom crossed the threshold producing the prize-winning roses from behind his back.

He had taken the flowers out of their wrappings and placed them in a vase he had brought; wider at the top than at the bottom with a shiny smooth metal rim. He had acquired the vase from a receptionist who had received one too many arrangements from an admirer. Tom would have re-used the flowers too, but they were already past their prime; however, the fern and frilly white embellishments were still in good shape. A little trim off the bottom and they were as good as new. He had washed out the vase in the office kitchenette; carefully drying it to remove fingerprints and smudges to make it appear new again. Betty could not take her eyes off the flowers in the vase as she escorted Tom into the living room.

"Tom, this is Jil's friend George...I'm sorry, George I don't remember your last name?"

George stood up sticking out a tan, manicured hand. Tom took the proffered hand and George pumped while grabbing Tom's elbow. Tom noticed the softness of a hand not used to doing anything more arduous then signing a business letter or contract.

"George Van Huesen. It's a pleasure to meet you Tom; you're all the girls have talked about for the past thirty minutes," George commented with a wry and now understanding tone.

"George is a banker, what is it...investments?" distracted by the flowers and Tom, Betty carelessly searched for the right word.

"I'm a fund manager over at Goldman Sachs, actually. Well, our dinner reservations are in fifteen minutes, we better get moving," said George.

Jil stood up and put her arm around George's. Tom could tell, now that they were standing next to each other, that George was older, maybe ten years older than Jil. Though he had only known Jil a short time, this did not seem to be her 'type' of date. George was too stuffy and formal for the fun loving adventurous Jil.

Dinner was at the Capital Grille. The tab was going to be a stretch for Tom this evening. On a first lieutenant's salary and the cost of living in the capital, it was all Tom could do to keep up with his new friends. He had stolen the vase and the flowers to cut costs, though he would pay for it later with a guilty conscience. The only way he was going to be able to pay for this dinner was with a tactical maneuver.

"Dinner is on me tonight," George announced as they were being seated.

Tom sighed relief, but this would put him at a disadvantage and appear to be a piker if he did not do something. "George, let me at least take care of the wine," Tom defended his honor.

Tom called the sommelier over, "Marcus, please bring us a 1985 Mondavi Cabernet Sauvignon from the locker." Tom knew his father well: The 1985 Mondavi while a nice red was below the normal quality Mr. Howell preferred for his dinners. Social climbers and bores did not deserve the finer wines from the wine locker and would not know any better. He would never miss the bottle. "I am sorry Lieutenant Howell, but your father took the last bottle not an hour ago. May I suggest the Opus One instead?" winked the all-knowing Marcus. Tom was trying to use discretion in taking wine from his father's locker at the Capital Grille. The Opus One was a very special wine. He would pay dearly for this indiscretion when his father found out later. At least he now had the advantage over George, the investment banker.

The dinner conversation was varied and delightful like the prime rib that evening. When it was time to go, George and Jil hailed a cab for a night of partying with the rich and famous. Tom knew when he was out of his league and begged off, claiming a meeting in the morning and he could not afford to lose too much sleep. "Generals, you know, are so demanding," said Tom.

Betty and Tom took a cab back to Betty's apartment; the conversation turned to Jil's date, George.

"I don't know where she met him, you know she is well connected with her family, but, I don't know Tom, the whole night seemed strange."

"How so?"

"Jil was giving George far more attention then she usually does with her dates."

"Yeah, you're right, usually she gets all of the attention—queen bee."

"Of course I'm right. George would be the type trying to impress Jil to get her father's business, not the other way around."

Tom looked at his hands, rough from military duty and pointed out, "George's hands were soft, and the difference in ages."

Betty looked sideways at Tom, "My, no details got by you, Mr. Observant."

There did not seem to be any answers that evening for the mystery behind George. At Betty's door, Tom begged off coming in to talk more, "I really do have a meeting with a general in the morning and I have to finish my report."

Betty stood on her toes reaching for Tom's lips. A delicate sweet kiss, just a little pressure, leaning in to let him know he did well tonight. "The flowers are beautiful," *though suspect!* "and the wine was amazing," *but obviously purloined from your father's locker.* She was going to have to keep a close eye on this resourceful first lieutenant.

TWENTY

SWIMMING WITH SHARKS

THE DAY AFTER the double date, Jil tried to hide the bruise on her face. Betty was already in the kitchen making coffee when Jil came into the room. *Do you think I'm an idiot? Your concealer doesn't fool me.* "Everything O.K.?" Betty prodded.

"Wasn't last night fun?" Jil deflected.

Yeah, I always enjoy a good beating by my date, don't you? Betty put on a goofy face to cover up her serious thoughts, "I'm sorry we were party poopers, Tom is dedicated to his work, though we all are. Did you and George do anything fun after we left?" Betty pared away at Jil's defenses.

"It was party, party, party! George can get into the best clubs. I'm sure I dumped a grand of liquor into the potted plants or I'd be in a coma this morning." She kept her right cheek turned away from Betty, but Jil was only delaying the inevitable. The bruise was a symptom, what led to the bruise was the problem.

Betty was no fool, she noticed Jil hiding the bruise with the cupboard and her general evasiveness of the past few weeks. *Jil always has money to spend, even when we were young. Folding money is what Larry calls it, just enough so his little girl would never be dependent on anyone, except of course, Larry.* "How is work going for you at the senator's office? Everything O.K.?" Betty pried a little harder.

"Oh, Bolden always has something for me to do. My work is changing, though." Jil did not really answer the question.

"You've been going out a lot lately during the week. Doesn't that make it hard to get through your workday at the Capitol Building?" Betty saw a crack in Jil's facade.

"Oh, I manage. Just some fun guys asking me out lately. Can't hardly turn down a good time, can I?" Jil's parries to Betty's thrusts were weak, but successful. "Besides, the senator doesn't pay me enough to mind a nap now and then."

Anything Jil needs or wants she only has to make a call. Her father is the only man she has ever cowed to! "Say, I want to take the rent check over a week early, maybe I can get Mr. Martin to remove that monstrosity of a brass bell by sweet talking him. Is that O.K. with you?"

"Oh, well, I kind of like that bell." Jil hemmed and hawed. "I won't be able to give you my half until after the first."

"Why, is something wrong? You always have 'folding money.'" Betty pressed harder.

"Daddy wants me to find a better paying job and my work with Bolden's office was arranged when Daddy was the senator's biggest bundler. Now he isn't raising any money, so my salary got cut to nothing." Jil conveniently forgot to mention being fired.

Betty knew the story well. Larry had raised a million dollars for the senator's re-election campaign by throwing a dinner party and inviting his well-heeled friends. The Harper jet had been ready on a moment's notice for any campaign trip the senator might need to take and there had always been a limo waiting for him at the airport courtesy of Larry. Senator Bolden may have been originally elected to the Senate without Larry's help, but his re-election was secured by the support of the Harper organization. There were whispers that perhaps in the next election cycle Bolden might be a long shot for president; running would at least test the waters for the vice presidency. Larry had wanted to make sure his horse was well positioned for that race.

Jil looked down at her leopard skin slippers and bit her lip. "Oh, fuck it! Bolden fired me because Daddy is broke." Real tears began to crest where only crocodile tears dare tread.

"Cut the crap! What's going on for real?" Betty was done beating around the bush.

"Daddy used to work just to maintain Grandpa Randall's fortune, but a year ago he tried to make a move to prove he was capable of succeeding on his own." Jil refilled her coffee cup and wiped her tears with the tissue offered by Betty.

"What did he do?"

"Daddy made a big bet, all of our fortune, on a merger deal with a manufacturing company. Betting on technology Initial Public Offerings just isn't good enough anymore with the downturn."

"It's not 1999 anymore, is it?" comforted Betty.

"There hasn't been a decent IPO for him to invest in for two years!" Jil sounded hurt, as if her father's failures were a personal affront.

"How did you find out?" Betty was seeing a new side of Jil, the desperate, moneygrubber underneath the thin veneer of lifelong wealth.

"Well, you know how we always fly home for Thanksgiving and this year we drove back?"

"Yes, you said we should take my car back because my dad wanted to have it serviced and you didn't mind taking the time off. Why?" Betty still was not sure where Jil was going with this.

"Daddy had to sell the jet. The maintenance costs and the staff payroll were too much to keep up with. When you mentioned your dad wanting the car back in Rochester for service, it gave me the excuse to not tell you about the jet." Jil was looking down at her coffee, her checks red with embarrassment. "Desperate times called for desperate measures."

"Why would you say that?" Betty tilted her head to the side slightly and squinted her eyes as if she might see into Jil's mind that way.

"Daddy says I'm on my own. He'll send money if and when he can, but that I need to come up with a better paying job. Senator Bolden, what a slime ball!"

"Slime ball? You've always talked positive about him!" Betty was confused.

"He wanted to give me a better paying job, all right! He wants to set me up in an apartment near his house so he can drop in on me at his leisure. Dirty old man!" Jil shivered as she emphasized the last point.

"What have you been doing the past few months? You've been leaving in the morning to go to the Capitol Building!" Betty was not sure how this could get any more bizarre.

"Well, I do go in from time to time. Most of the day I am shopping for outfits for my 'dates.'" Jil looked off into the distance as if she wanted to be anywhere but at the kitchen table explaining herself.

"Your dates? I've noticed you've had a lot of guys like this George guy coming around. They don't fit your normal type. What gives?" Betty thought back over the past month to the random well-healed yet slimy guys Jil had been seeing.

"I was getting desperate. You know I always have money to spend and I didn't want to disappoint you, the rent check. As it turns out, Sara, at the senator's office introduced me to a guy, John Spector." Jil sounded almost robotic talking about this new twist.

"What does this John do?" Betty was unrelenting, quickly jumping in with more questions to prod Jil.

"Mr. Spector runs an escort service. I'm doing the same work as Sara now, paid to entertain gentleman in town on business trips, keep them from being lonely is all."

"You're a hooker?" Betty was aghast and astonished.

"Not a sex job, not a hooker!" Jil looked aghast.

"Well then, what kind of job is this?"

"Just a well paid date to make the guy look good to his friends or just to keep him from sitting in a hotel room drinking from the mini bar, watching pay-per-view while he waits for the sun to come up." Jil defended her honor.

"You make it sound so, legit." Betty tersely responded.

"I wasn't going to take the job, but Sara seemed to think it was the easiest money she had ever made and she says she always has a great time."

"So, Sara recruited you?" Betty was trying to be sympathetic, but it was not easy.

"Sara chats endlessly at Bolden's office about her fantastic dates the previous weekend. Besides, she pointed out I would know how to fit in, I've been around these guys all my life." Jil seemed to be getting her footing again as she justified her work.

"I don't remember you meeting the type of guys who would pay for a date!" Betty was not letting her off easy.

"Oh, Betty, you'd be surprised how many guys have hired an escort or used a hooker. They're all bastards! Besides, John boasted he could charge a fifty percent premium for my services. Hell, I can make a thousand dollars a night if I treat the guy right and give him a happy ending," Jil blushed as she said the last part realizing she was contradicting herself on what she had previously claimed. "This is only temporary, until Daddy gets the deal done so he can sell off part of the company to fix his cash flow," she quickly added.

Betty was stunned by Jil's revelations. She had not seen it coming. *So that's why Jil is doing it! Money!* One detail seemed to be missing in the story. "So, uhm, how did you get that awful bruise?"

Jil touched her face, just below her right eye. "During the cab ride to the Apre', I commented about the wine, the Opus One, how it had really complimented the meal. George got mad. He said that the conversation had been about Tom all night and wasn't he paying good money for my attention?"

"He hit you, didn't he?" Betty crossed her arms and held her elbows, trying to protect herself from what Jil was revealing.

"Yes. That's when George swung and hit me on the right cheek with the back of his hand," Jil winced as she relived the moment. "The worst part was I had to take it. There is no way out. Spector won't give me anymore clients if I ever bail on a client, even if he's a bastard who hits."

"I thought pimps were there to protect you?" Betty derided Jil's position.

"Fuck you! John won't let George back if it matters to you, but I still have to take it or the business dries up. I needed the money to make this month's rent and to pay off my credit cards," Jil got up from the table and threw her mug into the dish drainer.

"So, two months ago Senator Bolden fired you to stem the damage caused by your dad's business problems?"

"He didn't fire me—he took me off the payroll." Jil's attitude turned. Now she was defending her family's honor, but there was nothing to defend. "Daddy tried to use Bolden's influence to finish the merger deal. A special tax break was attached to the omnibus spending bill to give daddy huge tax breaks he could sell to other companies to pay for the merger."

"Why does that matter? This town is filled with lobbyists pushing for this or that loophole." Betty was not seeing the connection.

"Someone leaked the deal to the press. This tax break only benefits one company," Jil looked ready to bolt from the room. "Even if it is an important military supplier, the impropriety of the quid pro quo, the obvious payout to a major contributor was too much for Bolden to face, what with his presidential aspirations and the ethics committee inquiry pending."

"That asshole!" Betty finally found something she could agree with Jil on.

"There was going to be blood in the water and it wasn't going to be Bolden's. He cut our ties quick, but he still needs me on some of our projects, so I come in as an unpaid consultant occasionally to tie things up. He promises he'll make things right later when the trouble settles down." Jil looked like she had a bad taste in her mouth. "That and he wants me to be his girl on the side."

"You have to stop this, now!" Betty got up from the table to give Jil a hug. "We can solve this. You don't need to be doing this."

"I can't pay the rent or my credit cards if I don't!" Jil protested.

"Mr. Martin will let things slide a little while on the rent and besides, we can always move to a cheaper place." Betty grabbed Jil's face and looked her in the eye. "We'll find a new job for you. We can get through this—together."

Jil began to sob softly.

"I may have only graduated last May, but I am doing really well at work." Betty did not normally boast, but now was not the time for modesty on her part. "I don't start paying back my student loans for a couple of months; besides, I can defer payment for a while."

"You're too good to me," Jil pushed her wet face into Betty's shoulder, snuggling into her friend's generosity.

"See, it will be OK. I know you are worried about your father and things look bleak right now, but you'll see, things always work out," said Betty as she patted Jil's back while Jil pulled her tight.

TWENTY-ONE

FETCHING, ISN'T SHE

TOM STIRRED HIS COFFEE SLOWLY as he listened to Betty. He nodded his head and encouraged her from time to time. The story that was unfolding was amazing. Jil's family was in deep trouble; their suspicions about George Van Huesen had been well grounded. It seemed strange to Betty not to have Jil around anymore. Jil went back to Rochester, New York, to be with her family in this time of crisis. The Harpers were all alone. The people they had counted on to support them in this hour of need had turned on them or, even worse, profited off their losses. Betty wished she could go back to help, but there really was not anything she could do. Her chosen career, immigration law, held little value in the fight the Harpers were going through.

Tom held Betty's hand, rubbing his thumbs gently over her smooth olive skin. He said, "I am so sorry for Jil and her family, if there was anything I could do I would. Do you want me to talk to my father?"

This amazed Betty; that Tom cared so much that he was willing to seek advice and help on behalf of the Harpers from his father. Tom had become estranged from his father at the end of high school. "What really happened between you and your dad?"

Tom hesitated before finally telling Betty the story. "I could have played football at any decent state college and even had partial scholarship offers—even a couple of Ivy League schools. Not that it would have mattered. My father could afford the tuition at any school, including the Ivy Leagues."

"You've never really talked about your parents before. Where did you father go to school?" Betty pressed gently, not wanting Tom to stop.

"Father was a Notre Dame graduate and wanted me to follow in his footsteps. The old man said, 'Hell, you can be a walk-on, make the team like that Rudy kid, but you'll certainly be joining my fraternity and the other clubs!'"

Betty laughed at Tom's impersonation of his father, giggling until Tom started to laugh too, but then he got serious. "We argued constantly during my senior year—mostly about college. I wanted to go to Annapolis or West Point."

"Don't you need a congressional nomination?"

Tom nodded slowly while staring at his coffee cup deep in thought. "Why couldn't he help me? He knows the senators and congressmen and with one call he could get me an appointment!"

"He didn't want you to go into the military?" Betty caressed Tom's hand, coaxing more from him. "Did he serve?"

"He told me it wasn't required anymore. 'Why put yourself through all that bullshit? There isn't a draft anymore, why take the risk?'"

Betty did not laugh this time at Tom's imitation. She had a somber look on her face. *Tom is still hurting.*

"Father had avoided combat; let alone any danger, but who knew? He never would tell me what he had been doing during WWII except that he was over in Europe for the duration. Some kind of aid agency."

"Maybe he just didn't want to lose his son or see you hurt?" queried Betty.

"He said 'You aren't interested in politics, so why take the chance? Hell, even if you were, Reagan made it all the way to president without front line experience, didn't he?' He just didn't understand me. I just wanted to serve my country, do my part. Maybe if he had done something important during the war he would have felt differently."

"What did you do after that?"

"I secretly applied to the military academies and even forged his signature on letters to the senators to get what I wanted. Ultimately, I went to Virginia State University and joined the ROTC program to pay my way. He cut me off and I wouldn't talk to him." Tom rubbed his face with the palm of his hand and took a sip of his Peruvian dark roast. "He discouraged me from coming home on holidays and breaks, which broke my mother's heart."

"What a jerk! I can't believe your mom let him get away with that!" Betty chided.

"After a few years, it became obvious to him I wasn't going to give in first. Mom finally prevailed on father to allow me to come home for extended visits," Tom sounded like a warrior retelling a well-worn war story.

"How did it go? The visits?"

"They tended to end sooner than planned. Very uncomfortable. I'd make excuses to head back to school early," Tom shrugged his shoulders as if to say what else could I have done?

"You were a good student, weren't you?"

"I graduated from VSU with honors. I had been an above average student in high school—the usual story, great in sports and the social scene, but not in the top twenty percent academically. In college, I took my studies seriously, more to bury myself in knowledge and keep my mind from wandering to my family."

"Well, you were paying for college with ROTC. How could you have any spare time?"

"I rarely left campus other than for ROTC related trips. I didn't date much and never had a serious girlfriend in college. I was on a mission to prove my father wrong."

The conversation stalled and both were quiet for a long time. Holding hands and sipping their coffees, they were just enjoying each other's closeness.

"You're the first girl I've been serious about since high school. Remember how we met?"

"I was walking Surry." Surry was an unusual mix of Weimaraner and Black Labrador. Betty liked to call Surry a *Black Wab* for short.

"I said to myself, wow, that is a gorgeous animal, fit, trim, and born to run!"

"You talking about me or my dog?" Betty playfully slapped Tom on the shoulder. Surry would go seven or even eight miles with Betty on their training runs and look at Betty as if to say, "Is that all?"

"Did you know my father obtained one of the first breeding pair of Weimaraners allowed to leave Germany? Just after WWII. When I was ten I was allowed to keep one of the puppies from a litter and named it Miles."

"You miss Miles, don't you?"

"I do, but my commitment to the military—I can't see having a dog," sighed Tom. "Guess I'm just lucky to have you and Surry."

"What happened to Miles when you went to VSU?" Betty was not sure if she should ask, but pushed on.

"My father put him down. Cold bastard, that one." Tom looked like a tear might creep out of his eye, but he forced a smile, "He was getting old." Tom was making an excuse for his father and shrugged the thought away.

"Weimers are such aristocratic dogs, but I had never seen one mixed like Surry, she is a beautiful dog, let alone such a beautiful owner!" Tom winked at his girlfriend. "You have a way of carrying yourself that says I know what I am doing and I know where I am going."

"I didn't notice my mittens though, did I?"

"Surry had picked one up off the ground and could not get the other one, her mouth was already occupied. I picked up the mitten and called out to the beautiful, purposeful owner—"

"That would be me!" Betty beamed brightly.

"—who seemed oblivious to her loss!"

"Oh, but what about your sappy line? 'She is quite fetching. Very beautiful. What's her breed?' I thought to myself, this guy is desperate!"

"Yeah, but you blushed and smiled. And I got you, didn't I?"

"Yeah, cause you were stalking me! Everywhere I turned, there you were!" Betty mocked Tom.

"I'd chat you up when I saw you, pet Surry. Sure." Tom looked down at his freshly empty mug.

"You borrowed your friend's dog to get a play date with Surry!" Betty wagged her finger. "You didn't need a dog to see me. You just needed to pick up the phone and ask me out."

Betty reached across the table, taking Tom's hands in hers just like that day long ago, interlacing her fingers with his and said, "It's really sweet of you to offer to call your father, but I don't know what he could do for the Harpers. I'm sure they'll figure things out on their own." Betty could not help but remember *Besides, Larry thought my family needed to find our own way to get me into a good school. Karma—what goes around comes around,* thought Betty.

TWENTY-TWO

OPERATOR!

THE PHONE RANG waking Betty. With one eye open, she read the glowing numbers on the clock. *Who the hell would be calling at three in the morning on a Tuesday?* thought Betty as she fumbled for her phone. *Someone on the west coast and oblivious to the time difference? Surry! You just had to eat the damn answering machine!* The phone kept ringing.

Well, I'm awake now, might as well answer the damn thing. "Who is this?" asked an annoyed and sleepy Betty.

"Hello?...Betty," a very shaky Jil was on the other end of the line.

Betty was really awake now. It had been several months since Jil had gone back to her parents. Betty had briefly taken on a roommate to help with the rent until Mr. Martin helped her find an efficiency apartment nearby and let her out of her lease.

"I'm in trouble...I need you to come get me," Jil pleaded.

Betty was confused. *Jil went back to Rochester, didn't she?* "Where are you Jil? What's wrong?"

"I'm at the payphone by the Washington Monument. I'm being chased. I don't have much..." pleaded Jil as a loud metallic bang resounded through the line.

Betty could hear that the phone must have been dropped at the other end. The loud *thud, thud, thud* of the receiver bouncing off the sides of the aluminum shell was followed by dead air. Betty could hear screaming in the distance cut off by the click of the handset being slammed onto the hook. The line went dead. Betty could not believe her ears. *Why is Jil in Washington, why is she being chased? What the hell is going on?*

Betty dialed *69 to call back, but there was no answer. She dialed 911.

"911 Operator, what's your emergency?"

"My friend has been kidnapped!" Betty screamed into the handset.

The operator took the details and said she would dispatch the Capitol Police immediately to the scene. "Stay on the line, please."

Betty heard a conversation with a policeman in the background. In a few minutes, the operator was back on the line.

"I have Officer Donnelly here on the line, Ms. Thursten; he is on site and has located your friend."

"Is she OK?"

"Everything is fine. She says to apologize to you."

"Apologize? Why, what did she do?"

"She says that she had a little too much to drink at the Smithsonian reception this evening. She is being given a ride home by the officer and she will call you in the morning," reported the operator before ending the call.

Click.

Betty was more confused now than when the phone rang the first time waking her. *My God,* thought Betty, *what has Jil gotten herself into?* Betty made a pot of coffee and sat at her kitchen table waiting for the sun to come up. *I can't go back to sleep and there isn't anything I can do until I know where Jil is staying—and grill her for some answers.*

Twenty-Three

Just for the Halibut

"**I** HAVE SENATOR BOLDEN'S office on line twelve," said Margaret, Betty's legal assistant. Betty took the call, half expecting someone from the senator's office to be calling to find out where or what was up with Jil, instead it was Jil herself.

"How are you?" started a way too chipper Jil. "I am so sorry I didn't let you know I was in town."

"What the hell, Jil? When did you get back into town?" Betty glared through the phone; annoyed that Jil was so chipper after such a late night.

"I just got back this last weekend and was going to call you as soon as I got settled," Jil was trying to smooth things over.

"Why didn't you call? You could have stayed at my place," Betty did not like being out of the loop. *I sound like I'm giving her a deposition. Take a deep breath!*

Jil stammered, "I've been on the run since I got here. I didn't think it would be fair to let you know I was back if I couldn't come over and at least have a cup of coffee with you."

"What's got you so busy? Did you have a job lined up?" Betty tried to turn down the inquisition, but Jil was being a little too secretive.

"I have been swamped getting back up to speed with the senator. Come meet me tomorrow for lunch, my treat," entreated Jil.

"What are you up to?"

"You aren't going to believe it."

"I don't believe you called at three a.m.!"

Jil rolled right along as if Betty was not baiting her. "Daddy's project worked out after all. Everything is going to be fine."

Betty was glad to hear the good news, but was not going to let Jil gloss over last night. "What the hell are you talking about Jil? Why were you calling me at three in the morning all frantic that you were being chased?"

Jil demurred, "Oh, I was drunk off my ass and was getting tired of being chased by the boys. You know how persistent they can be at times. I'm fine, really. Meet me for lunch tomorrow and I'll explain everything!" implored Jil.

Something isn't quite right with Jil's tone. The beauty pageant, I am perfect, ignore any flaws that you see, please, voice she reserves for meetings and events. "Where and when?" Betty did not like waiting.

"Le Bon Café at ten forty-five," Jil sounded rushed.

Betty thought the time was rather odd, "Ten forty-five?"

"To avoid the noon hour crush of bodies. You know how popular Le Bon Café is with the young staff on the hill."

"I suppose, it is usually packed by noon." Betty had met Jil there from time to time before when she had worked for Senator Bolden.

"I have to go! Toodles!" and Jil hung up without waiting for Betty's goodbye.

Betty yelled, "Margaret!" before looking at the door. Margaret was standing there with her pad and pen.

"Yes?"

"I hate it when you do that!"

"I heard you hang up; I just assumed you would need me." Margaret had an impish look on her face that turned to a slight pout.

Betty scanned her calendar for conflicts. "I need to clear my schedule from ten-twenty to twelve-thirty."

"Your meeting with the partners is from eleven to one, but Jan will reschedule everyone if I ask her to." Margaret looked proud that she had pull with the other staff.

"Do you know of anything I need to deal with before then?" Betty was not going to miss this lunch date.

"Maybe you should remind Mr. Donavan about his daughter's recital at school tomorrow? It's from eleven-thirty to twelve-thirty across town." Margaret had a concerned look on her face as if it was of the utmost importance for Mr. Donavan to attend his daughter's second grade music recital.

"Yes, that would be a good idea!" Betty made a mental note to give Margaret a favorable review next month.

"Oh, and Ms. Sullivan's aunt's funeral visitation is tomorrow. She was going to skip it for the meeting." Margaret was nodding her head as if to say she knew everything that was going on in the office.

"Anything else I need to be made aware of?" asked Betty.

Margaret's smile spread across her face before she could cover it with her hand. "Well, if a box of jelly filled donuts ended up in the conference room across from Millberg's office, well, can you say sugar coma by ten?"

"I assume you can take care of that. I'll remind the partners of their family responsibilities." Betty shooed Margaret out of her office with a wave of her hand.

✝

When Betty arrived, Jil to her astonishment had already ordered lunch and had it ready to go.

She offered two bags to Betty and asked, "Smoked turkey club on farm bread or grilled halibut Niçoise salad?"

Betty chose the salad with narrowed eyes to make sure Jil knew she did not know where Jil was going with this.

Jil grabbed her arm and said, "Let's walk, it will stimulate our appetites and the fresh air will do me good."

They walked down 2nd Street half a block and turned east on C Street toward Seward's Square. This was not unusual for them to do, but it was unusual for Jil to be so secretive. They chatted about nothing for a while as if to see what the other would bring up. When they got to the park, they sat down in the grassy triangle made up by Pennsylvania Avenue, North Carolina Avenue and 4th Street. The sky was an amazing azure blue with a slight wind that kept you from getting too hot in the late spring sun. Betty thought about taking her sweater off but the warmth of the sun felt nice.

As Jil took her first bite of the smoked turkey sandwich, Betty began to quiz her friend about this secrecy, "We've been living together since high school for God's sake, why are you keeping anything from me?"

Jil started by explaining, "Father's bet on the leveraged buyout was going very poorly. It looked like we were going to lose everything for a while."

"It sure sounded desperate."

Jil ignored her friends comment. "Then another company came in and helped him get the deal done."

"How did they do that? A loan or something?"

"I don't know all the details and he won't tell me, but he had to give up a significant piece of the ownership, but that was better than losing everything."

"I suppose he didn't have any better options."

Looking contemplative, Jil hesitated before continuing, "We're even going to have a jet again."

"Well, that certainly does sound like your dad got things squared away."

"We can go to the mountains skiing next winter as usual." Jil painted a rosy picture of the future. "I'm working for the senator again. He has me setup in an apartment near his townhouse."

Betty scowled at Jil, "Where is this going?"

"Don't look at me that way. Besides, Senator Bolden is a dear friend of Daddy's."

"You weren't so complimentary two months ago. 'Dirty old man', wasn't it?"

"Nothing is going to come of it, he just likes to stop by every once in a while when his wife is out of sorts."

"Out of sorts?"

"She can be so moody! We just sit and talk, that's all," said Jil while averting her eyes from Betty's.

Betty looked at Jil like she wanted to believe this, but it all seemed too innocent to believe. *A powerful man like the senator setting up a mistress in an apartment and all he wants to do is sit and talk? This is not making sense at all.* "Well, I guess you know what you are doing. What was the name of the company, the one who helped your dad?"

Jil wavered "It's something foreign, an investment house of some kind, maybe Danish. They don't own the new company directly; there's some special deal where they own an indirect stake—something about foreign ownership rules." Jil looked at her watch and said, "Time to pack up and head back to work." Jil to the senator's office to do public relations and Betty back to her office to figure out how to get a K-1 Fiancé Visa for an immigrant who had already been in the country past the 90 days allowed. The walk back to the Senate building was marred by large storm clouds coming in from the west. As Betty was about to cross the street to her law offices, Jil called out from the plaza leading to the Capital building "I'll call you this weekend, catch up, I promise." Betty was already planning on finding out more about this business deal Larry Harper had gotten himself into. Something smelled fishy in Denmark.

TWENTY-FOUR

OUT OF LEFT FIELD

HOWELL REACHED FOR HIS GUN, as he yelled out to Babs, "No! Back!" But it was too late. The shrapnel tore through her like rain through a screen door: bouncing off her helmet and flak jacket, but hitting her hard in the face and arms. He could see crimson seeping out everywhere. Blood flowing so fast it was already starting to drip from her chin. Her sunglasses split and shattered dangling from her ear and nose like a branch torn from a fir tree, but stopped by the other branches from making it to the ground. She spun to her left on her right foot as she was hit, but it was too late. Tom, turned away from Babs as a random piece of shrapnel tore through his right arm, just above the elbow, lodging into the meat of his bicep. It burned with heat as it sliced his muscle; Tom looked at the wound more with curiosity than concern. He moved his weapon from his right hand to his left; it did not feel very comfortable there, but would have to do.

Bzzzz Bzzzz Bzzzz Bzzzz went the alarm next to Howell's bed. *How many nights in a row must I have that dream?* Sometimes the dream made it through to the medic and the choppers. Sometimes it ended with the Bouncing Betty landmine going off just above him as he dove under the Humvee. Sometimes it was accurate down to the tiniest detail and other times it seemed all wrong, not that there was anything right about what really did happen. It took two years to find out what happened to Babs. She had vanished. There was no record of her getting to the hospital. Howell was not able to track down Gil Richardson the medic: The medic had been a ghost, a special operations soldier who just happened to be in the right place at the right time to save Howell and Babs. Howell considered moving on, but the dreams seemed to say he needed to know or they would haunt him to the end of his days. It was going to take time and energy to track down a man like Richardson. There was nothing special about that day to anyone but Howell, and maybe Babs, to make it stick out in their memories. If Babs was alive, she did not return to her teaching job or to her consulting job with the military contractor, Bethel Cronk & Martinsen: all possible sources of information only led to dead ends.

A lead finally came in a report on the turrets. While Howell recovered, Getner had shifted the responsibility for improving the turrets to a raw, new lieutenant, Jacobs. When Howell shifted to his new role in Control, it did not occur to him to check on things until a question came up about a report he had written in the field. Jacobs seemed like a decent guy, but he did not seem to have the same drive as Howell. Jacobs was more focused on crossing the *t's* and dotting the *i's*. Howell had forgotten to sign a report just before the "Babs incident." It had happened in the field, so who really cared? Jacobs the pencil pusher did. He did not want to have to sign off on it himself, so he tracked Howell down. They grabbed a cup of coffee and talked about the project. Howell to find out what had happened afterward and Jacobs to see if there was anything else he was missing.

"No," said Jacobs, "I hadn't heard a thing on that contractor, at least not until last week. It came over with this report, the one you forgot to sign." Jacobs handed Howell a pen to make sure he got the signature as if to say he was not going to give up anything else without that signature. With a scowl, Howell signed off and shoved it back to Jacobs.

"This document...." Jacobs pulled out a medium stack of paper, folded, spindled, and mutilated, "came from Dr. McGillicutty about three months after the incident. She wasn't going to get her last check or her medical bills paid if they didn't get this report from her."

The file indicated Babs had been taken to a private hospital in Denmark where extensive plastic surgery and skin grafts were performed. "It was a miracle she survived in the first place," stated Jacobs as Howell skimmed over Babs' report and file.

"She was inches from death when the choppers arrived at base camp. They had to pump her full of blood and fluids and stop the internal bleeding," said Jacobs pointing to the notes from the field hospital.

"She looks pretty torn up," Howell grimaced while looking at the official incident report photos of Babs' injuries. It stood in stark contrast to his memory of the base camp incident when she dropped her towel to reveal her full beauty as she tried to seduce him.

"The external stuff looked a lot worse than it was," said Jacobs as he pointed to the photos of Babs attached with a paperclip. "All that blood from so many small nicks and cuts. The worst was the large piece of shrapnel that penetrated her gut. The head trauma and the concussion from the explosion did something to her mind."

"What do you mean?" asked Howell as he flipped the papers looking for the diagnosis.

"She still had her higher functions, but her personality had definitely changed according to her co-workers," summarized Jacobs as if he had memorized the report.

"So she did return to work for Bethel Cronk & Martinsen, at least for a while. They were stonewalling me!" said Howell, pushing the report away in disgust.

"They stated that while the report should be treated as an accurate summation of the project, Dr. McGillicutty would not be continuing with this research project," finished Jacobs.

So, the trail was warmer, but it still came to a dead end. She had survived the blast and the surgeries, but she obviously was not the same person. The military report and the contractor's follow up report gave no indication where she went from Denmark. Maybe he would be able to sleep better anyway, just knowing she had survived.

TWENTY-FIVE

THE DEFENSIVE ATTORNEY

TOM HAD CONVINCED BETTY to take a self-defense class now that she was living alone. While her neighborhood was relatively safe, she did not have anyone to watch out for her, except Surry. A break in was not likely; the apartment was on the third floor, the only windows faced the building next door, and Surry was no push over as a home defender. Weimaraners were known for protecting their owners and Surry definitely inherited that trait from her mother. Her father was not known for sure, but her all black color, coat, and general disposition indicated the dad was a black Labrador.

Betty started with a general defense class designed to teach women how to survive a sexual assault or a date gone bad. She felt more powerful having learned the knowledge, though she did not feel a deeper appreciation for the art of self-defense itself. Having worked so hard on intellectual pursuits from high school to law school, it seemed strange to be striving so hard for physical prowess. Running did not count in this category. She did not run for time or for a special distance. She ran to feel better about herself and to stay in shape. Running helped her keep a positive mental attitude; however, Tom and a lot of other people started giving the matter of safety more thought after the attack on the central park jogger hit the news again. It had not been a gang of teenagers after all, but the act of a convicted rapist and murderer.

"Why take the chance of not being prepared?" lectured Tom and her parents.

So, after the basic self-defense class Betty began a karate class which led to a Brazilian jujitsu class. It reminded her of beating on her brothers Rob and Bill. They could hit harder, but she would get a chokehold with a ferocity that would sometimes scare her brothers. They would back down with their hands up and say, "OK, sis, you're trying to kill us, not fight us." Betty was surprised by her own intensity in those fights with her brothers. She got used to the taste of that feeling. The rise in her gut that said, *I'm taking anybody and anything on.* She learned to feel that way anytime someone told her she could not do something because she was a girl or that she was not good enough to hang with the best. Betty got the same feeling just before debates and arguments. She learned to control and use the feeling to her advantage, especially when practicing jujitsu. Betty was a shining example of how a small fighter could win against a much larger attacker. Her instructor, a graduate of the Gracie school of jujitsu, admonished others for not having her intensity, but her new sparring partners tended to ask that the intensity to be turned down after a few sessions. She moved up in belts quicker than normal due to her demonstrations of ability in competition. White led to blue, and a purple belt followed quickly.

Betty was on her way to a brown belt when a knee injury requiring arthroscopic surgery made her think about what she was trying to accomplish. She had learned enough to defend herself and decided to take some time off to heal and get back to her running.

Tom admired her new found physicality balanced by a deeper understanding of self. She had accomplished her objective and could let go of the bigger dream of a black or red belt. She could always go back and resume her training. Then again, he would not let her spar with him as it was; maybe it was a defensive move on Tom's part to keep her from being able to kick his butt.

Twenty-Six

Nestling

BETTY DID NOT SEE IT COMING. This bothered her. Her planned life had room for surprises, but this threatened to turn her world upside down. She had been in committed relationships before, but nothing too serious. The kind where if an interesting guy showed up, someone she would have liked to dance with or allowed him to buy her a drink, she would have to say, "Sorry, I'm in a relationship" *come back in a few months and try again.* Now she was in a committed relationship with Tom. She was not looking for the next best thing and she was not thinking about the next twenty years with Tom, she was just enjoying the ride, so to speak.

They had just left the Smithsonian on a Saturday afternoon. They had been to an art fair earlier in the morning. The sun was warming the earth in a way that made Betty feel like anything was possible. The world seemed to stand still just for them so they could pretend to be there for the exhibits when what they were really doing is just being close to each other. It seemed like they never stopped talking about things, but when they did, the silence seemed just right. Neither felt the need to fill a quiet moment with idle chatter. When either one had an important observation or just some item of whimsy that made sense at that very moment, they were able to express it without that void filling feeling that someone, either one or both, were uncomfortable because they were not talking. It was that kind of day.

Betty looked into the deep blue eyes of "her" man. Not any man, but her man. She realized at that moment that she could not envision a day without Tom. There were many days when they were apart physically but

Betty talked to Tom on the phone nearly every day. The rare days they did not talk, there were subtle reminders of him everywhere. The usual knickknacks purchased as mementos, or as a thank you for a nice meal, or I like you, or I really like you, or I miss you today kind of things... those where there. What really got to Betty today was that she started to see things, everyday kind of things as reminders of Tom. If she saw a man in uniform on the streets of the capital, it made her think of Tom. If she passed a military statue or memorial, it reminded her of Tom. She was constantly reminded that at any moment she could lose him to war. God forbid another great war should break out or that the war on terror should escalate. Afghanistan was a hot war now, but Tom was not to be going overseas anytime soon. He was not in a combat unit since he was on the research side of the military. He was the brainy soldier whose job it was to keep the other guys alive a little longer so they could do their job. At least that was the way Tom assured Betty he would be by her side for the duration.

She did not worry when she saw these soldiers on the street or the memorials to soldiers lost. She did not feel sad about Tom when she ran through the Vietnam Memorial, she felt proud: proud that "her" man was doing something to keep names off memorials. He was making a difference in the lives of not only soldiers but also the families of soldiers. Making a difference to women like herself, who cared about guys like Tom.

Tom waited until they were in the Mall outside the Smithsonian; as they walked toward the Washington Monument, just as the late afternoon sun was blocked for just a moment by that phallic symbol of conquest that Tom turned to Betty and said, "Why don't we move in together? You hate your efficiency, I know you miss the Martin House, the feeling of a real home. I need to move by the first anyway. Let's go find a place together, we'll look together to find something both of us like."

Betty could not believe her ears. She had been thinking about Tom for the past three weeks and how it was so crazy, the comings and goings of the two of them. The times when Tom had to quickly iron his uniform at her place, spritzing it with toilet water to mask the second day of wearing the uniform. He did not keep much at her place and she only had a few items stashed at his, sort of her claim on his space. A few weeks ago, he had cleared a drawer for her, but she had only just put a few things in it not wanting to make too big of a deal out of the gesture.

She put her head onto his chest and hugged him deeply. Taking a deep breath in, she savored his smell. That smell of his clothes, a little bit of sweat from their day of adventure and all those pheromones. She knew what she wanted and she knew what she was getting. *Am I ready for this step? What will my parents say? My God, I'm twenty-seven years old and worried about what my parents will say. Betty looked up at her man. What had taken him so long to ask?*

"Well, I don't know, I guess we could look and see what's out there...I guess I'm open to the idea...I don't know what my parents will say, of course," she answered.

Tom hugged her back and took a deep breath of Betty's hair. She used a Paul Mitchell shampoo, one with coconut in it. He could smell a faint note of lime behind the coconut.

The next day was Sunday. They got a *Washington Post* and a *Washington Times* to find out what was available. They had decided that they wanted to stay in Georgetown. Ideally, they would look for a loft apartment with a decent view of the street instead of something like Betty's current view of a wall. Tom's apartment was utilitarian at best, definitely a military man's bivouacs. Exposed brick walls would be a nice touch, but not mandatory. Not too close to nightlife, they were responsible, serious adults now. After a couple of hours of going over what was available, they agreed that there really was not anything worth a damn for them in that day's paper. Each secretly relieved that the commitment of moving in together was put off for another day. They decide to go get a cup of coffee nearby at Bonaparte's Cafe on Wisconsin Avenue. There was a simple ad, nothing special, on the bulletin board.

Loft apartment, view of the canal, must be willing to put some elbow grease into the place. Call Steve—(703) 555-1212

They ordered to go instead of staying in. Calling from Betty's cellphone they found out the manager was around and able to show the property right away. It was a dump. The last tenants had trashed the place. The plaster was falling from the walls, the hardwood floors needed refinishing, but there were twelve hundred square feet of space and huge windows overlooking the canal. If one stood on a ladder about four feet up you could see Theodore Roosevelt Island and the Potomac River.

They agreed to take it on the spot. The next weekend they were cleaning it up and planning for their move. Two weeks of chiseling mortar from walls, scrubbing and cleaning had paid off. By the beginning of November, they had moved what little Tom had and all of Betty's possessions into this large airy space. They now had one of the most desirable loft apartments in all of Georgetown and no one knew it. They needed Jil to be here to help them properly celebrate. Of course, that could be arranged.

Twenty-Seven

Did I Say Too Much?

"DEAREST BETTY," the letter dated November 11th, 2002, began.

Your father and I love you very much. We know that Jil's family has always been able to do more for her than we have been able to do for you financially. That is why, in part, we made your education so important in our lives. We can't begin to tell you how proud we are of your graduating from Georgetown Law School and beginning your career at such a prestigious firm in Washington. Your life seems to be quite idyllic from your letters and from what we saw on our last visit.

Your friend Tom seems very nice and well on his way to a fine career. While your brothers have not served and your father only just missed the draft by a few years, thanks to his graduate school deferment, we respect the service Tom is doing for our country. You know I'm against the war, but I want you to know I am for Tom. I just hope you know what you are doing. Just to be clear, we approve of Tom, but we don't approve of you two moving in together. We pray about this every day and keep hoping for the best.

Not to worry you too much, but we are very concerned about Jil and her family. Appearances would suggest that they have come out the other side of their financial straits, but there is a tension in that family that did not used to be there. Everyone seems to be on edge and hiding something. I can't put my finger on it. Did Rob tell you he broke up with Ruth? The engagement is off. He said it was his doing, but it doesn't seem right. He is crazy about her. I know Larry wasn't excited about the engagement. Larry would never approve of any man Ruth would marry but he does like to think of your brother as a son. Who knows, Rob isn't talking, but I know he and Ruth still see each other a bit over coffee or run into each other by "accident." I pray for both Rob and Ruth.

Did I tell you Bill got a promotion? He is now a manager of a small unit at IBM working on 'Artificial Intelligence.' They seem to think they have gotten somewhere new with their methods. I don't understand it really. He could tell me the company secrets and they would be safe. I wouldn't be able to repeat what he said anyway. I just nod my head and say uh-huh every once in a while. ☺

Rob is talking about going back for an MBA. I don't know why. I suppose it will help him rise farther at IBM, but I think it's just because of the breakup with Ruth that he is talking about it. It would give him an excuse to be busy I suppose and to be farther away.

Well, be good. Do good work. Visit when you can but plan on Thanksgiving. Tom can come with and use Bill's bedroom.

Love,

Mom & Dad

TWENTY-EIGHT

TE QUIERO (I WANT YOU)

"WHY ARE YOU SO DISTRACTED today?" Betty queried over coffee at Bonaparte's Cafe.

Now that they lived in the neighborhood, it had become a favorite haunt on the weekends. Betty would work on her briefs and Tom would study reports. Every once in a while they would look up from their reading and talk briefly about something that crossed their mind. "Oh, you know how I'm working for Colonel Getner now; we have that big field test coming up soon. He just has everyone twisted tight and on a short leash. He is way too worried about how this new equipment will perform. I think it will do just fine, but you never know. They say your battle plan is only good until the first contact with the enemy," explained Tom.

Betty reached out for his hands and gave them reassuring squeezes to say, I trust you; you will do a good job, there is nothing to worry about.

They had been living together now for three months. It took them six visits to five different furniture stores before they picked out a simple but large sofa to put in front of the large windows facing the canal. The sofa was large enough to compliment the twelve foot ceiling and long nature of the loft. The room was twenty feet wide by sixty feet long. The couch had become an anchor for the front of the space. In the back, the bathroom carved out a small area, but a large cast iron tub was conspicuously placed in the open with only a circular shower curtain to protect the privacy of a bather. Not that either one of them cared if the other watched while they bathed. The tub was just big enough for romantic interludes including champagne on ice and dozens of candles to light the loft. For parties the tub was filled with ice to keep the beer cold. Usually cans and bottles, but for the big parties like the house warming Jil threw, a keg fit nicely.

That was the only time Jil had visited. Betty and Jil frequently walked the Capitol Mall over lunch breaks, talking about relationships, work, and family. Rob and Ruth's failed engagement was one of the big topics. Betty and Jil had always considered themselves sisters, a marriage between Betty's brother and Jil's sister would have made them official sisters-in-law, almost as if the world was acknowledging what had been for many years already. The discussion of Rob and Ruth also brought home how Betty and Tom's relationship was moving forward. They had been seeing each other for over a year and living together the past three months. The obvious question was where is this going? Betty and Tom had talked about what it would be like if they were married, two children would be nice, a starter home in Virginia. It would be a better commute for Betty if they lived in Maryland, north of the district, but better for Tom if they were on the Virginia side of the Potomac to commute to the Pentagon—six of one, a half dozen of the other. They did not have to decide yet and both demurred to the wishes of the other at this point.

Frequently, Tom or Betty would reach out to touch one another. Tom insisted on limiting the PDA (public display of affection) such as kissing, but a peck now and again or a deep hug and smooch when parting seemed acceptable to both. It felt reassuring, as if to say, I am here with you and I will not be leaving you.

Tom worked on the research side of the Pentagon, but with the new War on Terror, he was in the field for brief visits to see how the real world affected new designs. Even when he visited bases around the United States, he was back within a few days. Betty traveled as well for her job as an immigration attorney. Her passport was riddled with stamps from the South American countries such as Chile, Argentina, Brazil, Nicaragua, Columbia, and Guatemala. She had studied four years of Spanish in high school and one year at Syracuse. This had been just enough to get her by, but now she was improving her Spanish using a self-paced study book and CD from a company claiming to be the "go to" product for the State Department. She did not know about that, but it certainly was tedious getting through the chapters without someone to practice with.

She had tried to get Tom to study Spanish with her, but he claimed he was way too far behind her skill level to keep up. To get back at him for not helping she would frequently tell Tom that she loved him "te quiero" or say to the Hispanic ladies they knew "Me gusta ese chico." She would look at Tom and say, "Quiero casarme con usted, pídale que me case contigo," *I want to marry you, ask me to marry you* when she especially felt romantic. Sometimes when she was in the big cast iron tub bathing, she would prop her elbows with her full breasts resting on the edge of the tub, chin in her hands and say in a deep sultry voice, "¡Quiero que ahora, en la bañera!"

Tom did not know what that translated to, but he certainly knew what it meant.

She also described their future children to him in Spanish, "Nuestro hijo va a ser guapo como tú con los ojos azules," *Our son, he will be handsome like you with blue eyes.* He did not know what she was saying and she thought it was a good subliminal tool.

Jil liked hearing about the latest phrases Betty was learning and the "hidden meanings." Their walks through the memorials were a good memory for Betty. Jil seemed to be on top of her world. She was not working for the escort service and had enough money thanks in part to a raise in her salary by Senator Bolden. Jil's love life was pretty hit or miss, she did not seem to have any relationships that lasted, but the ones she had were interesting. She would fly with the senator on his trips to New York, Europe, or the Middle East hot spots on fact-finding missions. Jil seemed to know a lot more about world politics and geography than ever before. Betty was amazed by the off-handed comments about meeting Senator so-and-so or being at the White House for such-and-such a meeting.

Betty perceived her world travels as mundane compared to the worldly circles and five star locations Jil bragged about. While Betty stayed in nice hotels while traveling, Jil stayed in the best, but this did not seem all that different from the way they grew up. Jil always had the nicer things like the latest designer clothes and too many shoes to pick from. While Betty had her cousin's hand-me-downs or made do with wearing the same dress a second or third time to formal events.

This was a happy time for all of them. The quiet time before everything got crazy. Or had it all been a mirage anyway?

Twenty-Nine

Dog Leg Left

BETTY HATED THE SECRECY. Tom would leave for a trip and he could not tell her more than a day in advance. He could not even tell her when he would be back. Usually he was only gone for a few days at a time, which made it difficult to plan for things. One of Tom's last minute trips made Betty reschedule an outing with friends for dinner and miss a gallery opening. It tended to make Betty think twice about planning anything and was creating a sense of uncertainty about their long term plans together.

One incident in particular bothered Betty. She had been planning a trip to Montevideo, Uruguay, for some time. A client needed assistance with the U.S. Embassy and a special request for her services had come from of all places, IBM. She felt a loyalty to the company that had supported her family and continued to be the employer of her father and brothers. There was not any direct connection between her work and her family but it made her feel good about her legal career. IBM had a long history of research projects using artificial intelligence to make the best supercomputer possible for playing chess. They had been quite successful with *Deep Blue*, a computer designed solely to play chess against Garry Kasparov, the reigning world champion. Now they were interested in the work of a young programmer from Uruguay who seemed to have a handle on artificial intelligence in a way that diverged from the mainstream research. Was he the path to the next great thinking computer? Montevideo was as far south as Betty had ever gone and she would be away for several weeks. She had counted on Tom to take care of Surry while she was gone—one of the benefits of living together.

Unfortunately, Tom ended up going on a trip for Colonel Getner while Betty was gone. He arranged for Surry to stay at the kennel next to her vet, but Surry was not quite the same when Betty got back.

"What the hell is wrong with you!" Betty exploded when Tom tried to explain. "It's OK, Surry, momma loves you!" Betty gave Tom the evil eye as she stroked Surry's head and hugged her close.

"But, sweetheart, I," Tom stuttered.

"You what? Left Surry in the apartment alone? Did you expect her to walk herself?"

"I was supposed to be back yesterday, Getner, he," Tom could not finish his sentences before Betty interrupted.

"Oh, so Colonel Getner ordered you to abandon our dog?" Betty was giving no quarter.

"Yes, no, I mean, he ordered me to stay late and I missed the last transport flight."

"So?"

"Jerry had already dropped Surry off and I couldn't reach him."

"I don't think you even tried." Betty glared at Tom with her arms crossed.

"He turns off his phone at night." Tom was digging his hole deeper by the moment.

"What the hell were you thinking?" asked Betty as she picked up and then dropped to the floor a broken lamp, a chewed up chair leg, and piles of torn up paperwork. "What about the dog shit and pee? It's going to take weeks to retrain her. *Ahhhgg!*"

Tom could only stammer excuses. Betty was watching a dying man gasping for air.

After a few weeks, Surry seemed to be back to her old self, but Betty was not going to let this one go easily. Tom tried to make it up to her, but he did not understand that it was a matter of trust, not how many flowers or little gifts he gave her that mattered. She had trusted him to take care of their dog—even if Surry had been her dog before they met: Surry was their trial child, at least for Betty. Tom did not pass that test and was one to be watched for a while. Tom must have sensed some of this because he made extra efforts to take Surry to the dog park between the Tenth Street Baptist Church and the Cardoza Playground. There were other places to go closer to the loft, but it was always nice to go where other dogs played together. Another favorite was down by the beltway at Founders Park next to the Potomac.

Tom was trying to get Betty's attention away from Surry after the incident so he could talk about his career. It took two weeks for him to finally find her in a receptive mood.

They were walking along the canal, Surry with them, when he said, "This project I'm working on with Colonel Getner, it's important. The generals liked our demonstration, not so much because it went right, but because of how we adapted and overcame. I don't know yet what they are planning, but Colonel Getner has something bigger for me to do. I won't know for a while and I won't be able to tell you much, but I want you to know I am excited about what is happening. I hope you can understand."

Betty was very confused by this. What was Tom trying to tell her? Not having security clearance frustrated Betty. With a security clearance, she could learn more about what he was up to and what was in store for them. She still had not quite forgiven him for the Surry incident and was having a hard time mustering the trust for this. *But God, I do love him, and hell, it's not really his fault his buddy screwed up.*

A week later, Tom took Betty to the Capital Grille. It seemed that important things were said here. Only good came from this restaurant, it was magical. Perhaps it was the attentiveness of the staff or the high standards of the food and wine. It never ceased to amaze her that Tom and his father both came here yet they barely talked to each other. They were so much alike, yet so different. Tom as usual pilfered a bottle of wine from his father's wine locker and for whatever reason, either from guilt or indifference, Mr. Howell never told the staff to cut him off.

Betty had a surprise for Tom that evening. She had planned to give it to him when she got back home from Uruguay, until the incident with Surry, but she felt that she could move on now and let it go. So, she had brought with her a small jewelry box. Wrapped in crimson ribbon, the cream-colored kid leather case had a gold hasp and hinges.

Tom greeted the staff warmly as he came in; Tom was their favorite that was for sure. The sommelier, Marcus, was quick to come over and find out what Tom wanted to pilfer from his father this time. A soap opera moment, would the son go long and take one of the good wines or just stay close with a basic red to match the meal. Tonight Tom went long. "Marcus, we are celebrating tonight, what should we have?"

Marcus began to ponder the consequences of pilfering a bottle for the young Mr. Howell yet again, but the fifty-dollar bill Tom had palmed him when he came over made him think no more. "Ah, I have just the right wine for you tonight, Mr. Howell."

Betty leaned in with her elbows on the table, her hands draped over each other to support her chin, "What are you up to you little scamp? Marcus seems eager to please tonight." That is when she slid the box to Tom: "I hope you don't mind, I got something for the both of us. I want you to know that I trust you, that everything is OK."

Tom opened the box to find two chains, each with a matching half of a broken heart pendant. Tom felt a love for Betty like at no other time. This would have been the perfect evening to propose to her. He intended to do just that, but not until he got back.

"Here, this is for you." Tom pushed a silver tray with a dome lid her way. The waiter had just dropped it off at the table. Her hand was shaking. *He isn't proposing, or he would be on one knee, right?*

Betty lifted the lid to see a ring box. *What is going on here?* she thought to herself. Half afraid to open the box, half dying to know what was inside, she slowly reached for the soft leather box trying to savor the moment. "What are you up to?" she said as she pried the lid back.

Inside was a promise ring. The 'X' shaped string of small diamonds set into the top of the white gold band set off the third of a carat large stone, giving the appearance of an 'XO'.

"I promise that when I finish the mission I am about to embark on, I will come back to you for good. This will be the only overseas mission I will ever take," said Tom as he slid the ring onto Betty's finger.

Betty was stunned. She did not know which stunned her more, that he was making this promise as a military man or that he was going away for some undetermined amount of time which surely indicated danger.

"What, what does this mean? Where are you going? I don't understand?" asked a startled Betty, unsure of the future.

"You know I can't tell you that, but what I can tell you is that I will be escorting a contractor to review some of our designs in the field. Anything more and I can get in trouble," said Tom as he grasped Betty's hand.

They ate their dinner mostly in silence. Betty, because there were so many questions she wanted to ask and Tom because there were so many questions he could not answer. They went on a long walk after dinner through the Mall, just holding hands. They stopped in front of the FDR Memorial and in an unusual departure from their self imposed ban on PDA, they gave each other perhaps the longest and most passionate kiss FDR ever witnessed. They took a cab ride home and made passionate love. Betty did not dare ask the question of when, because she already knew the answer. Tom never told her more than a day before traveling. *So this is it. I have to be patient...he is worth the wait.*

She did not sleep much that night and was a little miffed that Tom drifted off after sex. She elbowed him more than once to attempt to rouse him, but eventually just let him sleep. She would have gone off to the couch on any other night to sit and watch the skyline, but this was her last night to be by his side for who knew how long. She was not going to give up a moment of it. She finally found some semblance of sleep around 4 a.m. The alarm roused her to find that Tom had already left. She found a rose and a note on Tom's pillow.

Betty picked up the note and flower and rolled from her side to her back. Her anxiety diminished when she smelled the flower's deep penetrating fragrance, taking a deep slow inhalation with her eyes closed. *Tom loves me.* After hesitating for a moment, afraid to make Tom's departure a reality, Betty began to read the note out loud in a whisper, "My Dearest Betty, I love you. I will be thinking of you every day and in every way. I will keep myself safe and come back to you whole. Tom"

THIRTY

POWER EQUALS MONEY

BETTY HELD IT TOGETHER until her noon walk with Jil. They usually walked the Capitol Mall on Tuesdays, skipping lunch, but sometimes they would walk over to one of the restaurants frequented by the senate staffers to take in a quick bite. Getting together was simple. Betty's law offices on Constitution Avenue were kitty-corner from the Capitol Building. Just as the two had found a way to be together in college, it seemed life had provided a way for them to be together again.

"I feel like a prisoner!" declared Betty.

"Those horizontal stripes! Yes, I see what you mean." sniped Jil as she looked over Betty's outfit.

Betty frowned at her best friend. "I mean with Tom, in the sense like a prisoner who can handle any length of sentence as long as she knows how long the sentence is."

"Tom is your sentence and you got life without parole."

Betty giggled a little, but then got serious again. "The not knowing is tearing me apart. It could be a month or it could be a year."

"Speaking of a sentence, check him out!" Jil was looking at a man in a suit walking earnestly toward the Treasury Building while talking on his cellphone. His fine Italian suit jacket flapping open as he walked briskly, "Yummy! Throw away the key!" Jil pulled her focus back to Betty, "What did Tom tell you anyway?"

"Just that it is an important mission." Betty gave the Italian suit a quick once over, "Hmmm. You could do worse, but I've seen you do better."

"Aren't they all important missions? I mean, going shopping for new shoes is a mission," Jil looked at Betty's worn out walking shoes. "And honey, you need to go on a mission!"

"Hah!" Betty looked briefly at her well worn shoes. "He said this was important in part because it would be the only *long-term* overseas mission he will have to take, that it will lead to a big promotion."

"Since when can a military man dictate his deployments? He is the prisoner, jumping to the tune played by that Colonel," Jil waited for Betty to finish her comment.

"You mean General Getner?"

"Yes. General Getner is the one who is standing between you and Tom. Say, wasn't he just a colonel not too long ago?"

"You can't talk about any of this. I don't want to get Tom in trouble!"

"Do you mean Senator Bolden? Chairman of the Defense Appropriations Subcommittee?"

"Yes, him especially." Betty had a worried look in her eyes.

"Honey, you don't have a thing to worry about. The senator is only interested in four-star generals. Just like I am only interested in top dogs like that fella back there," Jil pointed with her thumb over her shoulder at the Italian suit that had passed by a moment before. "How long is Tom gone for anyway?"

"Oh, he didn't say, but by his past history it could be a couple of months or a year. I don't know."

"Maybe I could find out for you? Bolden won't know a thing."

"I don't know. He never said." Betty felt uncomfortable with Jil's persistence and tried to change the subject. "Any new parties coming up?"

"Everyday there seems to be something new! A girl could get downright fat in my job!" Jil stopped and turned to Betty, taking her hands in hers. "Bolden won't hear a thing."

"I know I can trust you."

"I won't make any waves for Tom."

"Of course you won't!"

"I'm just trying to help. What are friends for?" Jil smiled and gave Betty a quick hug.

That made Betty feel better, knowing that she had a friend that she could trust, had trusted for years, to confide her fears and feelings to without any qualms or inhibitions.

"So, tomorrow, you're coming to the reception for the Brazilian Ambassador?"

Betty cocked her head slightly as she checked her memory, "Seven, right?"

Jil nodded her head yes, but then looked at Betty as if she was critiquing her current outfit, "You do have something to wear besides a house dress, right?" Jil goaded Betty about her clothes constantly.

"I was thinking of wearing this," Betty pulled her skirt out and made a curtsey.

"Oh, please!"

"Thanks for being there for me. I know your work keeps you so busy these days."

"That's what I'm here for. That and to give you some fashion sense one of these days!"

"You make it easier for me to refocus on my own work." Betty paused as Jil ogled another male suit walking by. "Of course, when you need me to come to one of your social events, I'll always make time." Betty sighed loudly as if doing so was a great imposition. Betty gladly made time to hobnob with the rich and famous; actually, more to watch Jil at work than to be able to brag about who and where she had been. Her fellow lawyers were green with envy whenever they heard how plugged in Betty was to the Capitol. They marveled that she had not converted to lobbying for the big dollars.

"Why don't you become a lobbyist? Then you wouldn't have to count on me to go to the parties and I could come to yours!" Jil smiled broadly at that thought.

"Hah, you know I love immigration law."

"You like people and love solving problems."

"True."

"Well, lobbying is the same thing."

"No, I'm a lawyer and I wouldn't stoop to influence peddling," Betty winked at Jil to soften the jab. "I like my little bit of travel. The clients are rich, so getting paid is easy."

"True, now if you would just spend some of that on clothes!" Jil waived her hand in front of her nose as if a bad smell was emanating from Betty's outfit.

"Why would I want to spend my days cajoling people like you to do my bidding when I'm having fun doing what I love?" Betty could give as good as she could take.

"Well, I love what I do, too." Jil seemed to be in her own element on the hill. "You just need to be approachable and available, kind of like a magnet for lobbyists."

"Exactly! I'll stay in law, thank you very much." Betty saw what lobbyists did to get the attention of someone like Jil, the former beauty queen, socialite, and party girl. Jil was very hard to impress. "Senator Bolden is wise to use you for both PR and gatekeeper."

"I can smell a bad deal from a mile away!"

"You just have that sixth sense about people's intentions."

"You also have to know what needs to float up."

"Yep, you're savvy enough to know when the senator needs to be involved."

"The senator gets to maximize time with wealthy constituents while I take care of the common folk—and the lobbyists' gifts."

"Ooh-la-la! Minks? Diamonds? Chateaus?"

"That and more!" Jil wryly noted. "Of course, these 'gifts' can't come directly to the senator."

"Really, how does it work?" Betty furrowed her brow. For being so involved in the D.C. area, she did not truly know the inner workings of power.

"Don't speak a word or I'll rat out Tom!" Jil threatened in a light-hearted tone.

"Cross my heart and kiss my elbow!" Betty pantomimed the gestures, *I'm not sure if she is kidding or serious!*

"Lobbyists will make gifts to Bolden's business associates and large donors. Then the donors make loans to Senator Bolden's sister and brother-in-law—or make embarrassing trifles disappear."

"Loans?"

"His sister has a business that hasn't shown a profit in *years!*" Jil rolled her eyes.

"How does the senator know who to give favors to?"

"I discretely point out who the senator needs to give the most attention to, especially at the parties."

"That is so corrupt, Jil!" Betty looked displeased.

"Senator Bolden is fond of saying, 'You can have power or money, but you can't have both.'"

"Well, doesn't he benefit from the gifts?"

"Not really—but his sister does, that is the power, being able to say who is going to get the largesse of the lobbyists." Betty still frowned at Jil. "The money is going to go to someone! If he doesn't use his power, someone else will get elected to use it."

"I suppose you're correct, but that doesn't make it right."

Jill concluded as their walk ended, "The senator loves power and the office provides plenty of perks that make up for the lack of money. Besides, power is money and money is power."

Betty understood, *Jil has the power by being the gatekeeper to the senator.*

Thirty-One

Let's Split the Difference

"**N**OTHING! NOT A LETTER in two months." Betty decried the lack of attention from her busy boyfriend.

"Nothing?"

"Howell is such a jerk! The least he could do is say how the weather is." Betty pined for news from the front.

"Tom—Howell has some nerve! You deserve better treatment." Jil noticed that Betty no longer called him Tom. *Betty's way of dealing with the absence of her almost fiancé*, Jil supposed.

"I've been sending letters once a week or more to the address he gave me."

"Are you sure you have the right address, did he give you the wrong one, maybe?"

"I heard back from him a couple of times, but nothing has come back for two months," Betty looked tired and introspective. *That black void of not knowing!*

Betty seemed to be handling the situation well according to most of her friends and co-workers; Jil knew otherwise. Betty's all encompassing focus on work was driven by what could be happening somewhere half way around the world. Jil knew this about Betty and did what she could by making time for their walks; a relief valve for all of the pent up worrying Betty shunted aside during the workday. Meeting for lunch was becoming more difficult, especially when Congress was in session. There were too many meetings with lobbyists, constituents, and the media for Jil to stop midday. Instead, they made time at the end of the afternoon, which gave Jil time to prep for that evening's social gathering.

The late spring D.C. weather was just too much to bear; the heat off the concrete stored from the brutal sun was diminished somewhat by three or four o'clock, making their walks more comfortable.

Shortly after the equinox in June, they began jogging around the mall in the late evening after Jil's commitments or earlier if her schedule permitted. The sun was still above the horizon late into the evening, so their journey through the capital seemed safe enough; besides, Betty's martial arts skills would protect them from almost any predator. Jil was keeping the pounds off from all those lunch meetings, dinner meetings, and parties while Betty worked out her anxieties, frustrations, and nerves.

The lack of news from Howell was even starting to bother Jil; however, after so long without any information, there were suddenly two short letters in quick succession. Individually each letter gave little information, but when put together they gave far more than double the information.

My Dearest Betty,

The days here are productive, but long. I certainly wish I had taken your advice and packed more incidental items like baby wipes. There have been no surprises in my work, but I have been surprised by the friendly nature of my charge. No worries though, I will be keeping my promise, not out of obligation, but because I love you.

Tom

My Dearest Betty,

How strange it seems now, having been away for what on the calendar is a short time, but in mindset seems an eternity. Temptations are many here, but I am focused on the goal and will not wander from my ultimate destination. Half of a mind to set off anew, but time will tell. I know Jil must be a comfort to you and I am glad she is there with you. I only have my duffel and a photo of you to keep me company, but do not feel bad for me.

Love, Lieutenant Howell

Betty and Jil spent hours as if they were cryptographers, studying the letters. Jil scrutinized the words looking for meaning, "There is obviously a code here, but what is the key?"

"It seems to say that the contractor he was sent to mind and protect is constantly tempting him, trying to lure him into some compromised position." Betty was trying to sound unconcerned, but she doubted she was convincing.

"Maybe he is saying he's avoided temptation and looking to the future instead of short-term pleasure." Jil tried to spin the letters as positively as she could, but they seemed very odd. "I just can't figure out what he means by the different signatures."

Betty scrunched up her face, "Signing the second letter as Lieutenant Howell sure does seem cold!"

"I wouldn't focus on that as a negative, we just don't know what he means—yet." Jil stopped focusing on the letters and gave her gin and tonic the attention it deserved. After a long silence she refocused on the letters and Betty. "I'm certain that Tom is telling us that he is half way done with his tour!"

"Based on what?" asked Betty.

"Based on his comment about his mindset and being half minded. I'm sure of it."

"That would mean Tom will be back in a couple of months!" but Betty sighed and shook off the excitement "I know I should be excited, but I don't think I can go there and hold it together if he stays longer."

"I'm sure of it, he'll be home sooner than you think."

"You keep track of the time. I'm going to keep thinking that he won't be back early. It's the only way I can deal with the not knowing."

Jil took Betty into her arms and hugged her tight. "It's been a tough four months."

"The next few months will be tougher, especially if he doesn't come home like you think."

"I'm sure this means Tom will be back by fall," but she did not push the point too hard.

"I need to think of this as a sentence with no parole. That Tom is in for the duration of a tour and there is no early release."

To each their own, Jil thought.

Tom was wishing he had brought more of the wet wipes. He was able to trade for a couple of packs, but they were the baby-scented kind. He thought he had a line on the unscented, but the price was too high. He decided to split the difference and go with the scented. *I'm not trying to attract anyone out here, anyway; maybe it will repel Babs? Well, it is better than none,* he supposed. Sand and dust seemed to get into everything. Everything. Getting enough water was his first daily priority, followed by getting enough sleep: *if it isn't gunfire, it's Babs making a frontal assault. I just need to be strong, but sometimes I'm not sure who the enemy is, the Iranian IEDs or Babs.*

Thirty-Two

On the Rocks

JIL WAS CRYING, sobbing into Betty's shoulder.

"I can't believe it," said Betty. "I am so sorry, Jil. I've always thought of Ruth as my sister. I can't believe this has happened."

The devastating news had come over the phone to Betty an hour before from her mother, Beth. Betty rushed over to Jil's penthouse to be with her. Jil had already gotten the news from Janice, her mother. "Ruth was kidnapped at gunpoint as she was leaving her office."

"Why was she leaving so early? Did she have an appointment? Did the police question," Betty could not finish her sentence before Jil interrupted her.

"She was walking to the parking lot across the street to get her cellphone—she forgot it in the car, when a dark clothed man about five ten and around one hundred eighty-five pounds grabbed her." Jil's voice was shaky and her hands trembling.

"How did they get the description?" Betty checked herself; she was using her deposition voice. Jil needed a friend, not a lawyer.

"From witnesses. The getaway car was Ruth's black 2000 Audi A6, so no description to go on to track the kidnapper."

"Did he leave a ransom note?"

Jil shook her head no. "No ransom note and no call. Her car was found only a few miles away in an empty parking lot with no evidence of a struggle or means to track where they went next. They are searching the area."

"Rob is beside himself. I talked to Mom before coming here." Betty handed Jil a fresh tissue.

"When was the last time Rob saw her?" inquired Jil.

"Ruth and Rob tried to get back together—to work things out. They were at my parents' house for dinner three weeks ago. Mom said Ruth seemed distracted and despite Rob cajoling her to find out what was wrong, nothing he said or did seemed to work."

"Oh, he must have been frustrated," Jil blew her nose several times into the tissue before throwing it onto the coffee table. "She can be pretty tight lipped when she wants to be."

"Finally, enough was enough. Rob stayed behind and Ruth took off in that sports car of hers. I don't think Ruth even wanted to part as friends, which was very hard on Rob. I feel like Ruth is my older sister too!" Betty reminded Jil.

"I guess after fifteen years of living at each other's house, since that first camp out together at Lakeside Beach..." Jil did not finish her sentence and began to sob again.

Betty waited awhile and then cleared her throat. "It's been twelve hours since the first report. I guess with no new leads we have nothing to do but wait."

"Mom and Dad think it's that old boyfriend." Jil waved her hand dismissively.

"That guy with the goatee? The artist?" Betty tried to paint a picture in her mind of the last boyfriend she could remember at Thanksgiving dinner the previous year. "It was hard to like him after she broke up with Rob."

"Not that loser, he was just a phase! I'm talking about the salesman, the one that Ruth broke up with Rob to date about five months ago. She came home with a bruise under her left eye and wouldn't talk about it."

"What was his name?"

"Darryl, Darryl something." Jil seemed in too much of a daze to think clearly.

"Darryl? Not Darryl Hampton? He was that quarterback from Marshall High. He's a couple of years older, I think. Isn't he some hotshot salesman now?" Betty was picturing a Harley riding galoot, wearing a handlebar mustache who liked to talk big and spend big.

"Yes, that's the one. He has an alibi—out of town on a business trip."

Betty handed Jil another handful of tissues. "Where was he?"

"The police found him in Wichita, Kansas, making a sales call just two hours after the abduction." Jil looked disappointed.

"No way he could have gotten that far that quick." *It's funny how the police were interested in him when his name came up,* thought Betty. *He always did have a reputation of being rough with his girlfriends. Was Ruth trying to make Rob jealous?* Reviewing the evidence brought little new insight to Betty, so she worked at calming her friend down instead. Just as Jil had calmed down a little bit more, Jil's cellphone rang. Betty answered it, "Jil Harper's, Betty Thursten speaking...oh, Mr. Harper, I'm so sorry...oh, yes, she's here, let me get her on the phone."

Betty handed the phone over as Jil reached slowly to take it, seemingly reluctant to hear the news about to come.

"Yes, Daddy." The sound of Larry's deep baritone voice could be heard murmuring from the cellphone.

Jil's face went ashen.

She started to cry; then stopped the tears. Her face went tight. Jil was a skilled actress capable of going through four or five emotions in under a minute, but the first two emotions sure looked genuine to Betty. *The calm submissive look is the scariest. How can she be so calm now with what is happening?*

"Yes, of course, Daddy. I will let everyone know at this end." Jil carefully placed the cellphone on the coffee table as if she was using this moment to collect herself and put on her pageant face.

"Did the kidnapper call? What do the police know?" asked Betty.

"Betty," Jil awkwardly chuckled as she articulated her friends name, "You won't believe this, but Ruth went to Europe. There wasn't a kidnapping at all, apparently she has a new boyfriend, a European fellow—from Denmark. He asked her to go there this week and she simply forgot to mention it to Mom or Daddy. How silly this has all been. Oh, get me a stiff gin and tonic will you, Bets? I'm fixing to fall out."

Betty obliged by walking over to the bar, but she was not buying a syllable of that performance. Having watched Jil perform for the judges in pageants and the audiences at school plays, Betty did not believe this act. *Jil doesn't think she sold it either; that is why she asked for the G&T, to buy some time to compose herself.*

Betty slowly mixed the drinks as she pondered Jil's demeanor. *Of course, the police were called from the start, no wonder the Harpers are backtracking now to get them to leave. Damn rich people gallivanting off to Europe on a spur of the moment vacation. Who had time to investigate those kinds of abductions?* thought Betty.

Jil took the G&T from Betty, squeezing the lime just a little bit as if she needed a bitter pill at that moment, something to take her mind off acting and pull herself into character. She held the lime off to the side of the overstuffed brown leather couch dangling it between her third finger and thumb almost as if to say, oh, no cares in the world here, my sister is just off on vacation, no kidnapping to worry about, false alarm.

"Thank you, Betty. Oh, you had to have had such a scare there. I know I did. Ha, that sister of mine, Ruth." Jil shook her hair out as if she were a mother describing her rascal of a daughter. "She is in so much trouble when she gets back, double for not telling me she was invited to Europe. Maybe I would have liked to go too? Maybe Victor, that's his name, mind you, has a friend or a brother for me."

She was obviously trying too hard to laugh this off and she knew it. She bit her lip and looked at a frowning, disbelieving Betty.

"You're not buying it, are you?" Jil asked.

Betty looked Jil deep in the eye and stated matter-of-factly, "Not for a second, sister. Spill the beans."

Jil looked down at her Jimmy Choo pumps, kicking them off and curling her legs up under her. She sucked on the G&T for a moment through the straw like a little girl.

"Betty, you have to swear you will tell no one what I am about to tell you. No one. If you tell anyone about this, Ruth may be killed!"

"You know I won't!" insisted Betty. *Here comes another avalanche of bullshit!*

Jil placed the drink down on the side table as her cat, Steve, a gorgeous Persian with striking blue eyes, jumped into her lap. She began to stroke the fur of the feline when she looked over at Betty and said, "Daddy lost it all. Back, what two years ago? Remember when I...I... took that job with Spector? Daddy had bet everything and then some, leveraged to the gills, on a multinational manufacturing company. Widget something or other, I don't know, anyway,"

"I remember—go on," prodded Betty.

Jil took a deep breath and let out a sad sigh."He was able to make a deal with a Danish company to salvage something out of it...to finish the deal and walk away with his dignity and our house. He was not allowed to keep much else. A pawn! Daddy was king and now he is just a pawn of those bastards!"

"I don't understand," Betty squinted her eyes slightly as she tried to mentally visualize a chess set.

"Remember in *Good Fellas* when they robbed the restaurant blind by taking merchandise in the front and sold it out the back until they shut the place down and torched it?" asked Jil.

"Oh, I see," stated Betty.

"That's what they did to Daddy and his company. He had to take orders and like it. He was told to make bets against his own company, bets that if the SEC found out would put him in jail," Jil paused to take a drink from her glass.

"So he had to lose more money?" asked Betty.

"Well, no, he won big on those bets because they drove Daddy's company into the ground," said Jil pausing to look into her drink, the end was near. "Since then he has had to make trades when and how they tell him, he is the cat's paw, a tool of a hidden hand no one sees."

She leaned back into the chair, sucked on the G&T until the ice cubes rattled in the cut crystal glass. "Daddy thought he could end it, not do anymore trades for them."

"Did he stop?" asked Betty.

Jil shook her head no, "He did one last big one and that was going to be it." Jil paused to put her glass down, "Well, they aren't going to let that be it...they have taken Ruth to Denmark for 'safe keeping' until Daddy finishes what they want him to finish."

"What's he going to do? Who can help?" asked Betty.

"Oh, Betty, he's damned if he does and damned if he doesn't. He'll go to jail if he does the trades and they'll kill Ruth if he doesn't."

The cool character Jil, the former call girl and now mistress to Senator Bolden, actually did break down and Betty did not think this was acting.

What could she say? Betty went over to comfort her friend and tell her, "Don't worry. It will all work out. Ruth will be fine and your Dad will get out of this mess, you just wait and see." Betty felt like she was the one putting on a show now.

"How, Betty? I just don't see a way out of this mess. My family is at the edge of an abyss and there is a forest fire behind us!" said a despondent Jil.

"I bet your old Grandpa Randall is coming out of his grave to go handle these European mobsters. He won't put up with it, I tell you," Betty wryly predicted.

"I hope you're right, Betty. We're going to need all the help we can get," said Jil as she brightened just enough to lift her head up and smile a small smile.

I need a drink after that performance. Hell, I could use two stiff drinks about now.

THIRTY-THREE

THE NOW AND THEN AND BACK AGAIN

"**Y**OU, WHORE!" exclaimed Betty.

Slap. The burn on Betty's cheek stung not because of the impact and friction of Jil's hand across her face, but because she had come to the realization that her best friend, her surrogate sister, her confidant of the past sixteen years had been lying to her about everything. Betty's gut was churning as she realized the truth. She could not believe it at first, she would not believe it. Sara had called from Senator Bolden's office worried about Jil and turned to Betty for help. It did not matter to Betty why she had called—Jil was still working as an escort and was Senator Bolden's mistress as well. None of it would have made sense without the revelation a few months before about Harper, Inc. being busted, broke, and a sham for the past two or three years. Larry Harper was under the thumb of Danish businessmen who would stop at nothing to get what they wanted.

"I don't know you anymore."

"Did you ever!" Jil haughtily decried her former best friend.

"How could you?"

"I'm not a whore!"

"You sold yourself to those men—and Senator Bolden?" asked Betty.

Jil shrieked back, "You judgmental, bitch."

Jil reached back to slap again as Betty took a defensive jujitsu stance, "Try it again and I'll break your arm."

Jil looked like a possessed demon as she yelled, "Out of my house! I don't want to ever see you again."

Betty stood directly in front of Jil and calmly but sternly said, "No matter what you say or do I will always love you as my sister, but you will have to re-earn my respect and trust."

"I don't want either—get the hell out!"

"I won't be back as long as you do this to yourself and your family."

Betty strode purposefully out of the penthouse slamming the door behind her; she could still hear Jil screaming at her from behind the closed door as she got into the elevator in the foyer. Betty was grateful for the private elevator to the first floor, giving her time to compose herself. She was going to miss the old Jil, but did not relish the real Jil she had seen tonight. Betty felt betrayed in a way she had never thought possible. *None of this matters now! Tom is back!* Betty reassured herself.

Tom was back in the United States at the Walter Reed Physical Therapy Clinic and Betty was waiting for visiting hours to begin at 1100 hours. A call from Tom Howell Sr. had alerted her to Tom's return and location. Betty had never spoken to Tom's father before because of the estrangement, so it was a little awkward talking to the surly old man. *Tom is avoiding me for whatever reason; he probably had some minor injury and is too embarrassed for me to see it. I only want to be with him.* She was tired of waiting and ready to move on to the next phase of their lives. He had promised her that he would wait for her, that when he got back they would become engaged and then set a date for their wedding. Betty called him at the hospital incessantly for two days before deciding to stop by to see him but was turned away by the station nurse. The nurse claimed that since Tom and Betty were not married, Betty did not have the right to know any details of Tom's condition.

"I'm sorry, Miss...what was your name again?" the station nurse in Tom's unit seemed distracted, like she had better things to do than talk, yet again, to a patients girlfriend.

"Betty, Betty Thursten!" Betty's patience was thin as the vellum she had planned for their wedding stationary. Her grip on the counter turning her fingers white.

"Oh, yes, the one who has been calling multiple times per day," said the nurse looking up over her reading glasses.

"Excuse me?"

"Miss Thursten, unless you are married to Lieutenant Howell, I can't give you any information."

Betty lifted her hand to show the promise ring. "We are engaged... well, promised to be married. We were going to set the date when he got back." Betty smiled to show her pride.

"I don't see your name listed as spouse," the nurse began rustling the papers in front of her as if they were more important than Betty. Other nurses in the unit stood around talking about a bridal shower coming up on the weekend.

"What do you mean my name isn't listed?" Betty tried to smooth her voice and released her death grip on the counter. *Why didn't Tom tell them? Is he that hurt? Is he hiding something?* Betty girded her lawyer skills and struck back, "Your policy statement says you encourage visitation, why am I being denied?"

"Miss Thursten, Betty, the doctors sometimes discourage visitation; however, I can't speak to the particulars of this case."

"Particulars of the case?" Betty's face grew darker.

"Perhaps there is a misunderstanding. Lieutenant Howell will give you a call when he is ready. Have a nice day." The nurse turned away and began to ignore Betty. This infuriated Betty further, even though she knew they were right on the law. *Can't they understand I lived with Tom? That he was promised to me? Why doesn't he ask to see me!* Reluctantly, Betty turned and left without seeing Tom. It was not until the next day that he finally took Betty's call. "Sweetheart, how are you? I've missed you so much...when can I see you?"

"Oh, Betty, soon. These pain meds just make me loopy. The doctor is here, I have to go," and moments later Betty was talking to dead air.

Tom kept putting her off until suddenly he changed his tone and said he would meet her in two days at the Capital Grille. Betty was on cloud nine. She imagined that the rehabilitation from whatever injuries he had received was not nearly as tough as the psychological toll he suffered from the injury. Though her attitude deflated when she thought, *I wish I could call Jil and tell her the good news.*

The episode with Jil just a month before had been overwhelming—calling each other names, the accusations, revelations, and the slap. The revelations had been so large they were hard to digest. *Jil is a consort to the senator, plus the lies and deceptions about being an escort. Jil isn't the girl I grew up knowing. This isn't the same person I've lived with for almost half my life!*

Thirty-Four

Beware the Ides of March

I T HAD BEEN NEARLY A YEAR since the breakup with Howell. She had seen him in the distance several times but made no effort to catch up to him. The closest they had come was when Betty earned her black belt in jujitsu. Betty was surprised to see him there, but quickly realized Howell was there for his buddy, not her. Howell did not even acknowledge Betty except for a strange look in his eye, sadness perhaps. If Howell wanted to see her, he knew where she was.

More disquieting than seeing Howell again was who he was with. It was mid December, Howell was walking out of the Capitol Grille with his father as Betty was walking from her office, lost in thought. He walked somewhat stiffly, so Betty assumed his leg was still bothering him. *Men,* she thought. *How arrogant he is, thinking he can fix things by himself—by avoiding our relationship instead of working with me to heal whatever is eating at him. I could help him if he would only let me.* Betty spun away, harrumphed to no one in particular and began to take yoga breaths as she reminded herself that only she was in control of her mood. *I'll find a different Metro entrance, I guess.*

Today's tour of the penthouse in Old Town Alexandria, before signing the lease, felt like a new beginning. She was finally getting out of the loft. She hated to leave, but the memories were too raw, just as the memories of Howell were too painful for a new relationship. Friends had tried to set her up on several blind dates. She did not show up for the first two, so her friends dragged her to the third blind date with Ted. Ted was wonderful—Betty might have fallen for him, but the wounds from Howell were too fresh. Ted had been so sweet that Betty assumed he had been warned to be careful. *Had he been so kind and gentle for that reason?* Ted allowed Betty to turn the conversation back to Howell constantly: his injuries, the mysteries behind that man, and the pain Betty felt.

"Before Tom went to Iraq he had been so accessible. He had revealed so much of his inner self to me and now...nothing." Betty could not clear her head of Tom.

Ted had taken her to the Roof Terrace Restaurant for dinner to be followed by the opening of *Mame* at the Kennedy Center for the Performing Arts. The view of the harbor and Theodore Roosevelt Island were stunning as the sun began to set just before the performance.

"Ted, I'm sorry. I just can't seem to get my mind off my ex, can I?" sighed Betty as she turned to her date.

"It's OK, I'm sure *Mame* will tickle your funny bone enough to make you forget for at least a little while!" The ever cheerful Ted proffered his arm to Betty for the walk to the theater.

"You deserve my full attention," *but as nice as you are, you aren't grabbing it from me,* thought Betty as she forced a smile. The couple slowly walked with the crowd into the theater to find their seats, bumping gently into the mass of people as if they were on a bus or a train in motion.

After the first act and during the intermission, Betty found herself forgetting Tom and the past and began to focus on Ted. The play was just the tonic for her ills. By the end of the play, Betty's mind was on her date and the wonderful performance of Christine Baranski as the title character, Mame.

"Baranski's timing was perfect, don't you think?" declared Ted as they exited the theater. Betty nodded in agreement as the crowd pushed them gently forward. Exiting the Kennedy Center into the beautiful night, the skyline ablaze with the lights of the monuments, Betty sighed a satisfied sigh and Ted guided Betty on his elbow. "Let's walk a short bit, what do you think?"

"Oh, a short walk would be OK, but I'm not very good in heels," Betty minced around a puddle, clinging to Ted's arm to keep from falling.

"Good, a short walk, then a foot massage will be your reward!" Ted took a deep breath in, expanding his chest, looking proud as if he had just won an award for getting his date's mind off an ex.

The National Mall was a short walk south from the Kennedy Center. Rock Creek Park Trails followed the shoreline of the Potomac. Ted and Betty became engrossed in conversation, talking mostly about Ted's work as a botanist for the Department of Agriculture. He pointed out the different flora along the way.

"The cherry blossoms are gone now, but let's walk the basin—if your feet aren't too tired?" asked Ted anxiously.

"Oh, they are holding up OK, but you better not renege on your promise to give me a long foot massage!" Betty was warming up to Ted.

As they turned onto West Basin Drive, it dawned on Betty that they were entering the FDR Memorial. Suddenly, the past was present and the mood broken. The mirage that she could escape from Tom and her past evaporated as quickly as her good mood.

"Ted, I'm sorry, you've been absolutely wonderful, but I think I need to go home," Betty started to sniffle and pulled a tissue from her clutch.

"I don't understand. What, what's wrong?" Ted turned to Betty and gently held her bare arms underneath her shawl.

"Oh crap, Ted, I don't want to have to explain everything all over again."

"It's OK. I'll call a cab." Ted sounded deflated but supportive.

"Ted, this is the FDR Memorial. It's where Tom and I, it's where Tom is supposed to meet me one year after we broke up, next month on the 12th." Betty's gaze was on the ground. Her feet were hurting and she was not likely to get a foot massage tonight.

"Why are you going to meet?"

"Tom said—he said if I still loved him, we are to meet here to see if we can work things out."

"Are you going?" Ted seemed puzzled.

"I don't know. My heart says yes but my head says no way." Betty pulled the wrap tighter around her shoulders; the night suddenly seemed colder.

"Oh," was all Ted could muster. He whistled loudly with his fingers in his mouth to hail a passing cab.

"Ted, I'm so sorry. Can you forgive me?" Betty dried her eyes and tried to give her date the attention he was due.

"I forgive you, but you must forgive me for bringing you here. Let me make it up to you. We can go somewhere out of town." Ted pressed his fingers against Betty's lips to keep her from answering as the cab pulled up. "Don't answer now."

"Ted, you deserve better," Betty made room for Ted as he held the door to the cab.

"I think I'll walk a bit before going home, you don't mind, do you?" Ted handed the driver a twenty-dollar bill. "Keep the change," and Ted closed the door. The cab ride home was lonely as the tears fell from Betty's eyes. *Ted isn't going to call again, not after tonight. Damn it! He was so normal! Why can't I fall for the average nice guy?* Betty took off her shoes and rubbed her feet as the cab rocked on its ancient shocks over the streets of Washington, D. C.

✝

The rocking of the Metro train had lulled Betty into deep thoughts, but the shrill sound of the train coming to a stop at the Pentagon brought her out of rehashing the past. She was on her way to see the penthouse and if it looked as good in person as the website promised she would get the keys and start painting. What did it matter? She was not going to be at the FDR Memorial at 4 p.m. on April 12th. She was not going to give him the satisfaction of rejecting her a second time.

It's March 15th, thought Betty. "Beware the Ides of March," she blurted out to no one in particular.

The man next to her was startled and tried to shift slowly across the aisle as if he had dropped something.

"Oh, did I say that out loud?" Betty said as she looked sheepishly at the worried little bureaucrat. "Julius Caesar, that's what happened on March 15th, Julius Caesar was—oh never mind, I guess you've never seen Shakespeare's *Julius Caesar?*"

Betty was reminded of the movie *Point of No Return.* Looking at the man and quickly away, then back again with a smile, *What did Anne Bancroft tell Bridget Fonda's character, the assassin, to say in awkward moments?* Catching the scared little man's eye, she recalled wistfully aloud, "Oh, I never did really mind the little things," then looked straight ahead at nothing in particular. She tried to be serious at that point, but just started to uncontrollably giggle. The man across the way tried to shrink into his seat and looked like he could not wait to get off at the next stop, even if it was going to mean a long walk, he was getting off. As he rushed out the doors Betty's giggles began to subside. It felt good to let go for once. *It's been, what, almost two years since Tom went off to Iraq?* It was that way now; the before and the after times. Before he was Tom, now, he would always be Howell. Tom was a different person, warm, loving, caring. This man Howell had stolen Tom's body and locked away the man she loved. *I can never like or trust that doppelganger Howell.* She longed for the day she would see Tom again...then a serious look came over her face.

I won't ever get Tom back, I know that now. I need to move on; I hope the penthouse is what I'm looking for. Yes, a new place is the first step to my new life, thought Betty to herself.

She stopped being so serious and took a moment to look around the Metro car. *All these serious faces. Lost souls on their way home for sure but so serious. It's as if the work of the government went home with them and only in a secret room in their homes, after a few drinks and their overcoat in the closet, do they become human again. I am so thankful that my job is fulfilling, even if it means dealing with bureaucrats on a daily basis. I know I'm helping people become Americans or come to America: the greatest country and the greatest place on earth. OK, that was a little over the top,* thought Betty, *I'm getting sappy, time to get off this train and start anew.*

Thirty-Five

Ms. Thursten, I Presume

WHEN SHE ARRIVED at the rental agency, Betty felt very excited and nervous. She did not have a roommate so this was a big change from her past rental adventures. Well, to put a fine point on it, she had had only two roommates in her life: Jil and Tom. Even as a child, being the only girl, she had her own room. Her brothers Rob and Bill had shared a room when they were young. That room was now called "Bill's room," even though the same two beds were still there.

Thinking of Bill's room made her recall the time Tom had gone back to Rochester with her for Thanksgiving. Dealing with her parents on sleeping arrangements was stressful. Betty's mom insisted Tom sleep in a separate bedroom. *Hello. We are living together in a loft apartment with only one bed and a couch. Where do you think we sleep?* When Beth had told Betty that Tom would be sleeping in Bill's room, Betty got rather sassy. "Mom, Tom and I sleep together."

"Well, now Betty, you know your father's and my opinion on premarital living arrangements."

"We have sex several times a week. Sometimes it's even the mission position."

"Betty, I am so glad that you feel comfortable sharing these things with me. Tom will be in Bill's room. Our house, our rules."

That was the end of that conversation. Betty had tried to get a rise out of her mother and it did not work, but her sharp legal mind had seen a loophole. Her mother had not said where Betty would be sleeping. Betty went to her room as if she was going to sleep. After an eternity that lasted fifteen minutes, she thought her parents would be settled in. She could hear the TV on in their bedroom so she snuck over to Bill's room only to find her father sitting on the bed talking to Tom. Betty was wearing a pair of Tom's pajamas; the sleeves were too long, which kept her hands warm.

"Daddy!"

"Well, Bets. What a surprise, we were just talking about you. Sit down right here next to your dear old dad."

Betty tried to hide her surprise and chagrin at being found out. Her parents had known her better than she thought. *I wonder if mom set me up! Her way of getting back at me for sticking my sex life with Tom in her face? Oh, God, just thinking of mom and the sex talk! What a bizarre conversation! Going through puberty; having those talks with Mom.* Beth had been very open about sex, even masturbation. She laid it all out for Betty and finished by saying that she hoped Betty would wait until she was older to have sex, but realized that was probably too much to ask of any kid. She asked that Betty only have sex because she wanted to and not to let a boy pressure her. Listening to her mother talk about the pitfalls and joys of sex was at first traumatic then surreal.

Betty waited until well after two a.m. before she made her next rebel attempt at breaching her parents' perimeter. She knew which boards creaked, that the bedroom door handle had to be held hard to the left as you gently press your shoulder into the door to make it stay closed and to cover the vent with a pillow to keep sound from traveling between rooms. She even put pillows under her covers to make it look like she was still in bed should they check on their way to God knows where. Tom was her teddy bear, her nappy, her security blanket. Her world felt more complete with him by her side, especially in bed.

She lifted up the covers and slid into bed next to Tom, it was a tight fit in the old twin bed. Tom roused enough to move over; then realizing what was happening he picked her up and placed her on top of him under the covers. She could feel the warmth coming from his body, the firm taut muscles under the white t-shirt he was wearing. They began to kiss, Betty straddling her man at the waist, her knees resting gently on the mattress as she put her weight on Tom. She rubbed his chest with her left hand as she steadied herself with her right. The kissing was gentle at first and then Tom began to kiss her neck, slowly moving up to her earlobe.

"I don't want you to get in trouble with your parents," whispered Tom.

"You mean you don't want to get in trouble with my parents, right?" She slowly rubbed against his groin feeling the silk boxers he was wearing glide against her cotton pajama bottoms.

"I think I'm over dressed for the occasion," said Betty slyly as Tom's hands slid down her back, stroking her muscles as he descended to her hips. His meaty hands massaging her ass while gently rocking her hips forward and back. Betty reached down to remove her pajama bottoms, but Tom was already helping her with this nuisance. The bed creaked slightly as they shifted around but the TV was still on in her parent's room, so she was not too concerned. Betty was not wearing any panties under the bottoms, so now as she settled back on top of Tom she could feel the smooth silk of his boxers. Betty was not going to rush, though it pained her to go slow. Breaking the rules with her parents in the next room made sex in the tiny twin bed exciting, even dangerous. *Did Tom tighten the bolts like I asked him?* She could feel Tom's warm firm hands massaging her ass again, moving around softly and yet taking time to work her muscles. *God, that feels good,* thought Betty as they kissed deeper, longer, and fuller. His hands moved up her sides cupping her firm breasts as he pinched her nipples gently, rubbing them lightly. His hands were warm and sensuous on her smooth, firm skin.

Her hands rubbed his chest, stopping at his nipples to give him the same treatment. She pulled his shirt off and bent from the waist to kiss his chest, slowly moving from side to side and down his middle. Betty slid a hand slowly down Tom's chest until she could feel the band of the boxers—all that was separating the two of them from merging as one. She played around the edge both teasing Tom and checking once more with her conscience to see if she was going to go through with having sex in her parents' house on her brother's bed. Yes, she certainly was as the boxers slid down far enough for Betty to take control of the situation.

All of this flashed back to her as she walked into the Bosley Rental Agency because the rental agent looked so much like her mother. Grace read her nametag. Beth Thursten and the rental agent were probably about the same age, around that fifty-five to sixty gray area, Grace was dated more by her Farrah Fawcett hairstyle than how she looked. She was a fit woman who obviously cared about her figure and looks. Betty hoped she would be looking as good at Grace's age, but with a more modern hairstyle.

Grace took Betty's hand to shake it and stated her name, "Grace, Grace Arthur. We spoke on the phone I believe? Ms. Thursten, I presume?"

Betty was a little taken aback by Grace's formality and obvious foreknowledge of who she was until she remembered the extensive application form she had to fill out to get a chance at the penthouse. This penthouse had two bedrooms and two full baths in the old district of Alexandria. It had a view of the Potomac, which she found reassuring, her anchor point in the D.C. area. The King Street Metro Station was only a mile away, so on nice days she would walk and on bad days, she could take the bus. She did not have a car nor had she ever wanted one while living in the District. By not having a car, she saved almost enough each month to afford the upgrade to the penthouse without a roommate. The rent was steep at $3,500 per month, but by not paying parking at either end of her commute, the cost of insurance, gas, and maintenance she could afford it even if she did not find a roommate for a few months.

Tom was generous, too generous, about catching up on his half the rent. Betty had doubts about Howell's intentions, *that doppelganger Howell didn't have anything to say about Tom's generosity.* She envisioned the split person Tom and Howell fighting over her: *Tom wants to be with me, that bastard coward Howell running away; focus, Betty, focus* she could hear her jujitsu instructor say.

Grace looked at Betty a little oddly, tilting her head just a little to the right and said, "Ms. Thursten, is everything OK?"

Betty shook her head and realized that she was still holding Grace's hand; she released it and said, "Oh, I'm sorry, just that you remind me of my mother, sort of a younger sister," Betty quickly added to not be dating the older woman. "Please call me Betty."

Grace smiled and thanked Betty. "You shall call me Grace, then. Shall we go see the penthouse? The view is amazing."

"I can't wait to see it." The pair began walking across the street to the apartment building. Grace offered to take the elevator but said, "I usually take the stairs myself; it's the little things that matter, keeping in shape you know."

There were five flights of stairs to the top, Betty did not pause, "The stairs will be fine."

"I live on the fourth floor now," Grace pointed to her doorway across from the stairs.

"Was it your penthouse before?" Betty surmised from the conversation.

Rather mysteriously, not going into any great detail Grace explained, "I no longer need the second bedroom. I suppose I'm downsizing."

Betty jumped in, "Don't you mean rightsizing?" Grace smiled a small smile looking down slightly as if she were checking her footing.

Looking up she said in a silky smooth voice, "Yes, you're quite right, rightsizing."

The view from the dormer windows at the top of the stairs was amazing. Betty could smell the city, the Potomac and the faint smell of brine from the sea drifting through the open window. It was a glorious day. Dogs were allowed here, so Surry was welcome, even if she was a little large for the rules. Grace was willing to bend them on Betty's promise that she would behave, Surry that is, along with a small five hundred dollar deposit against any potential damage.

The main rooms were tastefully painted in light hues ranging from a light sage to lemon peel to dusty orange. Some rooms had an accent wall color that was in delightful contrast to the rest of the room. The ceilings were quite high, probably twelve feet at the peaks, but lower at the edges of the apartment due to the roofline. The woodwork was vast but painted white. Betty had expected eggshell white walls and had requested permission to immediately paint if the apartment had not been painted recently. Grace had said on the phone that the apartment had been painted only a year before, but if Betty had a different color pallet she liked she was welcome to paint away.

Some of Grace's moving boxes were in the foyer. "Oh, I'll have those out this afternoon, and you can start your painting as soon as you sign the lease."

Betty looked around then back at Grace, "This feels like home, I don't think I need to paint right now. I like your taste, Grace."

Thirty-Six

Patada en el Culo

THE *THUMP THUMP THUMP* of the helicopters usually calmed Betty. Sitting in the back with the thin padding of the seats and the smell of aviation fuel, grease, and gunpowder was somehow erotic to her. The adrenaline of action seemed to be the only thing she lived for these days. Mr. OMG you're tall, was sitting across from her with his feet stuck over on her side, not because he was trying to hit on her but because he could not stow them in the normal place. Slim took up a lot of space with his gangly frame; in these tight quarters, he looked like a spider forced into a corner, trying to avoid the swat of a rolled up newspaper.

The cowboy hat and boots were gone. He was wearing black garb and a knit cap to hide his shiny, baldhead during this sojourn into the Venezuelan countryside. As was his custom, Slim was chomping on an unlit Cuban cigar. They both had camouflage paint on their faces. Betty's hair was up in a knit cap. She kept her hair shorter these days but not military short. She had to be able to look certain parts at different times. Her olive toned skin and raven hair made the casual observer think she was Hispanic in one situation, Middle Eastern in another. It depended on the clothes, posture, and accent she took on. Her five foot eight frame gave her the advantage of seeing eye to eye with most men when she wore high heels. Even with all of her muscle, her lean frame made her look fifteen pounds slimmer than her one hundred and thirty pounds.

Back when she lived with Tom in Georgetown, she kept her hair just past shoulder length. It shined in the moonlight. In a light wind and afternoon sun, Betty looked like she could be in a shampoo commercial.

Now, her hair was kept to the bottom of her neck: easy to put up but long enough to show off. Tom had liked Betty's long hair. Howell liked her hair short so it would not get in the way on her missions.

Fuck Howell, I might just grow it out for a while. Betty paused for a second, realizing internal aggression was getting the better of her. She did some yoga breathing and calmed herself; emotions killed people, at least the ones who should have lived.

Twenty kilometers inland, after twenty minutes of a rollercoaster, tree-hugging flight, the landing site for the dam was near. The chopper would come close to touching down as it swooped over their mark. They were expected to drop out of the "nest" and be on the run before the bird was lifting up again. The *thump thump thump* was replaced with a whispering *whoosh whoosh whoosh* as the pilots switched to stealth mode two klicks out. The ropes were dropped, carabiners clipped on. Packs checked one more time. *Zipppp, thud, roll.*

Betty leapt to her feet and checked for anything broken, bent, or bruised. *Not easy to roll with thirty pounds of explosives on your back. Sure, they will only go off with the blasting caps armed, but that gives you little solace in the primeval corner of your mind.* They were blasting an earthen dam tonight to destroy a weapons factory run by terrorists supported by the Venezuelan government. The explosion would act as a diversion for the real mission: recovery of stolen Russian nuclear materials. Evidence from the resulting damage was supposed to look like the berm had failed. Traces of the explosives would wash away with the massive wall of water and end up thirty miles downriver. There could be no mistakes here. Slim was to place the explosive charges high on the earthen dam while Betty used a collapsible shovel to bury the charges in the low positions. She was to move down to the building to get the nuclear material while Slim remained on lookout, armed with a sniper's rifle and a scope. He would blow the dam on her signal or in fifteen minutes, whichever came first.

This amount of damage would normally be against Control's design parameters, but the illegal munitions plant was downstream. The whiz kids in intelligence traced several multi-million dollar payments for a dirty bomb being assembled by Al-Qaeda, as well as rocket launchers headed for Hamas and Hezbollah. The Venezuelan government headed by Hugo Chavez was no friend of Israel or America and was harboring the terrorist cell. Casualties were an option tonight, as long as it was blamed on the flooding. Next, they were to split up once the chaos of the flood ensued. Betty had to track down and interrogate Miguel at his plantation and operational headquarters for his militant rebel forces. It was time to determine if he was the mole. Slim was to stay behind to deal with any survivors of the flood and drop a few incendiaries at a nearby terrorist camp to remind them that they were being watched. Finally, just before dawn, they were to meet up at the chopper site one klick to the north of Miguel's plantation. The helicopter would continue south for several kilometers before beginning to turn east. Eventually the flight path would resemble a capital "G" starting north of the dam and ending just north of the plantation.

The two nondescript forms, differentiated mainly by their size, got to work setting the explosives. Somehow, Betty seemed to be getting way ahead of Slim. He was falling farther and farther behind her pace.

"Pick up the pace," Betty barked into her throat mic.

Slim stopped long enough spit out a bit of tobacco leaf before lighting the Cuban. "I'm doing just fine," taunted Slim.

"And get rid of that cigar, don't you know smoking kills," hissed Betty. *Jesus! He's going to get us killed! Where the hell did Howell get this guy?*

When she got to the other side, she paused long enough to see that Slim was checking her work. *What the hell? Where does that high and mighty walking stick get off checking my work?* She stowed the emotion and got ready for the next step of the mission. After inflating the portable raft, she quickly paddled for the munitions building. Checking for guards along the way, she silently moved to the wayward side of the building. There was a dock facing out over the slow moving part of the river, at least for the moment. She climbed out of the raft and headed for the backside where an infrequently used entrance would give her a line of sight of Slim's position. He was to be far enough away from the dam to avoid being hit by debris, but close enough to see through the night scope if anyone escaped. They had separated for the best odds of success.

Something was not right. Slim was not in position. She could see the ember of his cigar like a beacon in the night bouncing down a trail leading to the main road. Slim was supposed to be dealing with survivors, not headed to the next stage of his mission. Betty heard the explosives going off, but they were not supposed to go for another five minutes. *Slim is going to have hell to pay when I catch up to him. He better have a pretty damn good explanation for blowing the dam and leaving me exposed.* The primary mission was to secure the nuclear material to prevent a dirty bomb, *Is Slim the mole or is he off chasing a rabbit?* The plan was for Betty to get into position and determine if the material was accessible. If she did not signal Slim by throat mic, he was to blow the dam after fifteen minutes. Since Slim blew the charges early, Betty knew she had less than two minutes to find the material and get the hell out before a wall of water would reach the building. *There, in the corner! Thirty feet away, might as well be a thousand, with the crew around the bench and a wall of water on its way!* The workers had just gotten the material out and had turned to look where the noise of the explosives had come from.

They raced for the front exit while Betty raced to the material. Grabbing the canister, she threw it into her backpack that only a few minutes before carried explosives. *No small irony—I'm using explosives to stop a terrorist group from using explosives and dirty fissile material to kill.* As she ran back to the dock, the workers began firing AK47's at her moving target. Diving onto the raft, landing half in the water and half on the rubber surface, she quickly gained her balance and began to paddle like mad as bullets *zinged* into the water around her. *About the time they get to the dock they'll figure out they are screwed. I'll be out of range by then,* she hoped. *I want to survive this hell just so I can find Slim and wring his friggin' neck!* There was a roaring sound coming from behind her and the sounds of the workers and guards changed. Instead of being pissed at an attacker, they were now praying to Allah and looking to get their martyr card punched. *It's tough to fight an enemy who has no fear of death, who actually is glad to give up his life to go to the next existence. Then again, I'm one badass enemy of terrorists.*

The water came rushing up behind her. She could not stay on the raft unless she tied herself to it; yet, if she tied herself to it she could drown if it flipped. She did not have a life vest either. Her chances seemed to have gone from good to slim to none. She tied the rafts rope to her arm using a highwayman's hitch. She would be able to hang on if it got too rough and still release it if she flipped. The crest of the wave could not be made out, but she could hear the massive wall of water and feel the back draft as the undertow sucked the water back up the river. She stood up in the raft and got in her best boogie boarder's stance ready to do or die. She found herself in the curl before too long. She needed to ride this current for at least five miles to the rendezvous site; however, with the twists and turns of the river, that did not seem likely. *The trees! That's how I'm going to do this!* By watching the trees and not the water, she would be able to tell which way to go. By leaning just a little to each side, she could control the direction and by bending the raft a little with the rope attached to her arm, she could control the amplitude of her ride.

After three minutes of a harrowing ride, she knew she was getting close. *I don't want to overshoot the target, better to have to walk a klick than to shoot past into more trouble. There, that bend, if I lean far enough to the right I can get out of this wave.* She let go of the rope and grabbed onto a branch. She clung on for dear life for the few minutes it took for the massive wall of water to move beyond her. The lesser mass behind would be calmer. It took fifteen minutes for the river to subside, but she was way ahead of schedule for the rendezvous anyway. Her clothes were soaked and the canister had bruised her back and head pretty badly on that ride, but she felt good about preserving the mission and her life. *Not much farther*, she reminded herself. *Not much farther to the chopper and a chance to kick Mr. Slim's skinny ass from here to Caracas.*

THIRTY-SEVEN

NO SMOKING

THE RIDE DOWN THE RIVER had been exciting enough, but now Betty needed to cover about two kilometers in the dark to get to Miguel's plantation. Slim was to meet her at the pick up point a kilometer beyond Miguel's. There were likely hostile forces around but the locals would find her a curiosity, especially if she ditched some of her black garb. *Not much left of the night,* thought Betty as she used the cover of darkness to make up for lost time. Betty could run a 5K in about twenty minutes in her boots and gear, but the canister was not very tight to her back and that worried her. *This thing is going to bruise the hell out of my back! Hope the canister is still sealed and intact.* The backpack was designed to shield from possible radiation leakage, but she was not anxious to find out how good it was. She stopped long enough to ditch unnecessary equipment and to pad the canister. *Damn, those radiation symbols don't give you much comfort up close.*

Betty massaged her scalp after putting her knit cap in the bag. *God, it feels good to let my hair down. Off to the races!* thought Betty.

The trail was in pretty good shape, the light of the rising moon was OK in open ground but worthless in the shade of the trees. She managed until the gully wash. Betty tripped as she went down the embankment and landed face first into the mud and muck just missing a large sharp rock by inches. The rock would have crushed her face had she hit it at full speed, but she was able to soften the landing with her arms. Using a flashlight was out of the question; she would just have to slow down.

The ground was changing. Betty was now on the plantation; she was passing through what looked like coffee and cocoa. The concentric circles of low plants matched the aerial photos of Miguel's coffee plantation. *The rows are laid out in the wrong direction for quick movement, but I'm in the right place! At least I'm not climbing through ravines and creeks.* The cocoa trees were easier to move in, but her line of sight was limited.

I suppose if I can't see them, they can't see me! Betty thought to herself. She had her 9mm MAC-10 out just in case. The silencer made it the perfect weapon for this situation. Though originally an American made weapon, other countries such as Chile and Columbia would license the manufacturing process. Betty's was of Colombian origin. Control never wanted to leave a trace, if possible, as to where the damage came from. So far the evidence was dead or buried under the rushing water. Now Betty needed to remove any trace of herself from Venezuela before she was found. She could pass as a local but not dressed like this, let alone with the cargo in her backpack. If her reckoning was accurate, she was a kilometer from the rendezvous point. Dawn was coming soon and the workers would be getting into the fields. Betty had to get to the choppers. They would leave with her or without her before first light to avoid detection.

It would have been simpler to rendezvous in the rough terrain she had just come from, far from watching eyes, but there was one more target to take care of before leaving. A calling card, an F-U to the guerrilla who had turned on Control. Miguel had actually been the reason Howell had started to suspect a mole. The information coming from Miguel was accurate and designed to lure agents to their death. Miguel provided information that led to traps: the apartment above the bar in Caracas and the compound in the mountains between Columbia and Venezuela with the eco-terrorist. Ultimately, the information seemed designed to test or weaken Control.

It had been Slim's job to clean up any terrorists that might have survived the flood. He also was on this mission to start a rumor about giants stalking the terrorists should any survive and get away. *A little misdirection—makes people think in mythological terms instead of reality. Get them off balance and they start making mistakes. Mistakes can be leveraged.* Betty was still deeply troubled by Slim's messing with the charges. *Something just isn't right!*

Wait, what is that? thought Betty as she slowly approached the clearing to the main house. She spotted an impossibly tall figure crouched behind a shed smoking that damn cigar.

That bastard, thought Betty, *h*e *isn't supposed to be here!* Slim was to meet Betty at the rendezvous point and was not briefed on Miguel or the plantation. *This can only mean one thing: Slim is working with the Mole! He can't be the Mole—he joined Control too recently. What the hell is going on here?* Her orders were clear. If Slim deviated from the plan, she was to bring him in for questioning or shoot to kill. This posed a serious problem for Betty. She had no delusions of being able to carry a subdued Slim to the landing zone. *With a jujitsu chokehold I can have Slim out cold in under a minute. Capturing Slim is not going to be a problem. Transporting the big man, now that is going to be a problem. The question now is, do I just kill Slim or give it the old college try and capture him? Either of my brothers would be simple, but this guy's a giant!*

Her MAC-10 was lethal to fifty meters and accurate to one hundred meters. She was far from Slim now and it would be difficult to get within fifty meters without being noticed. She was not too worried about the sound of the MAC-10. The silencer was so effective that the mechanical action of the bolt could be heard over the sound of the bullet firing.

A fuel tank was between her and Slim. If she could get there she might have a kill shot; or if she thought she could take him, move in for a better chance of subduing the giant. He was not looking her way but that did not mean much. Crouching low and trying to keep her equipment from making noise, Betty slowly covered the ground to the tank. The clouds overhead blocked the coming dawn light. There were no lights on at the plantation except for a high-pressure sodium barnyard light about two hundred meters to the east. *Luckily, the light is more useful to me than to Slim right now.* She was able to spot Slim by his dark outline highlighted by the ground beyond him. It is tough to hide a seven foot tall giant.

She froze as he turned her way. *He's looking at his watch now. What is he waiting for besides me?* He was not really in the best position to find her or to even take action to stop her. *Is he waiting for me to interrogate Miguel before he acts? Maybe Miguel isn't the bad guy after all?*

Betty was at the fuel tank peering through the support structure pretending to be thinner than she was. She placed her backpack on the ground underneath the tank. *Not a particularly safe place for this item, but where else can I put it? If I'm going to subdue Slim, I certainly don't need this bulk on my back to give him any extra hand-holds. There, now!* Slim turned to look around the other side of the shed. This was the time to act. Betty sprinted the fifty meters to Slim's position like a cat bounding over a field, nearly silent on the grass. It would take Betty five seconds to get there. Four, three, two, *whomp whomp* went a metal cistern cover as Betty ran. *Shit!* Slim whirled around just in time to face Betty with a snarl and evil intent in his heart. *He wouldn't be ready to kill me if he was a good guy!* thought Betty.

Silently they each began to grapple. *Damn, the giant is strong*, but Betty was slippery, thanks to her wet and muddy body suit. Betty ducked under his legs and jumped onto Slim's back to get a chokehold on the beast. Slim tried to slam Betty with his elbows and bash her into the shed.

"Bad idea, Slim, we'll be found," Betty hissed into his ear. "Who's the mole Slim?"

She released her hold only long enough to give him a chance to speak.

That sounded like 'McF'...It couldn't be McFluffy!

"McFluffy?" Betty asked in a hushed tone.

Slim sort of nodded as she squeezed tighter on his larynx. It would be about thirty seconds before he passed out. She just needed to control him long enough to put him out. *I can hot-wire a car to haul his big ass to the choppers. He needs to be questioned properly.* Slim collapsed. She had finally put him out. *There's no way an operative would have given up the mole that easy. It has to be another misdirection. Well, if McFluffy is innocent, it'll be figured out pretty quickly. Still, the whole body scanning incident with Slim still bothers me. Why did McFluffy have us there together? Why did it seem like McFluffy owed something to Slim? I need answers, but now isn't the time to get them.* Reaching into her form-fitting bodysuit she pulled out a stunner, a needle tipped plastic vial, removed the cap with her teeth and stuck the needle into Slim's neck before rolling him over. *Crap!* His mouth was foaming. *That bastard had a cyanide capsule in his mouth. I was too slow!* He had killed himself and now there would be no way to get the answers she needed from this source. *No time to waste thinking about what could have been.*

She stripped him of his clothes, including the skintight bodysuit, to remove all the evidence and stuffed Slim's gear into her backpack except the slippery bodysuit. *His body doesn't matter as much as his possessions.* The cyanide would be a problem. *It's one thing to find a dead giant on your property, another to find a dead, naked, poisoned giant!* Betty used the slippery bodysuit as a sled and dragged his corpse to the fuel tank supported by an old wooden structure. On the side of the rusty metal drum was a hand painted sign "PROHIBIDO FUMAR — GASOLINA" in big red letters over a white background. She needed a distraction to get out of there and get to the chopper quickly. *Does removing evidence by blowing up a fuel tank cancel out the positives of Slim disappearing?* She was about to find out. *I hate explosions!* Betty used the tank's hose nozzle to spray Slim's body with a generous dousing of gasoline. Spraying the ground toward her getaway point lightly created a "fuse" of quickly evaporating fuel.

The smell of gasoline invaded the air of the plantation. Rivulets of highly flammable liquid reached out from the puddles below the flimsy tank. "Well, Slim, I told you smoking kills." Betty re-lit Slim's cigar with a long drag and tossed it on a trail of vaporizing gas. The gasoline vapor found the ember of Slim's cigar. With a *whoosh,* the fire ignited and began to rage below the tank. The dry, brittle wood was quickly engulfed and collapsed, placing the tank directly on the fire. *In a few minutes the whole tank will blow!* She did not stand around to count off the seconds. Grabbing her backpack, she sprinted to the protective cover of the cocoa trees.

It took about two minutes for the tank to explode which was enough time to get to the other side of the compound without being detected. *Too late to question Miguel. I have to keep moving or I'll be walking home.* As the tank lit up the predawn sky, a crowd of workers rushed over to see what had happened but stopped short when the heat of the funeral pyre grew too intense. Betty commandeered a just emptied, beat-up, old, Studebaker truck and rolled out of the compound heading to the chopper landing spot. She could have run there but she really could not afford to be late, walking home was not an option. *I should have had contact by now!* Toggling her throat mic brought a crackling sound to her earpiece. *Damn it! Wrestling with Slim broke my communications.*

The chopper had started to lift off, aborting the pickup. Betty gunned the Studebaker and used the headlights to flash the code name of the operation, Hydra, in Morse code.

$$\cdots\cdot \quad -\cdot-- \quad -\cdot\cdot \quad \cdot-\cdot \quad \cdot-$$

The gunner spotted her tearing down the road and pointed it out to the pilot who deciphered the code; he decided it had to be her, so they landed again. Betty had gotten there just in time. The look on their faces indicated they wondered where Slim was. She slashed her throat with her left hand to indicate the bastard was dead. The men on board nodded their heads in acknowledgment and they took off. The early dawn light rising over the ocean created a gleaming surface of water—a peaceful ending to a less than peaceful night. The *thump thump thump* of the helicopter was calming for Betty.

Thirty-Eight

Cab Ride With a Doppleganger

THIS TIME BETTY WAS READY to get in a bar fight. She thought of her real first covert mission, when she got her scar. How she had concocted the bar fight story to explain the scar to her family. Well, tonight she was ready to break some glasses and some heads; maybe leave a few scars herself. She was pissed—pissed at Slim for not only being the prick that he was but for killing himself before she could get proper intelligence out of him and then kill him herself. She was also sickened by the vision of what she had done. The explosion and the desire to be sure Slim was done for caused her to look back over her shoulder, searing the image into her brain. She needed to wash away these memories or wash out of Control.

Still, Slim deserved that ending after all! She had come across three dead dogs while running away from the exploding gas tank; on her way to the main clearing of the plantation to find a car to hot-wire. *Rottweilers! They must have found Slim and gotten their necks broken.* The dogs were lying awkwardly on the ground, necks bent at a severe angle. *It just wasn't right. Slim had stunners. He didn't have to kill the dogs.* Control had a policy of leaving the least amount of collateral damage and the least amount of trace possible. Betty had been sickened by the sight as she imagined Surry trying to defend her from Slim.

The ash pile that had been Slim left nothing to trace back to Control but gave Betty little solace from her gnawing memories of the mission. Evidence of Slim's existence and why he had been in Venezuela were either incinerated or removed by Betty: no cyanide residue, no clothes to trace back, no weapons, not even the soles of his shoes. The visceral images of what she had done were harder to dispose of than Slim. Betty tossed back another shot of whiskey, feeling the sting of the alcohol, letting it burn away the memory.

Betty was drunk now and talking shop with a couple of marines. The jukebox was playing so loud that only those right next to her could hear her loose tongue. Someone had queued up ZZ Top's *Bad and Nationwide* and the room was thumping.

"Forensics is amazing now," Betty thundered to be heard over the din of customers and the guitars. "You can vacuum fabric for pollen and dust to trace movements across continents. Databases are available for almost all the world. All that do good-er stuff out there in the wilds of Africa, South America, and even China is really about getting in depth information about the local flora and fauna. Some senator may have been trying to make his mistress happy, but the NSA, CIA, and twenty agencies you've never heard of are riding the coattails of the largesse for saving the blind wombats. You better believe it, baby. We're bad, we're worldwide. Yeah, ZZ Top has it right. No one's gonna give me trouble!" The marines were nodding in agreement; ready to back this badass woman up in any fight.

"So, dooo-gooders listen up, we're here to fuck-U-Up," Betty said a little too loudly. She was at the Froggy Bottom Bar in Georgetown. Her old haunt had a mix of graduate students, military types, and locals looking for interesting people to meet. The bar top itself was only about twenty feet long with room for seven or eight patrons. The rest of the room was small tables and places to stand. Froggy Bottom may be in the basement, but it is not a dive bar. Georgetown rent is too high for that kind of place. Just the same, events can still spiral out of control even in a place like the Froggy Bottom.

Betty was drinking with a couple of jarheads back from Iraq. Like Betty, they were ready for any and all comers. Fights were frowned upon here, but the furniture could take the abuse of the first round or two, after that it needed to go outside. The jarheads had tried to hit on Betty at first, but when a civilian came up behind Betty and put his hand on her shoulder, they watched in admiration as she took the guy down to his knees using the first finger and thumb of her left hand. She made the poor bastard lick her four-inch high heeled black leather boots before she would let go. With the boots, she was as tall as most of the guys in this joint but half the bulk; any woman who could handle a guy twice her weight with just two fingers had to be respected. They figured she was Special Ops, but they had no clue as to what depth she was in. They just knew she was itching for a fight and they wanted to be there when the hammer came down. The boot licker was too easy. If the guy had put up any kind of fight, it would have been more interesting for Betty and the two jarheads next to her. Betty was feeling like back in the day when her brothers told her she could not go fishing. Slim made her feel that way too, now that she thought back on it. He told her no, she was not going to catch any information from him.

"Fuck him," Betty said.

"Fuck who B?" the first marine slurred.

John B. Heinrich was from Fredericksburg, Iowa. He was six foot two and two hundred and twenty pounds of marine. He currently was a first lieutenant who had been busted down from captain for disorderly conduct. Heinrich was getting used to the idea of the tough chick by his side. He was asking whose ass should he kick and how hard? First Lieutenant Bobby Jetson was John's wingman and a real pretty boy. Bobby had hair too long for the marines and teeth so white you could drive on a moonless night. Bobby was another Iowa boy, born and raised. He planned on going back to Iowa City to live, paint, and maybe do a little sculpture for big bucks. Bobby was all pressed and looking good, but if you took him for granted in a fight, you were making the biggest mistake of your life. Fight him and you would get your blood painted on the wall and your face re-sculptured for free.

After the three new friends had the rest of the bar painfully aware of their existence, the bartender pointed out a couple of anti-war types, hipsters that were eying the gang at the bar. They did not seem to like how good of a time Betty and her boys were having. Perhaps they thought it was time to crash the party or maybe they just liked to get a good beat-down. Either way, the hipsters came over and instead of taking on the obviously superior fighters with their fists, they attempted to lure them into traps with their words.

The taller of the two greasy haired, former grunge band wannabees stepped up first. "Yo, meatheads! Why don't you go shoot a terrorist or kill some innocent civilians? We don't want you in our bar!"

"You look kind of like a terrorist. Maybe we should start with you? Then if you're innocent, mission accomplished!" Lieutenant John was ready to go. Bobby was off his stool before John finished, clenching his fists.

"Boys, these watermelons aren't worth your time," Betty coolly slid off her stool and stepped between the hipsters and her new friends.

"Watermelons?" the second hipster intoned.

"Green on the outside and red in the middle," Bobby was no stranger to this kind of harassment. "It's closing time anyway, so let's take it outside. Let's debate the war and what it takes to prosecute a terrorist, what do you say?" asked Lieutenant Bobby as he stepped up, shoulder to shoulder with Betty.

The hipsters turned meekly away while making their excuses as they headed for the rear exit as quickly as they could. Beauty and the beasts headed out into the evening with nowhere good to go but down. Betty was all set to go on an adventure with the two jarheads as a cab pulled up and the driver's window rolled down.

"Shit! Howell! How the hell did he get a cab?" said Betty to the marines as Howell pulled the bright yellow Skat Cab alongside the trio, now driving on the wrong side of Pennsylvania Avenue.

"Excuse me, miss, you called for a ride?" asked Howell.

"Sorry, boys, guess my ride is here and my time is up. You'll have to save America tonight without me," said Betty sliding into the back of the cab and closing the door. Before the jarheads could figure out what was going on, Howell roared off into the night.

"You know I'm not going to thank you for what you just did, I could handle that all by myself, thank you very much," Betty coyly chided the doppelganger who had taken over her onetime lover.

"We need to talk about what went down on the Venezuelan mission with Slim. Your debriefing seemed—how shall I say it, brief?" Howell steered the cab quickly through what little traffic was left on the streets of D. C. at two in the morning.

Betty had been short in her answers back at Control. Her mind kept racing back to Slim's corpse, the explosion, the foaming cyanide, and the dead Rottweilers.

"It was a bad scene at Miguel's. Slim shouldn't have been there. He shouldn't have killed the dogs," Betty had been looking out of the window, revisiting the horrors she had committed and seen. Looking straight into the mirror at Howell she continued more focused. "Slim said McFluffy was the mole before he killed himself. I didn't tell you before, because I don't believe it. Something funny was going on that day of the body suit scanning."

"Not by McFluffy. I think Slim was just messing with your mind. I told McFluffy to have both of you there to see how you and he would react," Howell explained.

"What the fuck, Howell!" exclaimed Betty.

"Settle down. There is another mission coming up. One you would have been on with Slim as his fiancé. I had to know how you two would react together."

Maybe the alcohol was finally depressing her system or maybe she had worked out her aggression already, but Betty calmed down and began retelling Howell the details from the beginning to make sure she did not skip anything: the muffled sound of McFluffy's name, Slim's appearance where he was not supposed to be, the dead dogs, the charges going off too soon, and Slim's tampering with her work. Howell did not speak for a long time. As he pulled up to Betty's apartment in Old Town Alexandria, he turned to look her in the eye.

"I waited for you at FDR for an hour. I figured if you didn't show by then, well, I guess I figured you had moved on. I'm mentioning it now, because there is a lot of bad shit about to come down on Control, and if you're not up to dealing with it, maybe you should move on again."

Betty about reached through the Plexiglas separating Howell from her wrath. She could not believe the arrogance of this man.

"You waited for me? Who the hell are you? What have you done with Tom? I was there Goddamn it! I waited in the cold rain for two hours for you that day. Fuck you, Howell! Go find yourself an agent you aren't gonna play mind games with. Fuck you and Tom too."

Betty stormed out of the cab and headed into her building. She did not look back at the dismayed Major Howell. She did not see the tear run down the face of the man who should have been her husband.

†

"It's done," declared Howell when his secure call was answered by dead air.

"Are you sure she won't quit?"

"You were the one who wanted to recruit her in the first place." Tom wiped the tear from his cheek and resisted the temptation to sniffle back the mucus in his nose.

"Yes, she is stubborn, I'll give you that. Do we need to move her?"

"Damn it, Bob! I told you I know what I'm doing!"

"Just to be clear, are you prepared to clean this up if she doesn't come back?" asked Bob.

Tom Howell wiped his face with his sleeve and the crook of his elbow at the thought of killing Betty himself. "I am prepared to do whatever is necessary and we will both burn in hell if it comes to that." Howell ended the call as he pulled over to the shoulder of the road and began to pound the steering wheel, dash, and roof of the cab with his bare fist. "Fuck, fuck, fuck!" Thirty seconds later the smell of the cab's exhaust and the smell of burnt rubber were the only evidence of Tom Howell Jr.'s passing.

THIRTY-NINE

WILL THE REAL TOM HOWELL PLEASE STAND UP?

FOUR P.M. APRIL 12TH, 2005, had come and gone leaving nothing but a dull ache clinging to her soul; just like the hangover from Froggy Bottom clung to her brain, that misty rain and heat of a greenhouse: Washington, D.C., Betty had waited for Howell for two hours in the rain; the light rain outside her bedroom window washed away the patina of time to reveal the memories of the past. Betty began to relive that fateful afternoon as she stared out the window.

She had arrived at the FDR Memorial an hour early. Betty was still enamored with the memorial as she walked the site for a half hour. Perhaps the anticipation of seeing Tom combined with the fear of his rejection was firing her imagination, but she could relate to the scenes of deprivation and sadness in front of her. The fireside chat, the breadline, all of these statues had a haunting effect on Betty.

She paused, perhaps a little longer than at the others, in front of Eleanor's statue. This was the first statue in honor of a first lady. While Betty had done nothing in her life that would deserve a statue nor could she envision doing anything extraordinary as an immigration attorney or when the time came as a mother, she thought, *perhaps, some day, a plaque might end up somewhere to commemorate my passing through this lifetime. Maybe I'll leave a large donation to the Georgetown Law School in my will, just to make sure. Yeah, the Betty Thursten Library Table. To commemorate the long hours of study that led to nothing more terribly remarkable than good grades.*

During the first half hour of wandering the four rooms of the FDR Memorial, Betty only paused briefly; she did not have enough time to view the whole site. To do it justice she needed at least four hours or even a whole day of picnicking to take in this vast tribute to not only

FDR, but also the strength and resiliency of the American people. The different rooms pay tribute to the four different terms of FDR and the vastly different situations the nation found itself in during those twelve years: *The Depression, The New Deal, WWII*, and though he did not live to see it, *Peace and Prosperity.*

At 3:30, she went over to the FDR statue. She touched the rough bronze of Fala, FDR's dog, and then the smooth bronze of FDR's cape. There had been controversy over this statue, whether or not FDR's wheelchair should be shown or hidden. To show the man as the world saw him or as the man who struggled every day with his ruined legs, who exuded confidence, strength, and determination. *Well, he had determination in spades; the rest was show,* thought Betty. She stood there as a light rain came down, waiting for her man to have the guts to show. She was waiting now, so that later in life she would have no regrets. *When I leave here it will be with Tom or on my own. Either way I'm determined to make the best of it.*

She gave him extra time; just in case something happened, like being run over by a bus. Tom would have dragged himself over here after being run over by one of the ubiquitous tour buses. The man she knew and loved would be here if it were not for that doppelganger Howell. She blamed General Getner, Howell's mentor, as well. He was the one who sent Tom on the mission. He was the one who convinced Tom that nothing bad would happen to him over there.

The constant rain felt like Chinese water torture. *Drip, drip, drip.* All the waterfalls surrounding this remarkable site had been favorite stopping points for Tom and Betty during their time together. Jil and Betty had sat ten if not twenty times in front of the WWII waterfall talking about what it must be like for Tom to be in Iraq. He had never said that he was there, but they both knew he was in the thick of it: sand storms, heat, and deprivation of all kinds. *Had he been sleeping in a tent or staying in one of the palaces? Did he ever get R&R or was it all business? Did that Babs get to him? Was it Babs holding him back today? Does he need my forgiveness and can't bring himself to ask for it? I don't think so, not the Tom I know. Howell? Yeah, that prick Howell would have gone there and done that, but not my Tom!*

It was almost 4:30. Around the corner she heard something, it sounded like "Tom, over here." Betty raced around the corner to see a woman running to a marine lieutenant in his dress whites. Hair so short she could see his scalp. *That's not my Tom!* It broke Betty's heart to see two lovers meet at her and Tom's memorial, another Tom no less, so Betty gave up. She turned away as the two lovers embraced each other and kissed for what was most likely the first time in over a year. The passion of that kiss, the embrace, she had deserved that after waiting for Tom to come back. Now a year later, she deserved at least a medal for having stuck it out. Her enlistment was over. Time to move on.

Betty exited the memorial site to the east and headed on over to the Jefferson Memorial. She held it together long enough to make it around the Tidal Basin to the steps of the founder's huge columned edifice. She collapsed just inside the entrance against the cold marble and began sobbing. A park ranger came over to see what he could do and she waved him off, gathering herself, Betty tried to rally, *I'm stronger than this!* Betty was not crying for Tom, she was crying for what she had allowed herself to hope for this past year, no two years. Betty took the tissue from the park ranger, thanked him and headed for the metro to go home to her penthouse in Old Town Alexandria. Not to start a new life, but to continue the life interrupted. No more military men for Betty. No men at all for a while. She was adrift. No Jil in her daily life, no Tom, just Surry. *Thank God for my Surry. Time to walk the old girl and do something, anything, to wash the bad taste of today out of my mind.*

Thirty minutes later at the penthouse, Surry pawed at Betty pulling her back to the present and the necessities of daily life. Surry had her leash in her mouth and her head titled to the side as if to ask, "Go for a walk? It will make you feel better."

"OK, Surry, good girl! That is just what I need right now." Walking Surry was usually a joyful time in the city. A chance to see things differently than before, meet new people and greet old friends. But today, the usual route just raised ghosts of Tom. Founders Park was just ahead and a favorite of Tom and Surry's. Betty was a hound sniffing out the past. She tried to not think of Tom, but imagining him here, walking Surry to make up for the kenneling incident brought it all back. Back where it all started. Now it was over. She mustered a false smile as Surry met up with her friends at the park as the light was fading on the end of a chapter in Betty's life.

FORTY

DOWN PAYMENT

"**B**UD," A DISTRACTED HOWELL acknowledged the head of his intelligence unit without looking up from the photos of Betty and her cohorts from the Froggy Bottom adventure, "Figure out if I need to know anything about these guys."

"Like what? They're just a couple of leathernecks." Bud had better things to do than to check up on his boss's old girlfriend, even if she was a hottie.

"Make sure Betty didn't tell them anything we don't want out there." Howell waved his hand dismissively, signaling he wanted to be alone. "Oh, Bud, good work on getting the stills from the hipster's Facebook account."

"Nothing, it was nothing." Bud smiled a self assured smirk; one that said *I am the best hacker in the world and I know it.*

"I don't know how you do this stuff, but I appreciate it." Howell tossed the pictures onto the growing pile of paperwork devouring his desk. Control's deep bunkers a mile below ground kept him from seeing the weather outside, but he knew it was raining in D.C. by the ticker tape weather report at the bottom of his screen. Just like that day, April 12, 2005; *Betty says she showed but I never saw her. How could I have missed her?*

As the rain dampened the ground, ten buses parked in a row belched diesel fumes, impatiently waiting for the obedient civilian passengers in long lines to board for their guided tour of the capital. A cacophony of umbrellas and expressionless cows were obediently waiting. Tom, dressed in his parade best, paused to look side to side before stepping off the wet curb just as the massive Tourmobile bus roared forward. With his artificial leg still on the sidewalk, he became unbalanced and slipped as he tried to jump back from the roaring diesel death trap that was about to take his remaining leg. The driver slammed on his brakes as he saw Tom fall to the sidewalk grabbing his stub as if it had been run over. The driver scurried out of the bus to see if he was now in big trouble, but Tom was back on his feet by the time the driver was there to dust him off.

"Hey, General, I didn't see you there stepping off...you got to use the crosswalks. I about killed you!" A worried looking round man wearing a bus driver's uniform pointed at the blank pavement in front of the bus with his black billed cap.

Tom could not believe that he had managed to survive Iraq only to come within inches of dying on the streets of D.C. Tom pinched the drivers name badge between his thumb and forefinger and said, "Dave, is it? Look down there," as he pointed to the crosswalk markings under the front of the bus.

Dave looked down at the white lines for a split second before he began his defense. "General, I can't see you if you're so close to the bus...."

"No problem, Dave, just my pride is hurt." Tom picked up the leg of his trouser to show his artificial leg to the stunned driver. "Not as quick as I used to be these days...and I am only an army captain," Tom said as he pointed to the gold oak leaf on his shoulder.

The driver quickly reached into his pocket and pulled out his wallet to give Tom a twenty for dry cleaning. "Captain, man, I am so sorry, buddy, let me pay for the dry-cleaning. My brother-in-law runs a dry-cleaner just a mile from here, Snooks Dry-Cleaning, he'll take good care of you."

They both jumped when the air horn of the Tourmobile sounded off. The tour guide was getting impatient to get the show on the road and was making hand gestures for Dave to come back to his job.

"Dave, it's all right. You better get back to your station; you have people counting on you."

Tom turned the driver by his shoulders and scooted him toward the bus. Dave looked over his shoulder pensively as he held the twenty in one hand and his wallet in the other. He shrugged his shoulders and shoved his wallet and the twenty deep into his pocket. As he grumbled to no one in particular he shook the water off his driver's cap. Still muttering as he entered the bus, he faked a smile and waved to Tom that it was safe for him to cross. Tom waved his arms as if he was passing a large ball from right to left to signal the bus had the right of way. He took a deep breath and waved as the bus roared off once again.

Tom did not have far to go to get to the FDR Memorial. He was early even after the delay of the bus incident. He wanted to be there before Betty, if she came. His gait was stronger now than it was a year ago. He had gotten used to the new leg and most people did not even notice the difference. He actually had two different artificial legs, one for walking and one for running. The running leg had a special flipper like foot that was made of extra springy carbon fiber material. He could almost run faster with the fake leg than he could with his real leg. Walking on the other hand still required a bit of concentration. He arrived at the entrance to the memorial at 3:45 sharp. He stood next to the FDR sculpture as nonchalantly as he could, fidgeting with the change in his pocket, his keys, and his cellphone.

General Getner was against Tom getting back together with Betty. Tom had important work to do at Control and did not need any apron strings to tie him down. Tom respectfully told the general he could shove it, that he was going. "If that means a change of duty, so be it."

The general harrumphed and said, "Your job is here and it will be waiting for you when you come back, today or tomorrow."

"If I have to choose between Control and Betty, I choose Betty." Tom sternly eyed his commander, daring Getner to stop him.

"Go get your head straightened out. I owe you at least that."

"Damn right you do! Sir," Tom added quickly, but softly.

Wagging his finger at Tom, Getner's face turned red as he stammered, "Your father would tell you to shove it and get back to work. I'm willing to let you figure this out, so you can let it go or get on with it. You owe yourself at least that much."

Tom leaned into the general's finger, forcing Getner to pull back, "Leave my father out of this! He may be able to pull your strings, but you better understand this—he doesn't pull mine!"

"Take as long as you need, but get back here, we have work to do, and that's an order." Getner winked to soften the sternness of his previous comments as he put his hands on Tom's arms, squeezing the meat of his biceps, smiling a grimace as if he was not sure how to smile and nodded his head in affirmation. After Tom left, Getner muttered to himself, "I don't think that little Jezebel will show anyway. Good agent material—sex kitten type maybe."

Tom stood at the FDR memorial for almost an hour. He had arrived at the outer area of the memorial site early. *Betty couldn't have already gone into the memorial, could she have?* thought Tom. That is when he remembered the other statue of FDR, the one in the back with his dog. *Crap. Is she waiting there?* The other statue was nearer to the waterfalls they had so loved to sit by. Tom scurried off as if he suddenly needed to find a bathroom. Heading into the memorial, he was near the FDR statue when he heard a women yell, "Tom, over here." A Marilyn Monroe wanna be blonde woman wearing three-inch heels was running to her marine first lieutenant in his dress whites. Tom paused for a moment to watch the embrace and kiss, thinking that it would be his turn in a moment. He turned the corner to the statue of FDR with his dog Fala and looked around. No Betty.

"Stick tight and wait for the other person to find you." Tom Howell Sr. had taught his son through stern lecturing at an early age.

Tom had camped out at the other statue; he would wait here as well. "Where are you? Why was I so dismissive at the Capital Grille? Didn't you know how much it hurt me to say that?" Tom mumbled to himself as he waited in the drizzle.

It was now 4:45 p.m.; *Betty is never late.* Tom looked at his watch for the tenth time in a minute, as if he could not believe it was so late or that the time of their meeting was so long past. *I was too hard on Betty, too standoffish, I wasn't fair to her—sending her away at the Capital Grille.* Tom looked at his watch again and slurred the word "fuck" to disguise it from the people within earshot. *I should have made a bigger effort to see her over the past year.* He had placed himself in her line of sight more than once to see if she would approach him. He set up meetings with friends in places near where Betty frequented hoping to bump into her, pretending to not know she was nearby. He knew that she had spotted him on at least one occasion, the day she got her black belt in jujitsu, but his ruse never panned out. He took a deep breath and sighed, "Damn."

He had been wrong to send her away and he had been wrong to come here today. *General Getner was right, time to get down to business. I still have work to do.* He would cast aside everything but work from now on. *I'm the property of Control. It isn't my place to decide my path. The president will decide what my life is worth, not me. The president and that prick, General Getner,* he thought as he walked out the front of the memorial.

Tom walked over to Arlington National Cemetery. The rain was light and he thought, *now would be a good time to walk amongst the dead soldiers who had paid the ultimate price for their country.* By losing his leg in Iraq, Tom had made a down payment on the farm; now was the time to see the parcel of land he was eventually going to own with his blood, sweat, and tears. Tears for Betty were coming down his face. The people walking by would assume they were tears for fallen comrades. They deserved his tears, but this day belonged to Betty. The tears mingled with the rain as they ran down his overcoat and soaked into the hallowed ground of a grateful nation.

FORTY-ONE

THE NEW BLACK IS BLACK

HOWELL SUBMERGED HIMSELF fully into the arcane world of spy-craft after the ill-fated non-meeting at the FDR Memorial. General Getner and Howell had been charged with taking over a special unit that was underachieving and to give it new legs. This special unit was at the beck and call of the president. General Getner worked directly with the president to set some of Control's objectives but it was up to Getner to decide on methods. No bureaucracy to meander through, no branch of the military to wait for, no agency like the CIA or NSA that was in the cross-hairs of Congress and the press. This unit was self-funded and self-contained. An income stream from a legitimate corporation that had been given sole rights to new medical technologies created by research labs of the military was all they needed; millions of dollars and free access to the world through salesmen and remote offices. They had special privileges with any military base or equipment. If they needed a MH-60K Special Ops Night Tactical Black Hawk Helicopter and flight crew for a special op, they got it. If they needed a SEAL team deployed off the coast to pull in an agent, no problem. The actual missions were strictly run by the agents with no documentation to finger the U.S. Government, much less the president. This was black on black need to know basis. This was Control.

The unit was put on ice previously because of an incident that started in Somalia, went through Sudan, and nearly ended up where the buck stops: the president's desk. The Chinese were infiltrating Sudan to take control of the oil rich country. The "Cold War" may have been over, but the Chinese did not get the memo. With approximately a hundred thousand alleged visitors and tourists, observers, handlers, and military advisers on the ground in Somalia and Sudan, it was hard not to see how big the Chinese presence was, even with the diversity of insertions. State Department policy was to look the other way because the Pentagon has a million men and women spread around the globe, let alone one hundred thousand troops in Germany and South Korea. The cold war was still on but it was by proxy: Afghanistan, Vietnam, Korea, Kosovo, Ethiopia, Sudan, Iraq, Israel, and so on. Like a gang leader having to prove his machismo on a daily basis, someone was always waiting to line up toe to toe with the U.S. on neutral ground.

A Chinese freighter delivering weapons under the cover of grain and a humanitarian aid mission for the Sudanese in the Darfur tent villages was a problem. The refuges had been forced to relocate from their homelands so the oil could be confiscated. China was growing and needed that oil like a sailor needs a drink on shore leave. The hands of U.S. Diplomats were tied by the vast quantity of U.S. debt owned by the Chinese. For that reason, they could not just come out and say what the Chinese were doing, but the president was not about to stand by. The Chinese freighter rounding the Horn of Africa was filled with weapons veiled by a pile of humanitarian grain. Because the president could not afford to be caught acting directly against the Chinese, a message was sent through a former intelligence officer to a secret organization that did not seem to exist: the old Control. A clandestine operation was devised to destroy the arms in a way that would prevent China from complaining and still allow the grain to be delivered to feed the starving people of Darfur. The arms had been sabotaged to blow up when the crates were opened up on shore.

Chinese intelligence caught wind of the intended operation as it was unfolding. As a counter measure, the Chinese triggered the munitions in transit, blowing up the grain and the crew aboard. The Communist party leadership valued the public relations coup over the lives lost. The crew was expendable. The Chinese intelligence officers left the crew on the freighter to make the explosion believable as an act of humanitarian sabotage. The outcry was enormous from the far left who were fed propaganda that a special operation from the Nimitz Class U.S. Aircraft Carrier *Abraham Lincoln* had caused the freighter to blow up in a horrific shower of crew and burning rice.

Check and mate thought the Chinese spymasters. China reaped huge PR points for shipping rice to the region as a humanitarian effort. They had avoided the PR nightmare of their true intent being thrust into the light of day. Even though China was known by the international intelligence community to be mucking about Sudan and Somalia; yet, the headlines emphasized the humanitarian disaster caused by supposed U.S. intelligence assets.

General Getner and the newly minted Major Howell were to never let this kind of debacle happen again, let alone allow it to taint the president. Howell wanted to believe he had earned his promotion to major, but he had an uneasy feeling he had been promoted for walking away from Betty after the failed meeting at the FDR Memorial. Getner hinted that because the job Howell performed would normally be held by a colonel, a field promotion was close at hand for his exceptional performance at Control. The general had bigger fish to fry and he needed good men in charge. Men who did what needed to be done and no one would notice except for the general and the president. Men willing to die for their country. Men who did not need medals or praise to get the job done or keep going. Men like Thomas Alvin Howell IV.

Forty-Two

Premeditated Success

KEEPING INFORMATION from Howell was not new; Betty had hidden details from him starting early in their relationship. *He isn't on a need to know basis* was her usual thought processes.

Betty never told Tom any details about her trip to Uruguay, to arrange José's student visa in early 2003 because she was too angry about the kenneling fiasco while Tom was on a last minute mission for General Getner. Besides, the client asked Betty to keep the trip quiet, like a furtive spy operation. The IBM recruitment of the artificial intelligence prodigy was the cover for the meeting with José. The secrecy seemed extreme, but Betty was willing to go along since no one was getting hurt and the fee was large. Pulling strings with IBM to cover her real mission was a snap for Mr. Silva; they had a large financial stake in the Latin American division of IBM. Mr. Silva explained that it was merely a favor to smooth over the ruffled feathers of the local bureaucrats.

She flew into the capital of Uruguay, Montevideo, unsure of how to hide her real purpose or what might be waiting for her. Back then Betty would not have known clandestine if it came up and introduced itself to her. José Eduardo Santos Almeida Melo Silva was from an important Brazilian family that controlled huge tracts of land. They were influential in the politics of Brazil and wanted their son groomed to be a leader. Therefore, it was imperative that José come to the United States to study at a premier university. Preferably an Ivy League school so that he would have connections to future leaders of the United States. The problem was that José's academic career at Universidade Federal do Rio de Janeiro up to that point was less than stellar and he had caused a little mischief with a gang of fellow students. A misunderstanding really. They had targeted José because of his family and his major, chemical engineering. He had been conned into joining what later became classified as a terrorist group. José had learned how to make explosives in chemistry class, nothing sophisticated, but because of his interest in the subject he did a lot of independent study. His family had land that was isolated and rocky, so naturally he did some experiments.

Being a bit of a showboat, he took some friends out to his family's remote farmland twenty miles outside of São Paulo and demonstrated the explosives on some jagged rock formations. The demonstration included different types of explosives and different methods of delivery such as pipe bombs and a few mortar rounds. Some were very effective at removing rock while others were great at creating dramatic booms with large puffs of smoke.

The situation escalated when the group wanted José's creations to blow up part of the Parque Nacional da Tijuca, a beautiful hand planted forest surrounded by Rio de Janeiro. A portion of the Favela da Rocinha bairro, the group's neighborhood, was slated for demolition to make way for a new shopping mall. The leader was willing to destroy part of the park to achieve his goal. The twelve square mile area had been deforested two hundred years before for coffee production. Cultivation led to wide spread erosion and damage to Rio de Janeiro's water supply. The forest was replanted in the late eighteen hundreds by Major Manuel Gomes Archer to protect the water supply.

"José, you're going to help us save our neighborhood," boldly stated the leader of the group as if he was doing José a grand favor.

"I won't do it. These are just for fun, like fireworks. Besides, you might accidentally blow yourself up," José tried to reason with the anarchists, now regretting his decision to impress them with his toys.

"You'll do it, José, or Rual here will knock your sister up. Wouldn't that be a shame, such a young sweet thing, embarrassed?" The leader made a puffing sound with his mouth and gestured a womb filling up with his hands while he extended his belly.

"You bastard. You wouldn't. Fuck you!"

"Now, José, be reasonable. Just give us what we want and no one gets hurt, no one is embarrassed."

"OK—OK. But you touch her and there will be consequences. Do you understand?" José capitulated, knowing he had options. A plan was developing in José's mind. Giving the devices to them would allow him time to expose them to the authorities. Arming the bombs improperly to prevent the thugs from following through with their extortion plan was easy. Not getting himself caught in the same net—that was the hard part.

The horror and indignation of the local government landed on José when the hoodlums preemptively announced they had planted bombs in the Cascatinha da Tijuca, a beautiful cascading waterfall. The ransom note warned of extensive damage if their demand to end the development of the bairro was not met.

In the end, José was painted with the broad brush of terrorism despite his heroic effort to prevent the extortion. The authorities agreed that if José were to pursue his higher education overseas, certain aspects of the investigation were likely to have no fruition. That and some minor donations by Juan Silva to local causes like the Policeman's Benefit and the new fire station in the Favela da Rocinha bairro.

Betty's trip was made secretly to prevent any further notoriety for the Silva family. The trip was long and hot from Montevideo to Rio de Janeiro; however, Betty was arriving just in time for Carnival, so there was some benefit to the long and arduous journey. The Silva's connections also gave her special access to the parades and the samba competitions, which she especially enjoyed.

Betty was torn about this trip because she was not to share any of her adventures with Tom. It was unusual for a client to require such secrecy, but they paid well. The secrecy was liberating in a way, but strangely it constrained her actions in a yin and yang dualistic tension. The desire for hedonism was balanced with dire guilt should she indulge in taboo activities; even though she was not engaged to Tom and the activities were really pretty tame.

Thanks to the hard work of Betty and her successful interventions with the State Department, including suitable sponsors for José in the United States, accommodations were made and the bomb-making episode was overlooked. José's father took care of the Brazilian side. Should undue scrutiny ever uncover commissions or lack of due diligence, the Brazilian bureaucrats were given a bail bond of sorts, the type that was never expected to be returned.

José's application to Princeton University was immediately

accepted, in no small way, due to the kind letter of recommendation by Senator Bolden, conveniently provided by Jil Harper. José would have his MBA in short order and Betty had a client for life.

FORTY-THREE

CANNED

BETTY JAMMED THE HARD metal cylinder object into her bag. Her eyes did not waver from her quarry. A few steps forward and Betty jammed another can into the bag without looking as she quickly turned her back to avoid eye contact. Betty's hair was now shorter with a hint of ginger color that evoked Betty's childhood look. Her hair was hard to define back then. There was the black and then there was the deep velvety red depending on the light. In the bright midsummer sun, Betty looked like maybe she could be a redhead. In a dark corner, Betty surely had a raven's mane.

He began to move again, away from Betty. He had picked up some papers, holding them in his left hand. This could be important. Betty needed to see which papers he picked up: She would have to get closer to him to find out. His last position imparted no worthwhile information; she would have to get closer. She jammed another object into her bag and got in line behind the mystery man. He was six foot one inch tall, blonde hair and had a strange scar on his left hand that looked like a stab wound. The papers were curled up in his hand, so Betty could not tell which they were, but he would have to lay them down in a moment for the woman to check them. Betty dumped her bag out onto the belt rather abruptly, one of the cans rolled off to the floor catching the man's attention. He graciously bent down to pick it up for her, dropping the papers on the belt to grab hold of the counter with his right hand as he reached down for the can with his left.

Damn it, Betty thought to herself, *The Washington Times and the Post. No way to know his political bent from that, though it says he likes* to read a balanced opinion of the District and the world. *That check out girl is checking out Mr. Helpful's butt! Yes, a truly splendid example.* Mr. Helpful stood up to put the can back on the belt.

"That one about got away," he said with a smile.

"Yes." Betty anxiously giggled like a little schoolgirl, which bothered her. "Yes it did didn't it."

"Dick," said Mr. Awkward as he stuck out his hand. "Dick Thomas, it's my name."

Betty took Dick's hand while she blushed and said, "Betty."

Dick Thomas turned back to the cashier to pay for his papers, his sourdough batard, raspberry jam, and half pound of aged cheddar cheese. Perhaps a continental picnic? Much stranger were the four cans of food Betty had managed to collect while tailing the man now known as Dick Thomas. She had one can each of oysters, green beans (French cut), mixed olives (pitted), and spicy enchilada sauce.

"I would love to know what you're making for dinner," said Dick as he pointed to the sundry items.

This was Betty's chance. *I don't want to look desperate—put Dick in charge from the start. No, that wouldn't do.* "Wouldn't you like to know!" said Betty slyly. *Oh, God, I am so over doing this! Turn away! Don't let him think you're interested.* Betty began going through her purse, acting dismissive of Dick and his groceries. "Where is that coupon?"

The cashier began to scan Betty's items as Dick, looking perplexed and intrigued, picked up his bag and headed out of the store.

Joan, the name on the cashier's badge, made the sound of a cat and clawed her hands in the air as Dick left. "Girl, that man was so into you."

Betty handed the clerk a ten dollar bill for her odd variety of items and with an air of a woman on a mission headed out the door without her change to see what kind of transportation Dick was using, but he was already gone. She looked around the Trader Joe's to see if she could spot the potential date, but he was nowhere to be seen. Betty headed back to her penthouse to see what she could make for dinner, without any of these future food pantry donation items. *Dating post-Tom is going to be difficult,* thought Betty. *How am I supposed to find a good way of meeting men? My work is filled with exotic foreigners and boring lawyers. I need to find someone in Old Town who is somewhere in between. Missed my chance today; thankfully I'm not that desperate, but will have to shop Trader Joe's more frequently for the next few weeks. Maybe bump into him again. I need to come up with a better shopping list!*

Forty-Four

New Memories

BETTY MISSED JIL. She missed Tom. She missed the loft. Had it really been that good or had it all been an illusion? Betty began writing a short letter to her older brother Rob:

Rob-

Jil was a call girl and Tom is off the reservation. Now Jil is worse than a call girl, she is a lobbyist. And Tom? He's been General Getner's errand boy...and now? He is some unfeeling, uncaring soldier who has given up his past and his future—for what? I've been there for both of them. I haven't done anything wrong. I surrounded myself with quality people or so I thought. I have desires just like other people, but I've been burned by those I love. I still have my family, but that is my only sanctuary of loyalty and trust.

Rob, what am I to do?

Betty

The letter was cathartic, but not worth sending. She balled it up and threw it away.

Betty had tried to date. They had all been Dicks. Guys who had the lines and the looks or schmucks who were trying to get back at all the women in the world for some perceived wrong by a woman in their past. The odds seemed stacked against Betty.

José was in her office again, the bad boy from Brazil. He needed her to extend his visa. He was finished with his MBA and now he wanted to start his doctorate in economics. Something was different about José. Not just in the karmic sense, but José had grown up. He was much more serious now about his studies and his future. He was not out partying with the wild things and he was not a wild thing himself. Betty felt she needed to find out what had changed in José, just like things had changed with her friend Jil and that beast Howell. What could cause someone to become better instead of worse? This was worth pursuing further, but she had to be careful. She needed to maintain her distance from José to protect their attorney client relationship, but her office was too formal, he would never truly reveal himself here. *Dinner? Too intimate. Lunch? If it is for business...I can do that. Besides, the partners say I need more expense items to balance my billable time. OK, let's do this!*

FORTY-FIVE

EXCELLENT

I WANT TO GET TO KNOW you better before I allow myself to be vulnerable again, is what Betty wanted to say. Instead, she said, "My schedule is really full right now, José, but let's meet over lunch to talk about your situation."

Updating José's status and renewing his F1 Visa only required perfunctory paperwork. He had been accepted at Georgetown University to earn his doctorate in economics despite his lack of credentials. Getting in was not a problem with his family's money and connections. José's GRE test scores were excellent, especially the quantitative section, which made up for his lack of a masters in economics. He had hired a tutor and studied heavily all summer after graduating from Princeton in May of 2004 with his MBA. José worked hard to get into Georgetown and rewarded himself with a trip to the Futsal (indoor soccer) World Cup, spending November and December in Asia. He was back now and needed to straighten out his visa for the fall semester.

"We should meet at Ceiba on 14th street," José spoke with a certainty and conviction—confidence that exuded over the phone line to Betty.

Two blocks from the White House? That's only five minutes by cab, Betty was calculating the angles, how to make this an accidental date. "That would be convenient and an easy ride on the Metro for you from Georgetown."

"I like Ceiba because of the Latin menu. They specialize in São Paulo type cuisine."

"Like we had when I visited?" inquired Betty, surprised that the food she had in Brazil was all that great to José.

"No, not at all!" José insisted. "That food during your visit is not what we would call local delicacies. It is time to remedy this deficiency!"

Betty wanted to go now to meet up with her Latin prospect. She paused and made noises as if she was checking her calendar. "I have an opening a week from today, noon—a cancellation, the ambassador was called home." Betty lied to make her schedule seem more important and busier than it was.

"Yes, that will work. I will make the reservation. See you then! Thank you Ms. Thursten." José's politeness and good manners had always been perfect with Betty.

"José, call me Betty, lunch is on me, you are my client after all," Betty sent a mixed message by telling José to use her first name, but this was a business lunch. *Yellow light: move slowly, keep him wondering, and make him think it was his idea to ask me out,* thought Betty manipulatively.

Time could not go by fast enough for Betty. She had been intrigued by José when she first met him. Betty thought she might have acted on the temptation of José during Carnival, had she not been living with Tom, not to mention the minor detail of being José's lawyer. It had been a great time getting to know José's family and his native Brazil.

Ceiba had a high ceiling and murals of the ceiba tree throughout. Together these made Betty feel like she was in a very large space. The high backed chairs and furniture were made in Brazil and the mosaic tile came from the Yucatan. The wait staff was attentive and seemed to come in waves. The food was authentic and plenty.

"What should I have for my 'first' real Brazilian meal?" Betty circled the menu with her index finger as if she was waiting for José to say stop.

"Begin with the lamb empanadas and the pork feijoada," José said without pausing to look at the menu.

Over this fare, the two became better acquainted, with José talking the lion's share in response to questions from Betty.

"The trip to Taipei, Taiwan, was amazing. Brazil demolished its competition in the first two rounds, including the United States." José darted his dinner fork at Betty to emphasize his point. "The food there was interesting but not to my taste."

Betty giggled at the darting fork in José's hand. "Where did you stay?"

"I stayed with a college friend, a native of Taipei. Taiwan has the same incredibly dense feeling as Rio and the incredible tension of being under siege from China." José was very flamboyant with his hands as he spoke.

"I suppose you have a sense of that tension because of Argentina?" inquired Betty.

"Uruguay was created from a disputed part of Brazil and Argentina and resentment still exists! Yes, I understand that tension." José had Betty's attention with his colorful descriptions of the localities, smells, and geopolitical intrigues of neighboring countries; not to mention the excitement of the Futsal crowds.

"Tell me more about the Brazilian squad."

"Three of the top five Futsal World Cup scorers were Brazilians: Falcão, Indio and Simi." José began to smile broadly when he mentioned Falcão. "I grew up with Falcão in São Paulo. We played many games with and against each other. Now, he is the star of Brazilian Fustal."

"Why aren't you playing on the squad?"

"Well, you are familiar with my history. Had it not been for the explosives and my father's desire for me to go to graduate school, perhaps I would be still playing with Falcão."

"Oh, well, yes. Graduate school is very important." Betty smiled while pointing her index finger at her chest. "Just look at me, I wouldn't have been able to help you without graduate school, but tell me more about the game."

José seemed to glow as he described the thrill of being there, even if Brazil was cheated out of first place. "In the semi-final game, the score was tied with regulation and extra time expired, Spain won a penalty shootout five to four. Spain went on to win the World Cup and Brazil— took third."

"So close!"

"An impartial observer would argue that Brazil dominated the semi-final match. A yellow card penalty in the first extra time was the difference between Brazil winning and tying."

"They were cheated! Was anything done about it? Did Brazil lodge a complaint?"

"No, there was nothing more to do, but this will be hotly debated over many beers for many years in São Paulo and the rest of Brazil."

"What are you going to do now, I mean in graduate school?"

"Economics. It will allow me to make a difference in the world affairs of Brazil. I will have to work my way up in the Brazilian government, of course, but I am confident and sure of myself."

"Yes, you are!" Betty was confident that José would succeed.

"Someday, I will head up Brazil's economy to ensure stability and growth, but that is many years away."

"Where would you start? In the government that is."

"I am only talking about myself. Tell me about your graduate school experience." Every time José tried to steer the conversation to Betty's life, she would deflect it back to him.

"Oh, just a bunch of boring books on law and the usual late night papers. How was Princeton?" Her past was closed as far as she was concerned. Betty was only interested in José's past and her future.

"Oh, just a bunch of boring books and late night papers," José jabbed back.

"Tell me more about your hometown, São Paulo. Did I see most of your old turf?"

He gave up trying to pry information from Betty and instead enjoyed telling her stories of his hometown, travels, and future plans. Betty brightened visibly when he talked of his home. She thought she was looking through a peephole into the future; a thread lay there waiting to be picked up. A thread that would lead Betty into a possible future if only she were to follow the thread. *I hadn't visualized myself living abroad. I'm not looking to be José's girlfriend,* but she could see that possibility. She just as quickly closed that thought and tucked it away. She felt vulnerable in a way she did not like when she thought her future like that, especially after what had happened with Tom.

Betty believed that someday the right man would come into her life, that she would settle down with two beautiful children and live that fulfilling life of a wife, mother, and career lawyer. *I can still have it all, just not with Tom.* Talking to José gave her the comfort and feeling like it could happen to her someday, that there were men she could trust with her heart. Eventually.

Betty felt a slight tingle up her arm as José kissed her hand at the taxi stand. "Thank you for a lovely lunch." *Damn, it! I want to ask him to have coffee. To keep this going.*

"We must do this again, but next time it will be dinner and my treat!"

"Are there other restaurants like Ceiba?"

"Of course, but none so authentic."

"Well, yes, I would like that." Betty tried to look simultaneously like she wanted to be kissed while trying to appear aloof at the same time.

"Adeus, my fair lady. I will call you next week." José turned abruptly and walked towards his home.

"Miss, miss!" Betty turned to the sound of the male voice behind her. "Do you need a cab?"

"I need something," Betty stammered.

"What?"

"Oh, yes, a cab, thank you." Betty refocused from José's fading image to the open door of the cab. *Strange, this is the cab company I usually use from home.* "Funny, I usually call you guys for a cab. I don't usually see you on the street."

"Yes, miss, Skat Cab is growing but still a small company," the driver winked as he turned to drive off. "Now, where am I taking such a fine woman as yourself?"

Forty-Six

Surprise, Surprise

IT WAS A BEAUTIFUL DAY. The rain had washed away the grit and grime of the capital. It seemed to sparkle with a wetness like in some movies where they hose down the streets and buildings to make everything shiny. There had been a lot of rain the past week, so everything had already been cleaned off, the morning rain just touched up the look. It gave Jil the feeling that anything was possible in the most important city of the most important country in the world. That power was available to anyone who happened on the right bit of information at the right time. Jil had that information and she was willing to use it to her advantage. No, she had to use it to her advantage. Not only her life, but also her family's lives depended on her success.

A deal had been made. Expectations set. They all would go back to their former lifestyles, except for Ruth of course, back into their comfort zones so to speak. Their debts would be paid in full, if they performed as required. If not, the debt was due immediately. In rather explicit terms it had been explained to Jil that the first installment on the note, should the family fail to make their "payments," would be Mrs. Harper's life. Next, Ruth Harper, then Mr. Harper, and finally, if she had not taken her own life by then, Jil Harper. If Larry would not perform as required, the pressure was ratcheted up. Abduction, murder Janice, then Ruth (she would be a nuisance at that point), and if he was not motivated by then, well, they would use Jil in their own sordid way until she held no value to them.

They had proven they could get past any security, any defense, any counteroffer, or any subterfuge. Larry and Jil had both tried in their own ways to worm out of the situation. Janice, Ruth, and Jil were all culpable because they had all owned a share in the business run by Larry Harper. They had lived off the ups and now they were paying for the downs. If Jil was not in hell, she was headed there.

It did not matter that she did not know what her father had been doing. These people had no conscience. They had no morals or scruples. They only knew the bottom line and it was written in blood. Jil had tried to seduce her way out this predicament. The awful little man sent to enforce the will of the Cabal took what she offered and then told her the bad news. She was still on the hook. Larry had tried in vain to protect his family from these monsters. He anguished over having allowed it to get this far. When he first resisted they took his ring finger, including his wedding band. The second time they were about to take his class ring in the same way, but instead they just broke the finger. The class ring had to be cut off later when the finger was set. The missing ring finger on his left hand was explained as a sailing accident, a warning to others that rings needed to come off before you sailed or they could come off while you sailed. Friends felt sorry and acquaintances felt pity for the once great man.

Jil threw up the first time she saw her father's hand with the gaping hole between his middle finger and pinky. A stark reminder of what powerful people were capable of and willing to do. Of course, as her father pointed out, this gruesome punishment was not meted out by the powerful but by their henchmen. Thugs who must either enjoy their brutality or thieves who made poor choices and now must pay their master in the only currency they had—pain. That thought, that her tormentors were in the same position as Jil and her father, gave little comfort. She imagined the debts the hoodlums owed were of a different kind. Some who faced certain death or incarceration? Was a family member being held to coerce them, like Ruth was being held as collateral in Europe? She recalled how Ruth's engagement to Betty's brother Rob was called off suddenly and then Ruth's sudden trip and marriage in Denmark. Jil was not to ask about the marriage or Ruth's situation directly. Ruth was in a secure location and details could lead to an unseemly attempt at rescue, though she could call Ruth anytime she wanted. The vacation story was meant to redirect the authorities to keep them from prying any deeper. Victor made it clear that Ruth was a captive through marriage.

She would not be going anywhere without her husband's approval. A gilded cage as it were, only the dungeon master, Victor, had conjugal privileges.

The men outside Jil's apartment building seemed ever present with not enough to do each day. These strategically placed guards were meant to look like maintenance or gardening staff. The entrance was a little too neat and a little too perfect. Whenever Jil needed to go somewhere, a driver would appear to take her. He would follow her like a valet. It gave the appearance of a very wealthy household from the outside. The constant supervision was becoming a strain on Jil. Just a week before, Jil bailed out of the "limo" at a red light yelling to the befuddled driver "I'm going to the coffee shop, do you want anything, Michel?" Michel bolted out of the car, but the drivers behind him began honking and pointing at the green light. So, he circled around until she came back. Jil handed him a tall coffee "Black, no cream or sugar, right?"

"You're not so bad after all, Ms. Harper," the driver said with his heavy Eastern European accent. His grin disappeared when the hot coffee spilled all over his shirt when the loose fitting lid failed on his first sip. "You bitch! I'm going to make you pay!" he exclaimed as he locked the doors and scowled in the mirror.

"Really, Michel, that is no way to speak to a lady!" reprimanded Jil. "Personally, I always check the lid; they tend to be so loose at these cheaper coffee shops." The beauty of the day and the success of her small act of rebellion made her briefly forget the horrors of her imprisonment and focus on what she needed to accomplish that day.

Senator Bolden, Jil's onetime lover and employer, was up for re-election. Bolden's support of the Cabal's agenda was required or the next election would go poorly for him. He did not have to publicly back their pet projects, but he had to guarantee his positions to get their political backing. These foreign nationals were controlling Jil and, by extension, controlling the senator. No one was to know who these shadowy figures were, lest any red flags be raised. Her lobbying firm's finances were layered many times to hide where the contributions came from; everything was legitimate, on paper. Unfortunately, Senator Bolden was publicly talking about using his Chairmanship on the Finance Committee to stake out a position contrary to where the Cabal wanted him to be. He needed to back off on taking a hard line on naked short selling.

A naked short sale is a bet. If the stock's price drops after the bet is made, a profit is earned. The investor does not even need to own the stock to cash in. By betting that a stock will decrease in value, naked short sellers can cause a large drop in the value of a stock; especially, if it was already headed down. SEC regulation SHO is supposed to prevent this behavior. Senator Bolden was rightfully against the abuse of short selling; nevertheless, the powers, the true powers wanted to be able to continue this sort of investment vehicle for their own purposes: right, wrong, or be damned.

Jil's job was to twist a promise out of the senator, something that would stick should he conveniently forget. Holding a failed businessman's daughter hostage in Europe and threatening to kill his family was one thing, but a senator had the FBI, CIA, NSA and who knows what else at his disposal to take care of problems like this. No, it had to be a cat's paw. Blind control no one could see, feel, or touch. It had to be a scandal that would take away the one thing a man of power covets most. Power.

Jil had some dirt on the senator, but their affair was not a showstopper for Bolden. He had enough support that he could go back home and throw himself on his constituents as a fallen man worthy of redemption. Even the quid pro quo legislation did not matter as Larry's company never profited from the tax loophole. Campaign contributions in exchange for favored legislative action were just par for the course. Larry had lost that bet, so with no gain, no pain for Senator Bolden.

Jil had something much better. A year earlier, while still working for the senator, she had arranged a meeting with a Jim Tulner, CEO of Park Place Bank of New York. The bank was in dire straits. They had made some very bad bets in a hedge fund that put the bank technically insolvent and if not fixed in a matter of days would lead to closure by the FDIC. Foreclosure would expose the past manipulation of funds by Tulner for the benefit of Bolden. Stocks had been shorted without delivery to the hedge fund per SEC regulation SHO. Bolden earned hundreds of thousands of dollars from his "investments" with the bank while other customers showed losses on similar investments. The hole for Bolden would get deeper if regulators delved into the banks falsified accounting. He could not allow such a bright light to be shown on his shady dealings. Could Jil do something for him?

Of course, the situation Park Place Bank found itself in had been arranged by the Cabal. The fix as well. Would the senator be willing to help intercede on the bank's behalf? Not only could Bolden keep his profits, but certain loans to the senator's family would be forgiven as well, loans amounting in the millions. Loans for failed businesses of the senator's sister and her husband, Bolden's campaign manager. These types of scandals, if they were helped to spiral out of control, would cost him his seat of power. How could he help his sister then? She faced bankruptcy, divorce, and social isolation—how could the senator stand by and not help?

All he had to do was pick up the phone as Chairman of the Finance Committee and make some inquiries. The bureaucrats who enforced the banking laws would know what he wanted even if he just asked for background information on the situation. A nod and a wink was all the FDIC and fellow Senate Finance Committee members wanted. Bolden would keep his seat, his sister would still be in business and his campaign manager brother-in-law would get him re-elected with a hefty war chest at his disposal.

The senator did not realize that by keeping himself in power he was on the hook as well. They could ask anything of him as long as it was not too obvious, otherwise he might lose his seat to a challenger. These people were all about subtle. They made large profits based on advanced knowledge of very small changes in the value of stocks, currencies, and commodities. They made the unlikely and the impossible happen at will. Jil and her family were part of the structure that insured their power and control. Jil knew all too well the price of not doing as she was told. She rubbed her left ring finger where a wedding band would go someday. She was not about to say no to the little things they asked, let alone the big things.

Forty-Seven

Spiral of Hell

THE SUN GLINTED off the Capital Reflecting Pool in the National Mall. There was just enough of a breeze to disturb the surface of the water, breaking it into a multifaceted mirror. The same breeze gave the crowd a sense of relief from the heat of the noon sun. Refracting light off the water raised havoc for anyone not wearing polarized sunglasses. Secret Service agents mingled amongst the crowd, some in the usual business suits and others who blended in, while the Capitol Police patrolled the perimeter. Tensions were high amongst the law enforcement types. A large crowd had formed to rage against the Federal Reserve. All types of people were in the crowd. Tattoo laced hipsters who felt it was their duty to finish what the hippies had started. Motorcycle gang types who tried to put on a softer, less intimidating look for this event, but Richardson could smell the beer and blood of the bikers over the patchouli of the hipsters. There were gaunt looking vegans and vegetarians who looked like they could use a juicy hamburger, but would go on a hunger strike before they would let that evil food past their lips. They seemed normal compared to the oddest, most striking person in the crowd, an army major who just seemed to be there, not so much to observe, just to be. He was almost Zen-like amongst the throng of hipsters and Neanderthals.

Gil was bored out of his mind. As a Secret Service Agent, he had the prestige but the Rangers and Special Ops were where the real action was. *Why the hell am I here? I should be in some ditch watching terrorists settle down so I can call in a drone and a smart bomb. Why? Oh, yeah, Sally.* Sally was the girl he met after his last tour as a Special

Forces medic in Iraq. Sally was all that and a bag of chips: five foot seven inches, big chested, and a redhead. *Man, is she ever a redhead. Full of spit and vinegar if you cross her the wrong way or sweet and hot if you treat her right.* She had talked him into settling down; to get out of the military before he was killed in the field or worthless to normal society, unable to walk the streets without spotting safe zones for cover. He had been tired, worn out, and ready for anything beside sand and dirt for his main course. She was soft and supple, tender and loving; she was everything that Afghanistan was missing. He was a man and he had needs, one was that rush of adrenaline he got in the field, the other was the rush Sally gave him in bed.

It had been time to re-up for another tour. He had planned on it and even told his buddies he would see them next time around. He had been sure of it, being half way to twenty years and a great pension. One, maybe two more tours in the mountains or in the desert of Iraq and he would rotate to a training slot. *No, that was not good enough for Sally. She was a woman with needs. Her man was not going to be in the desert or in the mountains while she pined at home!* So, he cashed out of the Special Forces and signed up for a slot in the Secret Service. He had the credentials, the training, and the patience. He was just finishing up this rotation and would soon be in one of the special units, Counter Sniper or Emergency Response Team (ERT). Then at least he would have a chance at some adrenaline. *This current duty is bullshit and a waste of my talents. A bunch of loud-mouthed malcontents who don't know how good they have it or what I went through to protect their right to shout out crap like this. If it wasn't against regulations, I'd give these bums a piece of my mind right now. Frigging ingrates.*

The problem was that he caught Sally cheating on him. After leaving the Special Forces and getting into the Secret Service for her, Gil was saddened to see that Sally needed a little adrenaline of her own. He came home early on a Thursday because he had twisted his ankle on a loose rock in the mocked up town they used for training. Sally and some jarhead were in the bedroom making a racket so loud Gil was able to appear in the doorway of their bedroom hobbling on his crutch before being noticed. He did not blame the marine; he probably did not know any better or was not smart enough to see the pictures on the wall. Besides, even if he was on crutches he could kick this guy's ass ten out of ten times so why bother? Sally was the problem. She was the tip of a spiral down into hell if he allowed her to suck him down. He was not going to let her get away with this and he was not going to lose his control either.

Gil gave her ten minutes to pack and get out. She could text him a message if she forgot anything and he would put it outside the door. This girl, who he had changed his life for was not worth going to jail over. Not now, not ever. So, here he was on a duty he did not want to be on when he could be making a difference in the world by killing terrorists. *Right or fair did not matter,* his drill instructor had drummed into his head, *doing what needed to be done did matter.* He would get his turn. This was not a dead end for him. *Maybe I'll sign up with an outfit like Blackwater, go back in as a contractor. Damn good money in that.* Only, he was not in it for the money. He was not in it for the prestige. If you boil it down, he was in this fight to make the world a better place and feel good about what he did on that journey. Karma.

There was something better waiting for Gil, and it was not watching over a bunch of poorly dressed idiots sucking at the teat of the government while complaining about that same government. He had patience. It would come. *Where'd the Zen guy go? Damn, I didn't see him leave. Got to get back on the ball!*

FORTY-EIGHT

SOMETHING FISHY

GIL COULD NOT SMELL IT. He could not taste it. Gil probably was seeing it, but he did not recognize it. It made the hair on the back of his neck stand up and adrenaline start to course through his body. Gil knew someone was watching him. The watcher had been there for days. He had not called it in yet because it was just a feeling. Not a trace of anything, not even a misplaced object in his apartment. For the past week, Gil locked the door to his apartment and placed a hair across the doorjamb so he could tell if the door had been opened. Today, the hair was still there, but Gil was not one hundred percent sure it was still in the same place. He had wiped the doorknob to leave a blank slate for an intruder, but it seemed even cleaner now than when he had left. Everything was just a little too much as it had been, yet somehow out of place.

Gil opened the door quickly slamming the heavy hard wood door into the wall while he pressed his back into the wall on the other side. He had his SIG Sauer P229 loaded and the safety off. He peeked around the corner of the door quickly to see if anyone was there waiting to blow his head off. There was, but he was not waiting to shoot Gil. He was sitting in the kitchen area of the studio apartment with his hands facing up, one on top of the other, thumbs touching. His forearms were on his knees and he looked really bored.

"Sergeant Richardson. I won't shoot and feel free to frisk me," said the same suspicious major from the demonstration in the Mall, the Zen guy.

"Who the hell are you and why are you in my apartment?" demanded Gil.

"I'm Major Tom Howell. I'm here to offer you a job, if you want it and if you pass our training."

Gil smirked. He could pass any training, mental or physical, and had the fruit salad to prove it. He had made it through the Army Rangers, medic school, Special Forces training, Special Ops training, and survived in some of the most hostile terrain anyone could imagine with terrorists itching to take him out. *Who the hell is this army major—something too tough for Gil Richardson? Yeah, right.*

Gil motioned for the major to stand up and raise his arms up for frisking, signaling that he should turn around. Gil stowed his gun as he frisked the major, finding nothing but a wallet and some keys. "Apartment key—landlords tend to use the same cheap locks, a Ford, and what appears to be a Suzuki motorcycle." Gil tossed the keys on the table and began to rifle through the wallet. Library card, insurance card, government ID, parking stub, MasterCard, ten crisp sequentially numbered twenty dollar bills, and a driver's license. Thomas Alvin Howell IV read the drivers license. *What a pretentious name,* thought Gil.

"So tell me, Thomas Alvin Howell 'the IV,' why are you in my kitchen and how did you lose your leg?"

Gil pushed the major back down into his chair and pointed his SIG Sauer P229 at Major Howell's forehead from five feet away; far enough away so he could react if the Zen Master came unglued.

Tom slowly crossed his legs and leaned back into the hard wooden chair making it creak.

"I am from an organization that doesn't exist. My uniform is real; officially, I am an army major. My service record is real. I lost the leg in Iraq while saving a contractor. You were the medic who saved my life," said Howell with a slight nod of his head.

"You're the asshole who pulled a gun on me?" Gil shook his head in astonishment. His pistol hand dropped a few millimeters. Suddenly feeling defensive again he raised the P229 level with Howell's eyes and asked, "What the hell are you doing in my kitchen?"

"I've noticed you are bored in your current service to your country. I am here to offer you a job, a job that doesn't exist, fighting problems the world won't admit exist and the people of our country will never thank you for—if you do it right," said a smug looking Howell.

"Sounds a lot like what I used to do. Why would I go back to that shit?" asked Gil with a dismissive wave of his gun hand.

"You will be paid better than a typical government job of this type, but not extravagantly so. If you ever turn on us or go rogue you will be cleaned. If you survive long enough to retire, you will be taken care of for the rest of your life," stated Howell with a sweeping gesture.

"Well, since you put it that way, how could I turn you down?" asked Gil satirically. "Buddy, I know you have to be a decent guy. You told me to save that contractor's life when I told you that you would lose your leg. See, I was right," Gil pointed at Howell's leg with the pistol.

"I take care of my people. I'm expendable, just like everyone else." Howell looked down at his shoes and then back up at Gil. "Are you ready to do what you were born to do, Gilbert Bradford Richardson, son of Edward Bradford Richardson?"

Forty-Nine

Down the Rabbit Hole

"**Y**OU'RE EITHER INSANE or one hundred percent for real. I'd vote for insane if I hadn't seen you in the field." Gil sat down in the overstuffed black leather chair seven feet from the major and held the SIG Sauer P229 pistol casually in his lap. He was not worried about being attacked, but he was in the unknown, so he kept the P229 ready just in case. "Keep talking."

"We have been watching you for some time. Our recruitment committee has gathered a nice crop of reports on your work, I can personally attest to your ability as a medic in Iraq," said Howell with a slight smirk.

"You got lucky. I just happened to be in the area," boasted Gil.

"From your first tour in Afghanistan as Special Ops to off the record in Iran, we are aware of your special talent for entering and exiting an area undetected. We especially like the fact that you didn't have to fire your weapon during your last three insertions. Our organization doesn't like to leave any noticeable evidence of our presence," continued Howell.

"So, I don't like to draw attention to myself. That is why I'm in the Secret Service, right?" asked Gil.

The major paused for a moment and looked at the closed front door of the apartment. "You paused for two minutes outside your own door because you had a feeling but could not figure out what was bothering you. You knew you were being watched, but you couldn't prove it or you would have made a report. We noticed your backtracking, checking twice, and especially the hair on your door acting as a seal. Only a covert special operations type would be so paranoid or even notice our observation; we don't like to be noticed."

"I knew it!" Gil raised his hand as if to say slow down–pause. "You keep saying 'we'. How many are you?"

"Special Agent Richardson, I think you know. Search your memory. If you are as good as we think you are, you will be able to tell me how many have been watching you this week."

Gil thought for a moment and itched at the spots in his memory that had bothered him recently. "The flower vendor outside the Willard Hotel. The taxi driver, but it was a different cab every time. I thought I was profiling, but he was the same guy, different cabs. Umm, the traffic cop giving out parking tickets. The drunk on the Metro with the beer can in a paper sack. I don't know, others I guess, but maybe I was just getting paranoid."

"Very good, I would be impressed, but I wouldn't be here if you weren't good enough to see these. You are right about those observers. Now comes the question: am I right about you? If you need to know more before making your decision, don't. Either join us or forget we exist. I wouldn't have come here if I didn't believe strongly that you would join us." Major Howell stood up, slightly favoring his real leg as he picked up his wallet and keys and pointed to a card on the table that Gil had not noticed. "If you want to join us be at this address at exactly 9:07 a.m. tomorrow. Otherwise, do yourself a favor and forget we ever met. You only know enough about me to get yourself fired from the Secret Service for being paranoid. You can't do me or my organization any harm. The people observing you won't be there and there are no traces of me in this apartment for you to even prove I was here. Oh, and Gil," Major Howell turned slightly. "Sally was a spy. Not for us. For the Venezuelans." He walked out, spinning on his false leg while stabilizing himself with the doorknob he held with a handkerchief.

It took a moment for Gil to realize he was alone in his apartment. He put the P229 away and sat down in the other chair at the table looking at the spot Major Howell had just occupied. "What the fuck am I getting myself into?" Gil asked the empty chair.

Fifty

Something Undone

THE EMPTY CHAIR did not have any answers and Major Howell was out the door before Gil could ask any more questions. Questions that he needed answered; however, the answers required Gil to take this meeting. Gil walked back and forth in three strides from his living room to his kitchen; there was nothing keeping him here or with the Secret Service, especially after Sally's departure. The apartment was nothing special. Being a Secret Service agent for the Treasury Department held prestige, but he did not have a decent assignment and would not get one for some time. Not to mention, the travel could be murder on a relationship. Gil stopped in front of the kitchen cabinet where he stored his liquor.

Was Sally a spy when I first met her or was she turned when she became my girlfriend? Was she using me or did she get used? Who was the scumbag banging her when I walked in? Was he the handler? Who, what, where, when, why, and how: I want to know it all and forget it all. Gil reached for the bottle of scotch in the cupboard, a twelve-year-old single malt of no great quality but no mean character. He splashed the caramel colored liquor into the glass and onto the counter. Suddenly, in a fit of rage, Gil threw the glass and the bottle against the far wall of the living room, shattering the glass all over the apartment. Initially he believed he threw it because he had spilled the scotch, but upon reflection, he had been fooled. He had been a fool to believe Sally. He never should have left Special Ops for the Secret Service. He only did it to be with Sally. He should be in the desert right now taking out terrorists. Instead, here he was about to dive into a bottle of scotch to drown his anger, frustration, hurt feelings, and fear; fear of the unknown.

Gil swept up the broken glass with the straw broom from the closet. Now the apartment reeked of mediocre scotch. He began to treat the next twenty-four hours as an operation, planning how and when he would act. He started cleaning the apartment to remove any trace of his fingerprints, but then realized that he was really cleaning any trace of Sally. Checking for bugs left behind by Sally or by Major Howell proved fruitless except for a pair of Sally's panties hiding under the couch cushion. These were from the night he came home and told her he had been accepted as an agent for the Secret Service. They had a little celebratory sex on the couch and then went out for dinner. Finishing with dessert in bed, including whipped cream and Baileys on ice. Some whipped cream even made it on top of the Baileys. Sally certainly knew how to give a man pleasure and by the expression on Sally's face that night, Gil knew how to drive Sally crazy.

Gil's running shoes were in the closet with his surveillance gear. He took the small binoculars and stuffed them into the fanny pack. His SIG Sauer P229 went into the shoulder holster. It had taken a while to get used to carrying the piece under his arm and hidden by his clothing. He did not want to go out without protection. Who knew what was going on since he kicked Sally out and now he had this other group keeping an eye on him.

Hitting Glebe Road outside his crappy apartment, Gil turned east on Lee Highway to get to the Mount Vernon Trail. The trail led to Theodore Roosevelt Island, the site of the meeting in the morning. He was to be there at 9:07 a.m., a strange time for a meeting. They were to meet under the Teddy Roosevelt statue. This would be a very lonely spot on a Tuesday morning. No tourists, no runners, no one to see what they were doing or saying. Gil stopped at the footbridge peak to see if anyone was following him. He scanned the sky and the surrounding land for signs of being followed. Surely, anyone close enough to keep an eye on him would have to pause to keep from being noticed. No one. Was he being paranoid or cautious? No way to know right now.

Gil circled the island to make sure he knew the lay of the land. He went under the Theodore Roosevelt Memorial Bridge to check for vagrants and any hidden agendas. Nothing out of the ordinary. Time to head back to his apartment and find something to occupy his mind for the next fifteen hours. The jog back was uninteresting so Gil pushed himself a little harder, going a fast seven minute mile clip to wear himself out a little and make it easier to fall asleep. With the loop around the island, he had run about ten miles. Not a bad workout.

He grabbed a Coors Light from the fridge to reward himself for pushing the run back to the apartment. This reminded him of how good the first beer tasted when he got back from overseas. *Only one tonight,* he had to be sharp in the morning for this meeting.

Gil started to clean all his weapons, even though they did not need it. Gil's meditation: the soothing click of metal on metal and the smell of gun oil. He even sharpened the knives that had not been used since their last go at the whetstone. Around midnight he finally found some peace and laid his head on the pillow.

Fifty-One

Wall of Darkness

THE D.C. METRO AREA IS DECEPTIVELY quiet at 4 a.m. The stillness of the five million residents in the fifth largest populated city in the United States and the political center of the world was masked by marble, limestone, and pavement. There was far more activity than met the eye but hidden mainly in buildings and underground facilities. The streets were quiet except for the occasional cab zooming by ghostly empty or stridently purposeful depending on the occupancy of the back seat.

This particular Tuesday morning did not have much to recommend for itself. Thunderstorm clouds, cumulonimbus, had formed to the west and were headed toward the D.C. metro area. If they held off it would be a dry meeting in the park. Gil planned for a wet one. He normally would have worn a poncho, but the Secret Service job required him to purchase a very serviceable raincoat. He brought the poncho anyway and wore it over the raincoat to keep his head dry and the wind from chilling his bones. He was not worried about how much noise he would make wearing the poncho just yet, though he did want to make sure he was not being followed. *I can ditch the poncho for a different look if I need to,* thought Gil.

Gil's plan was to go under the bridge on Roosevelt Island and stash some gear. He did not know what he was getting into and wanted to make sure he had a backup plan. Maybe it was just a pointless mind trick, but it was going to make him feel calmer and more in control; that would make those around him feel more at ease as well. *If the guy in the center of attention is calm, everyone else follows.* He learned that from guarding dignitaries.

An instructor once told Gil, "If the dignitary is jumpy it makes you jumpy. If you are jumpy it makes them jumpy sometimes, but if they are calm despite your demeanor, it tends to straighten everybody out."

Gil placed a rolled up canvas oil cloth in a high spot out of sight and placed a stone in front of the roll to keep anyone from noticing it. Inside was a six-inch hunting knife and a survival kit. Nothing he would miss if the authorities found it or a vagrant rummaged through the space. It should still be there in a few hours if he needed it.

Gil's watch showed 7:45 a.m. Gil was supposed to report to work at 8:00. He dialed the office with his cellphone and spoke with the receptionist, "Marty please." There was silence and then a half second ring before the handset was picked up, "Marty Fieldman." Marty did not care for fools and anyone calling him at this hour was either a fool taking the day off or sick enough to stay in bed. The fools he allowed a day off from time to time. These men and women had to be sharp. If they did not think they could do the job that day, he would rather rearrange the schedule than take a chance on an underperforming agent. Gil, in a hushed voice said, "Marty, something has come up. If I come in it will be at noon. If I don't, have someone check my apartment. I'll fill you in at noon." Marty hung up. There was not anything else to say and he did not have time for fools. This fool was taking on something bigger than himself.

The squall line of the thunderstorm approached quickly. The sheet of rain came at him like a predator as he walked up the path in the densely wooded park toward the central open area where the statue of President Theodore Roosevelt stood. Roosevelt had initiated the park system and it seemed simultaneously poetic and unfortunate that the man who inscribed the park system into the soul of the nation was honored in such a remote location accessible only by footbridge or boat. Although tens of thousands of cars crossed the Roosevelt Memorial Bridge each day, it did not have an exit ramp to the small island. *Just as well,* thought Gil darkly, *they will have to carry me out on a stretcher if things go poorly. Nice to know someone will have to work a little to make me disappear.*

Gil waited for an hour in the brush. The rain soaked the ground around him making a mess of the muddy spots. He was glad he had his poncho. The rain would muffle most sounds and make visibility limited, but he felt confident that he had covered his bases as best he could. Gil was restless but stationary, waiting until his watch glowed 9:05 a.m. before moving toward the statue. The rain parted like a curtain as Gil came closer and there was Major Howell in the middle of what had just been an empty paved area. *Was that a magic trick or just the low light level?*

Major Howell howled over the thunder as lightning lit the sky, "Are you ready to give up your life for your country?"

"Sure, just like in Iraq and Afghanistan," Gil shrugged his shoulders.

"Will you submit to our training without question?"

"Why not?" Gil sounded a little bored and was tempted to roll his eyes.

"Are you willing to kill the enemies of the United States of America, no matter where that takes you?"

Gil solemnly nodded "yes".

He had already signed up for these kinds of duties and expectations by being a Special Ops soldier. This was just a new level.

Darkness. The storm had covered the movement of Howell's men from behind the monument, allowing them to get behind Gil without his noticing as he was concentrating on hearing Howell over the raging storm: lightning flashing like a strobe and thunder repeating like artillery fire. They had pulled a smelly burlap bag over his face and grabbed his wrists at the same time. He was now secured by cable ties, just like the ones he had used on terrorists in Afghanistan. The journey to hell had begun. He had to trust these men and he had no reason to do so. *Howell trusted me with his life, I guess I can trust him with mine,* thought Gil.

Three hours later, Marty Fieldman pounded his desk and flipped open a file labeled Richardson, Gilbert. "That stupid SOB!"

FIFTY-TWO

SPARKLING

THE SUN CAME THROUGH the gap in the curtain of the east bedroom window and caressed Betty's forehead with its warm fingers. The bright sparkling light prying her eyes open at an hour far too early for civilized human beings. The night before had been glorious and filled with champagne. José had proposed to Betty on one knee at the Ceiba restaurant, the site of their first lunch date that was not a date, two years before. The courtship had been slow and gentle. Betty had been weary of letting anyone new into her heart. There was room for José there, but Tom still held a corner of her heart; the corner with an ache that would not go away, not even with José's tender love. Betty was resigned to knowing she could never nurture that lost love into full bloom. It was over, yet she could not let go.

José had presented to her a beautiful diamond engagement ring with a platinum band and a six-prong setting to hold the princess cut one and a half carat perfect diamond. José had said that a larger diamond would have been pretentious, yet a smaller diamond would be unworthy of resting on her finger. José was ever the economist, looking for balance between cost and benefit.

They had gone to Ceiba for their usual Brazilian fare and as had become the custom, Betty used her now nearly flawless Portuguese to order for both of them. He did it to make her work on her pronunciation, to prove to her that it was not just his discerning ear that cringed at her early attempts. "You sound Italian, darling, I won't order here again until Rafael tells me he understands you." Rafael was their usual waiter;

they enjoyed his banter and his interest in Betty's earnest attempts at the language.

Rafael brought out the dessert tray and on it was a jewelry box. "Senorita Betty, qual sobremesa que você gostaria?"

José's look in his eye made it obvious which dessert he wanted Betty to choose. She felt a chill and a desire to reach for the white kid leather box in the middle. Rafael could not suppress his smile and his secret knowledge of what was happening. José spoke up, "I said I would not order again until you could speak Portuguese flawlessly. That day has come and I wish to give you a special dessert. A dessert to share with you for the rest of my life." José reached for the box as Rafael held the tray steady. Opening the box as he went down on one knee, José continued, "I have waited two years to be able to say this and know you would understand perfectly what I am saying, 'Betty, você vai ser minha companheira, minha amada, minha mulher para sempre?'" (Betty, will you be my partner, my beloved, my wife forever more?).

Betty placed her right hand to her bosom as she put out her left hand, "Sim, José, Sim." (Yes, José, Yes.). That night she made love to José like a tigress. In the elevator up to his apartment, she unbuttoned José's shirt. She began to run her fingers along his finely shaped chest muscles and began to imagine them as hers to possess, hers to caress and kiss. She began to think of all the things she was about to do to and for the man she loved. They made wild love until the early hours of the morning and cuddled until they could not resist the hug of the night any longer, slipping into a deep and restful slumber.

Light from the window played over the ring on Betty's finger, the natural light sparkling as it danced inside the perfection of carbon atoms. It certainly was large enough, but not pretentious. The white gold was more subtle and allowed the diamond to be bright without looking like an island on her ring finger. Betty was as happy as she had ever been. This was the beginning of the dream, even if it was not the one she originally envisioned. That perfect life. She had found a beautiful man with a beautiful soul. She was content.

Fifty-Three

Perfection Lost

I T HAD BEEN FOUR WEEKS since the engagement. José's family was coming up from São Paulo to give their blessings and celebrate with the happy couple. They were a pragmatic family who knew the best way forward for their family and country was for their son to be able to cross into both worlds: Washington D. C. and Brazil. José would be finishing his dissertation soon and graduate with his doctorate in economics. As soon as the newlyweds picked a home in São Paulo, Betty would start packing and wind down her work. Her family had graciously agreed to allow the wedding to be in Brazil and José's father, Juan, had arranged a small fortune for Betty's father, Robert, to pay for the trip and the wedding, sort of a reverse dowry. It made Betty feel both odd and special. Odd, that once again, her dream was being altered now that she had committed to moving to Brazil. Special, because José's family was making such a big deal about him marrying this middle class woman from a distant land. The Silva's could not be more excited. The caterer and florist were chosen for their native Brazilian food and flowers.

Juan was calling Betty's cellphone from his limo, "We are delayed, the luggage—it is lost; would you please run a couple of small errands to help speed things up?" Juan's voice seemed shaken, odd, really, but who would not be out of sorts upon losing their luggage?

"Of course!" Betty was anxious to help her future in-laws. "What can I do?" Juan paused, Betty could hear another male voice in the background but could not make out the words.

"Correto, aprovado—não!" Juan was talking to the male voice with the mouthpiece of the phone only partially covered. "I am sorry.

Excuse me for a momento," he hurriedly spoke into the phone before covering it again.

Betty was fluent in Portuguese thanks to José's tutalage. Juan was clearly agreeing with the male voice but then interjecting a stern dissapproval. *What is going on?* thought Betty.

"Betty? If it were just me, I would wait for the luggage to show up but, eh. We need some items right away. Peço desculpas, I appologize, can you do this? Right away?" Juan seemed very sorry to be putting Betty to any trouble.

"Of course, Juan, I will get you everything, right away," Betty giggled a little. *How could I say no? They just traveled across the globe!*

"Wonderful! Here is what I need you to get." Juan listed the usual toletries, except these were expensive versions including a perfume from Bloomingdales.

"Yes, Juan. I will go right now. I just have to put my files away, I'm at the office catching up." *This is going to take all day! Argh, damn airlines!*

Betty spent the morning collecting the necessary items and delivered them to the hotel. The Silva's valet, Michel, was in the lobby to meet her. Michel was a tall Slavic looking man. His hair cropped within a few millimeters of his scalp to hide the bald spot on top. He had the air of a military man, retired now, but still running a tight operation as the chief member of the Silva's personal staff.

"Ms. Betty, it is a pleasure to meet you. I am looking forward to your wedding with great interest." Michel's Slavic accent was obvious but not overbearing.

"Why thank you, Michel. Here are the items; I added a few extra things I thought the Silva's might need." Betty handed the precise man the bags she had accumulated.

When she got back to José's apartment, the door was bolted shut and the chain was set. *What's going on? He never chains the door!* This could only mean José was still in the apartment, but no one was answering the doorbell. Betty called through the crack of the door, "José?" but no answer. *Is he in the shower?* She could not hear any running water. *What is that noise? Something is really wrong; none of this makes any sense!* She could hear the city now. "José? Come open the door. What are you doing in there?" Betty dialed his cellphone and could hear it ringing in the apartment, or rather the shrill sound of a phone playing the Brazilian national anthem. The flourish of horns and the snap of the snare drum emphasized José's lack of response. The music stopped and Betty heard José's voicemail message so she hung up. *That noise, is that a window opening on its rollers?* "José? Damn it! Open this door!" Betty was now more worried than angry.

She put her shoulder into the door and broke the chain after several hard runs at the door. Bursting into the apartment she could see drapes fluttering in the wind from the open living room window. She rushed to the window, but no one was there. "José? José!" Betty called out. Feeling silly, rushing about the apartment, because, of course, there was an explanation for this; she suddenly came up short upon entering the bedroom. On the bed was a grotesque site, a brutal lie. The tangled body of an imposter——her fiancé. This could not be. There were documents and pictures strewn about the bed. José's calm face belied the tremendous pain he must have experienced prior to being shot in the forehead. His beautiful sensuous fingers were broken and mangled. His wrists tied to the bedposts. His head rested on his shoulder at an awkward angle, which directed her attention to the blood spattered wall. Betty was overwhelmed by her discovery. She collapsed into a heap at the foot of the bed and began to sob uncontrollably. Her heart was torn into shredded pieces and she thought she was going to die.

Betty gathered her wits and looked closer at the documents. *It doesn't make sense!* They showed the Silva family fortune in ruins. Huge loans past due, investment portfolios looted, and bank accounts near zero. The pictures showed José in compromising positions with other women. This could not be the man she knew and loved. They had spent almost every day together for the past two years. She knew almost everything about José or so she thought. She called Juan but Michel, the valet, answered instead. "I am so sorry but I am the only one here to speak with you."

"José has been murdered!" screamed Betty. "Where is Juan?"

"José murdered? How is this possible?" asked Michel in his distinct European cadence.

"How the hell should I know how this is possible? Where is Juan?"

"Is there any evidence?" asked Michel as if he did not believe Betty's assertion—that she might be joking about her fiancé being murdered.

"Only his dead body and some paperwork" shot back a pissed off Betty.

"I see, yes, I understand. This is very bad news, Ms. Betty; I cannot tell you my sorrow for you and José's family." Michel took the news as if he was just told he could not get the tickets he ordered for the opera.

"Juan? Where is Juan?" persisted Betty.

"Mister Silva is not available right now. Have you called the police?" Michel sounded like he was asking for the manager, perhaps he could find the missing opera tickets.

Betty had been in too much shock to call 911, not that it would have helped anyway. "No, I haven't. I suppose I should, it's too late for an ambulance." Betty hung up on the valet and dialed 911.

While she was waiting, it dawned on her she had time to remove the documents from the bedroom. The Silva's did not need the public humiliation of these documents getting out. She knew she was tampering with evidence and could get in trouble, but the police were not going to find out. She stored the damaging papers in her briefcase and went to the living room couch to have a good cry before the police arrived. She looked down at her left ring finger and contemplated the perfection the stone evoked, what had taken a million years to create and now was a symbol of the flawed human drama before her. Betty willed the magic of the stone, the bright flashing light, to somehow conjure her fiancé from the dead. What some evil bastard had undone in a moment was beyond the power of her will and the hard carbon of the diamond. Betty walked to the bedroom door to look upon José on last time; she clenched the ring in both hands, looked at the wrecked body of her love and said, "José, I promise I will avenge your death." *Even if it means losing my own life, wherever this leads, I will follow the path to your killer!*

FIFTY-FOUR

MESSAGE IN A FLOWER

T HE MESSAGE COULD NOT BE clearer yet she was completely befuddled as to why Major Howell would know anything about José's death or why it was of national importance. Yes, José was important in Brazil or rather would have been had he lived. His family was influential. She had experienced it first hand from her very first contact with them about getting José to Princeton. *What on Earth did an army major, let alone my former, almost fiancé, have to do with my now dead fiancé?* It had been a year since José's death and five years since Howell had sent her away. *Why now? Why did he suddenly feel the need to console me?*

She crumpled the note attached to the flowers and threw the vase against the wall, shattering the thin glass into hundreds of pieces. *Who the hell does he think he is?* Margaret, her administrative assistant, came in to find out what the noise was and covered a wry smile while pretending to be shocked. She had signed for the flowers, but there had been no name on them.

"Who the hell does Howell think he is?" screamed Betty at the remains of the flowers.

Margaret had guessed correctly who the flowers were from. Tom had frequently sent flowers years before. *Mostly sorry looking flowers, poorly arranged, and these are more of the same; I need to post a bad review on Angie's list—if I can figure out who his florist is!* She would be the one to clean up the mess, but considering what Betty had been through the past few years, Margaret did not mind so much.

The flowers arrived shortly before noon, just as Betty was headed to her daily lunch hour workout at the gym. Without a backward glance at the mess on the floor, she picked up her workout bag and headed out with a head full of steam barely acknowledging Margaret as she stormed out. She had some lunchtime sparring partners to brutalize. Her jujitsu master had warned her about going over the edge. Letting her emotions run rampant was bad juju. Betty needed to control the emotion and use its energy as a weapon, not blindly let it control her. Today, she did not care: People were going to go home with bruises and hurt pride; she was in the mood to kick some ass.

Margaret gathered up the glass and flowers. A pity, but they had to go in the trash. She only got flowers on Administrative Assistants' Day. Her husband did not understand the importance of flowers let alone that there was a right way and a wrong way to do it. Margaret picked up the card that had come with the flowers. She knew the right thing to do was to place it on Betty's desk, but she also wanted to protect Betty. Margaret overcame her misgivings as she turned the wrinkled, discarded note over in her hands several times and decided to read it.

Instead of the usual business card size florists typically use, the note came on a 3x5 card stuffed inside an ivory envelope attached to flowers of sympathy. The note was cryptic. It simply said:

> I know who did it and why. 9:07 a.m.
> tomorrow at the Theodore Roosevelt
> Memorial – by the statue. T. H.

The flowers were cheap and the vase cheaper. Margaret had known José and the circumstances of his death; however, this note made no sense to her. She placed it on Betty's desk, fretting that she was doing the right thing. Obviously, Betty knew whom the message was from. That part was certain.

When Betty returned from her work out, Margaret made a point of intercepting her at the door.

"Ms. Thursten, you know I don't pry...."

Betty noticeably rolled her eyes. *Margaret is always prying into my life. She seems to live vicariously through my travels and relationships. She stalks information in the office like a lioness collecting food for her young but if you only knew her by the way she describes her home life—a docile, subservient woman afraid of adventure and is no doubt still having sex in the missionary position. Margaret is not the type to rock the boat—at home, so of course she has to get involved in my life here at the office.* Betty picked up the note and turned it over several times before tossing it back onto the desk before deciding how much to confide in Margaret.

Margaret pried, "The note, I opened it only to see who to send a thank you card to, but it doesn't say who the flowers are from...other than the initials T.H. on the card." *She needs to let me help her!*

Betty paused, looking down at the clean floor where there had been glass shards only an hour before. *Margaret does a good job, even if she is a pain in the ass sometimes.*

"Margaret, I uh," Betty looked the frumpy, middle-aged, glorified secretary in the eye, "those flowers were from Tom Howell."

Margaret pretended ignorance, shrugging her shoulders as if she had never heard the name.

"Remember, five years ago, he was to be my fiancé." Betty pointed to her ring finger to emphasize the relationship to her legal secretary. "He broke off our relationship and his promise to propose when he came back from Iraq injured." *I can't believe she doesn't remember this!*

"Oh, that Tom Howell. Now I think I remember." *Like I'm not going to remember a hunk like that! Even if he couldn't send decent flowers, at least he sends them.* "You haven't talked about him for a long time though."

"We were supposed to meet a year later if I still wanted him."

"Did you?" Margaret pretended she had not hashed over this story with the other clerical staff many times.

"He didn't show." Betty cast her eyes down at the note, thinking back to that day wistfully, pining for what might have been.

"That pig!" squealed Margaret.

"I wouldn't cross the street for him if he was the last man on earth." Betty looked at the floor like she was going to spit on the spot where she had thrown the flowers but held back.

"Ms. Thursten, Betty, the note says he knows who did it. I can only assume he means...what happened to José."

Betty glared at Margaret, *So you do remember!* She picked up the note and read it again.

> I know who did it and why. 9:07 a.m.
> tomorrow at the Theodore Roosevelt
> Memorial – by the statue. *T. H.*

Betty could not care a lick what Howell had to say about anything. Except, what if he really did know something about what those bastards did to José. That would be the only reason she would want to talk to the S.O.B.—for revenge!

Fifty-Five

Introspection

B ETTY ARRIVED AT THE FOOTBRIDGE at 8:55 just as the latest D.C. thunderstorm threatened to roll in. By car, she could have driven herself in twenty minutes, but she did not own a car. By public transportation, her preferred method, it would have taken an hour and a half. She took choice number three, a thirty-minute cab ride instead. The cabbie was familiar. Betty did not like to flag down random cabs, *You never know what you're going to get and they might not be there right when you want them,* so she frequently called Skat Cab Company ahead of time, *but what are the odds? They always send the same driver!* She had never considered this before, but today it seemed more obvious. He never really spoke to her. He seemed to barely know English. Betty would casually go about her business using her cellphone during the rides, assuming she had privacy, but now she wondered.

The footbridge was empty except for a couple racing off the bridge to get back to their car before the rain hit. She had been here many times with Tom and Surry for walks and occasionally as tour guide for her family and friends. The impending thunderstorm guaranteed the island was empty at this hour on a weekday. *Why that damn Howell can't meet at a Starbucks like everyone else is beyond me!* As she approached the statue, there was no one there in the foggy mist. Suddenly, as if a lace curtain was parted by a puff of wind, there he was.

Betty coldly eyed Howell through the misty rain and firmly stated, "I expect some answers and I don't want any of your bullshit!"

Major Howell began his story, "José was used as a tool to get to his father. Juan Silva was forced to listen on a speakerphone while they tried to break José. He heard every snap of José's fingers as they were broken; yet, José refused to give in to their demands and Juan was powerless in persuading José to do as he was told."

"Why didn't Juan do something? Call someone!" demanded Betty.

"Juan didn't believe they would kill him, nonetheless, he had tried to get his son to bend. José said they were asking for too much," continued Howell.

"Too much? What did they want?" asked Betty as she leaned in closer.

"They wanted him to manipulate the Brazilian currency, the 'real'. José agreed that stabilizing the economy of his country should be rewarded, but he wouldn't be party to a worldwide Cabal of sadistic manipulative bastards," declared Howell, raising his arms palm up, signifying the futility of the situation.

"No, José wouldn't have agreed to their demands. He was very proud and held tight to his convictions." *Unlike you!* Betty glared at Howell, but softened slightly as she reminded herself, *don't shoot the messenger.*

"They heard you coming and killed José as they escaped out the balcony window. I know about the evidence you hid," commented Howell.

"Here comes an avalanche of bullshit! How the hell do you know all this? Were you the bastard who did this?" She avoided thinking about her part in José's death by fixating on Howell. *How could he possibly know I gathered up the photos and documents before the police arrived?* Betty started to move into a ready stance—ready to kick Howell's ass.

Howell put up his hands as if to fend her off. "We intercepted their communication over the cell network. These photos are from José's security system and crime scene photos." He removed black and white photos from a Mylar envelope showing the same sanitized bedroom scene that Betty remembered. "It took several hours for the system to kick it out to us. As soon as I heard the communications, I secured the security camera footage to discern the killers and look for possible leads back to the Cabal. They mentioned damaging evidence that is missing in these photos."

"Who the hell do you think you are? You can't do this. I'm a private citizen, I have rights!" raged Betty.

"I had a watch on you in case someone tried to get to me through you. I had cleaned my trail enough that no one would think you meant anything to me any longer so they wouldn't go after you," said a castigated Howell.

Betty thought about kicking Howell where it would hurt most. "You certainly left me with that impression too."

"I am working on the assumption that you are now on their list because of José. I want you to join us and get the men who did this to José."

"I don't need your help!" sneered Betty.

"I can help you with information, training, and equipment. I want you to join our operation—to take out terrorists. The kind that did this to José and the kind that takes people like Jil hostage via economics."

"What does Jil have to do with this?" Betty was surprised by this turn in the conversation.

"Yes, they also have you linked to Jil. You have been manipulated in the past in subtle ways. In the future, it won't be so subtle. Your parents and brothers will be next," stated Howell.

Betty was stunned. "This is too much." *The rain isn't helping, the thunderstorm is rolling in.* She muttered to herself, "What am I supposed to do?" *I want out of this conversation and out of this weather!* Betty looked at Howell, trying to read his mind, to see behind the cold eyes that had replaced her lover's warm look. *Howell is offering a way out, a path to revenge. Is this what I want?*

"Come with me now and I can show you things I can't show you here. I can tell you things I can't tell you here; however, there is no turning back. You can leave now and I will never contact you again, though I will do my best to protect you in a limited fashion. If you come, we will train and arm you to go after the merchants of death who have taken control of the Silvas and Harpers. It is too late for José, but there is still time to save Jil. Maybe."

"You bastard! You aren't giving me an option, you've boxed me in," Betty spat at Howell's feet.

"Good. My men are going to blindfold you when we get on the boat. Please don't resist—for their sake." Major Howell turned to his left slightly to point toward two awaiting agents and, maybe, the path to knowledge and vengeance. *He's an angel of death offering me a path to revenge.* Betty looked back to the bridge, the path to freedom. B*ut it wouldn't truly be freedom. I would always wonder what Howell knows, what I could have done with that knowledge. I would never know peace. I can't go back to ignorance.* "You are a real bastard, Howell. You aren't leaving me any choice. You know that, don't you?"

"I know."

"Now I have to know or I'll always be angry at you, at José for choosing death, and Juan for not saving him." *And what the fuck! Even Jil! How is her family part of this hell?* There was only one path for Betty and Howell knew the way.

Howell apologetically handed Betty a dark blindfold, the sort you might wear on an international flight to sleep. "Please wear this; we can't let you know where we are taking you."

Betty glared at her former lover. She was about two seconds away from bailing on what seemed to be more like a hazing than a recruitment when the words of Margaret echoed in her head. It had absolutely nothing to do with the current situation. Her assistant had been talking about a previous boss and a case that was dismissed. The client stood to gain millions from a copyright lawsuit, including damages; however, the client died of a heart attack just hours before the case was to begin. The fiancé had no standing so the case was tossed. They had planned to marry after the case was decided win, lose, or draw. Nothing is one hundred percent certain in court, but this would have been golden. All the "widow" really wanted was closure. Now, she would never get it from the courts or the defendant. Just as José's murder would never be avenged in a court of law. It was up to Betty to be the judge, jury, and executioner. She took the blindfold and placed it over her eyes. "Get it over with before I change my mind," the words hissing out through gritted teeth.

Fifty-Six

Shaken, Not Stirred

BETTY WAS STILL SHAKEN UP by the harrowing flight to Control. The journey had begun at Roosevelt Island aboard a skiff transferring to a SUV then a helicopter and finally a propjet with the final leg a nearly vertical descent into what was the headquarters of Control. Sitting in a conference room while recovering gave her a chance to think twice about what she had just gotten herself into.

"I need someone like you to be the eyes and ears of Control in the D.C. area. Your offices are so close to the Capitol and you have access to foreigners, including the upper echelon." Howell used a laser pointer to circle all of the embassies concentrated within a mile of her office on a large map projected on the wall across from the table.

"It isn't like I have dinner with these people every day," chided Betty, although she could already visualize how to infiltrate these sources, even if she lacked daily contact with the foreign embassies.

"You are perfectly positioned to collect intel and you have the assets for the clandestine work. You will be able to gain access to areas through the front door," continued Howell, barely acknowledging her concern with a wave of his hands above the hard wood surface.

"But surely my prodding will arouse suspicion, maybe expose my intentions. They'll know I'm a spy," said Betty as she poked her finger into the mirror like finish of the table.

"Our first priority will always be to maintain your cover, but your access is undeniably a valuable asset," Howell was not going to take any excuses.

"I don't trust you completely. How am I to believe you when you were dishonest with me about why you couldn't keep your promise? Why? Why did you dump me like that?" Betty's face was scrunched up, a tear glistening in the corner of her eye and her finger pointing at Howell. *God, I hate this! I don't want him to see me cry, suck it up!*

Howell leaned back, as if the force from Betty's accusatory finger was enough to push him to the back of his chair. "It's complicated, but I will try to answer your question." He paused to draw in his breath and gain a moment to collect his thoughts. "General Getner and I were tasked with reforming, no, rebirthing a secret espionage group known as Control. Due to a botched mission in 1996 involving a Chinese freighter, the operations of Control were mothballed to protect remaining assets. We needed to act quickly and as silently as possible to avoid attracting attention to our operations."

"What kind of operations? What kind of assets are you talking about? Mothballing?" Betty's mind was racing to the future, when she might be the one to be mothballed.

"There are facets of this I can't explain now, but in time it will become all clear," Howell forced himself to stay focused and maintain eye contact with Betty.

"There is nothing clear about what you did or what you are doing now. I don't understand how you wound up here. I thought you were doing research." Betty's perplexed expression tore at Howell.

"My time in Iraq made me think deeply about what my purpose in life is. How situations can become out of control in a split second. Babs did not listen to me when I told her to wait until the turret was checked out by the bomb unit." Howell paused and looked down at his hands resting on the darkened mirror image of himself. "Had she listened to me...well she wouldn't have been blown up and I wouldn't have been injured."

"You're telling me that a little shrapnel in your leg was a life altering experience, one so drastic that you threw our future away to become a spy?" asked a frazzled Betty, unaware of the full extent of damage to Howell's leg.

"No, I'm telling you that my eyes were opened to the frailty of life and the potential for one person to make a significant difference. I couldn't do what I am doing if I married you." Howell looked almost angry, unwilling to reveal to Betty his prosthetic leg.

"Are you trying to say I was holding you back? Maybe if you had talked to me about this," Betty felt the tears welling up again, *I can't let Tom know how much Howell is hurting me!* Betty vainly wished her former lover to retake the body of the doppelganger before her.

"I should have died in Iraq, I didn't. I'm not the same man who left you. I know I promised I would come back whole. I couldn't keep that promise. If I had walked away from saving Babs, well, I would have become a different kind of man. Maybe whole but always wondering if I could have done more. It would have haunted me," Howell sounded almost hollow saying this, as if the effort of revealing himself was exhausting.

Betty could see a glimmer of Tom in the man before her. *Maybe there's hope. Maybe Howell does have a soul. Maybe I can work with him after all.*

"I want to see everything you have on José; don't hold anything back or I'm out of here. If you ever screw with me, I'm out of here. If you ever lie to me, I am out of here. You messed with me once and I let you live, do it a second time and I doubt you would be so lucky." Betty slammed her fist into the hard wooden surface to make her point. The heavy table shook.

Howell did not consider this a death threat. He knew Betty well enough to know it was a promise. Yes, if he ever crossed her, she would make him pay dearly, especially with the training they were about to give her. Howell glanced up as the lights dimmed slightly twice, as if someone double tapped a dimmer switch for the room. "Wait here. I'll be back in a few minutes. We have an operation going right now and I need to answer a question."

Betty's patience was running thin waiting in the conference room. The eight-foot mirror on the wall told her that someone was watching. *They are probably talking about my impatience, debating if I'm made of the right stuff for the job. I just want closure on José's murder. That and the satisfaction of beating the crap out of the SOB who ordered it. I'll rest when I know who did it and why.* She was not a widow, but close enough, just like the woman Margaret had described.

Howell is the only available path to closure on José, that thought again echoing through her mind as she scratched her nail into the polished wood table, engraving an ever so faint 'Betty is pissed!' into the dark wood. Howell being the only route to revenge did not seem fair or right, but it was what it was. Betty could either go back to not knowing and wondering if José would have survived if she had not shown up at the apartment when she did or dive blindly into the abyss Howell offered: purgatory or revenge and knowing.

If Betty's glare was any hotter there would be two holes burned through the mirror on the wall. Waiting for Howell yet again seemed not only unfair but a sign of his indifference to her feelings. *That bastard! I should have included not having to wait as one of my stipulations.*

Before Howell had left the room, he explained that she would continue her legal work as a cover for her travels and to provide access to important people in the world. She would infiltrate the capital's power structure and act as a spy in distant lands. She had to be comfortable in these roles or Howell would have to reconsider how she would fit in.

Howell re-entered the conference room just as Betty was ready to bolt.

"You'll start training immediately," stated a serious looking Major Howell. "Here," he handed Betty a cellphone, "don't worry, it's encrypted."

She dialed her direct office number, "Margaret?"

"I've been worried sick, where are you?"

"I'm going to be taking a couple weeks off—for personal reasons." Betty was sworn to secrecy. *It has already started. The lies and cover-ups!*

"OK, I can handle that."

"I'm pursuing information about the murder of José," *at least this isn't a lie.*

"Oh, Betty! Those thugs are ruthless! Be careful." Margaret sounded truly worried.

"There is nothing to worry about. It's an academic search, no hunting down criminals in dark alleys." Betty forced a light laugh at the preposterous notion of her personally chasing the bad guys.

"Don't do something stupid," Margaret ruffled the pages of the appointment calendar. "You don't have anything pressing, but if something comes up I will have Mark take care of it. Hey, Betty, nail the bastards!"

FIFTY-SEVEN

PRINCES OF DARKNESS

BETTY WAS SITTING IN A STERILE ROOM in the bunker of Control. Sitting near her at the only other student's desk was another new agent named Gil. Both were being indoctrinated by Howell in the dark ways of their enemy. With the lights low, he ran through an audio visual presentation of information defining their enemy and its methods. *Is this the table that will end up with my name on a plaque?* thought Betty. *This table no one will see instead of the law library at Georgetown? Will I pay with my blood instead of writing a check?*

Howell droned on, "The Cabal membership tends to travel in pairs. Control has identified some of the families who have the means to influence governments, but it is difficult to trace actual events and transfers to these people."

"You mean people like Gates and Buffet?" asked the roguishly handsome Gil.

"Billionaires like Bill Gates and the Oracle of Omaha, Warren Buffet, are pikers compared to the ultra wealthy of Europe." Howell dismissed these candidates with a wave of his hand.

"What about the Russians or the Mandarins?" inquired Betty.

"The oligarchs of Russia and China are up and comers, but they need many more generations of refinement and sophistication before they will be able to sustain their power. Some conspiracy theorists call the Cabal 'Illuminati' or the 'New World Order'. They are neither. They have been, are now, and will continue to be the World Order, the hidden power behind countries, the true masters of the planet." Howell kept flipping through a series of images by pressing a button on a remote.

"Why not just confiscate their money?" Gil posed the obvious solution.

"Their vast wealth is hidden from the normal, trivial measurements like bank balances and retirement funds. Power is wealth. Wealth is power. Some are princes and princesses, but most are just noble families who have purchased their peerage during one historical turning point or another." Howell seemed to enjoy lecturing his new pupils as he slowly opened their eyes to the vastness of the problem.

"How are they protecting themselves?" Betty also was beginning to enjoy the "class"; it was like being in graduate school again. Something she excelled at.

"These families control governments through subtle moves, sort of a jujitsu on a national scale. By using pressure points, they prevent up and coming political powers from usurping their control. The governments in turn protect the Cabal." Howell looked at his nails, inspecting them for dirt, as if he was waiting for his students to ask a question, one less obvious.

"What sort of pressure points?" *This is starting to get interesting,* mused Betty. *Not so bad when you get to sit next to a hottie like Gil.*

"Pressure points like greed, hunger for power, lust, envy, and pride. If the politicians can't be corrupted they are compromised. If they can't be caught in a compromising position they are enlightened with the knowledge that they will be replaced or killed. Brute force is rarely used, though examples have been made of recalcitrant public figures, but only in extreme cases."

"Any examples?" pressed Gil, looking for the low-down dirt of history.

"Possibly a few popes, one for sure, and various early European governments. And recently, well, JFK was supposed to be a warning," Howell paused and turned his eyes to the ceiling as if he was deep in thought.

"JFK? I thought that was a Communist thing?" opined Betty.

"Yeah, right, Oswald! The Warren Commission confirmed it, the magic bullet theory." chimed in Gil.

"Slow down, you're going to sidetrack us. Wait. OK, five minutes then back to where we left off."

"This is going to be good, I just know it!" blurted Betty, her face expressing the anticipation of learning something new.

"The Cabal likes to put a scare into a head of state every once in a while, to keep them 'honest'. Kennedy was pushing to end the Federal Reserve System. We think he was just using it to push the Cabal back, but they weren't too pleased with the brush back," Howell, while talking, changed the presentation to the relevant information on JFK.

"Here you can see the extra shots fired or rather the botched autopsy showing extra shots that lead to the magic bullet theory. Oswald wasn't supposed to be good enough of a shot to take JFK out in a moving car from the Book Depository."

"Yeah, so what if he made the shot, that is what the Warren Commission claimed. You're just saying the conspiracy nuts were wrong!" interrupted Gil.

"In case someone found the connection, the Cabal introduced extraneous evidence that would lead a reasonable person to conclude a conspiracy had occurred."

"That's crazy! Why would they do that?" interjected Betty.

"Oh, I see, cover your trail by sending anyone with half a brain down the wrong trails, multiple ones: the mob, the CIA, the magic bullet, Castro, the industrial military complex," chimed in Gil.

"Exactly. Confuse your adversaries by giving too much information," concurred Howell as he returned his presentation to where they had left it, popes and European princes.

"Oh, a document dump—overload them with meaningless documents and depositions, old lawyer's trick." *Smart*, thought Betty.

"As a government becomes aware of the Cabal's manipulations, they have a choice of becoming corrupt enough to ignore the string pulling or be overthrown. Whole governments have been replaced while wars and revolutions have been started or ended per the wishes of these Machiavellian charmers," Howell stopped on an image of a Serbian general and his men standing over a trench of bodies; then flipped it to the genocide in Rwanda. "They show no mercy in picking the puppets who slaughter the innocents to cover the bodies of the nonconforming politicians."

Gil and Betty had nothing to add to the gruesome pictures before them, not even a wry comment.

"The Cabal does not exist in the minds of most people. Their wealth is too immense to imagine and their power too vast to resist. They don't care if you want to make stop signs purple or give away money to the poor. They only need stable, manageable governments to engineer astounding new profits from the masses." Howell turned from his pupils to look at the image depicting an aristocratic and wealthy looking man holding a wooden cane with a golden dragon's head handle standing tall amongst a group of coarse looking ruffians. He cocked his head slightly as if he somehow recognized the man but could not remember why.

"How does their operation pay off?" Gil's interest was becoming more intense by the moment.

Howell pulled his thoughts from the image and clicked his remote to move several images ahead. "Their take, in countries they control, averages one dollar of value per person per day. This is accomplished by controlling the monetary supply. By taking a cut off the top, they get their money tax-free. That works out to a profit of three and a half billion dollars per day and one and a third trillion dollars per year. Compare that in contrast to, say, Russia who generates that much each year in gross domestic product (GDP)." The still image changed again to an animated picture of a pile of money growing in size every second until it filled the screen. "Is it any wonder they control the world when they have collected this "tax" for hundreds of years?"

"That's a lot of money!" exclaimed Betty.

"Mind you, we only have guesstimates, it works out to three to five hundred million per year per member of the Cabal," Howell started looking for the bar graph to represent this information but changed his mind.

"I'm surprised it's so much per member, what, around three to five thousand Cabali?" Gil had been a good student as well; the army likes sharp, intelligent, adaptive kids for their special operations track.

"The Cabal tries to keep their numbers in that range. During the plague years, they lost a few extra. Yes, between three and five thousand would be correct." Howell obviously knew the number by memory, but he seemed to be calculating it in his head again to be sure.

"How did this all start? I mean, every 'business' has a beginning," Betty cut through the meat and went for the bone.

"It all started with the Hundred-Year War in 1337," Howell started looking for the pertinent information to present.

"Who was that war between?" Betty showed her weakness in middle European history.

"France and England, of course, the House of Valois and the House of Plantagenet. Really both French, but Plantagenet also controlled England." Gil's knowledge of history included all of the great wars due to his military training and personal interest combined.

Betty still looked uncertain, "Who? What?" *So the big gorilla has a brain to match his looks after all!*

"Joan of Arc. She brought it to an end. Crazy feminist." Gil looked at his new partner with feigned disgust.

"Yes, that is right, Gil. Someone had to finance the wars between countries and provide liquidity in times of stress." Howell's map showed a stain spreading across a map of the world, starting in Central Europe and spreading across half of the globe while a calendar flipped years.

"Controlling the currency insured that no one would notice the breadth and depth of the Cabal's operations as they expanded. It started with one family and grew. Control of the Cabal changed over the centuries but solidified with Mayer Rothschild around eighteen hundred. Each of his five sons moved to a new region to open a bank branch and control center. There was no need to sell anything or do an hour of manual labor. Control the money supply and you control the rate of inflation and, ultimately, the stability of a currency."

"That's a long time between the Hundred Year War and eighteen hundred," commented Betty.

"Yes, it took a long time to build their base of power. Then it took a visionary like Rothschild to take it to the next level. Three hundred years to develop a system but only a hundred and fifty years to dominate over sixty percent of the world. In another forty years, they will control ninety percent of the world, if we don't stop them." Howell used his index finger to stab at the remote button to make his point with the next image of the world slowly being enveloped with a red ooze.

"A monopoly!" concluded Betty.

"World domination without an army," observed Gil.

"Well, they have an army of accountants. Men and women who cause more damage with a computer than I could ever hope to in the battlefield," corrected Howell.

"Why hasn't anyone seen this end game and stopped it?" Betty had a look on her face that said *I have almost all the puzzle pieces, what is left?*

"By allowing a small fraction of the world to have power over their own destiny, the ultra wealthy make it appear that they aren't a 'monopoly'. This perpetuates the belief that individual nations control their own future. Nothing could be further from the truth." Howell began the wrap up and turned the video screen off.

"Any questions?" Howell looked at his watch. "You have range practice in fifteen minutes."

Gil closed his notebook to signify he did not have any questions.

"How does a family like José's or Jil's fit into this?" Betty had a hurt look on her face. *Don't think I really want to ask this question, but I need to know.*

Howell looked closely at Betty as if he needed to confirm something before continuing. "They are merely pawns. José was to join the army of accountants, lead the Latin Branch as it were, once he rose high enough in the Brazilian government. The Harpers tried to rise above their station and, like a prairie dog sticking its head up out of the burrow, got caught. They had the option of dying or submitting. Once you submit you are a pawn."

"What about Gates, Buffet, and the rest of the new billionaires? Why are they allowed to have so much money?"

"The total net worth of the all the world's billionaires only equals three years of income for the Cabal. They allow some successes to give the appearance that they aren't in control of the world. That and the computer companies provide back doors into the world's data systems for the Cabal." Gil and Betty gave him blank stares. "To monitor the situation, keep an eye on things—spy."

"Son of a bitch!" exclaimed Gil.

"They are so dead!" concluded Betty.

"Right, off to target practice for you two. Gil, don't let Betty show you up this time, OK?" Howell finally seemed to find something to laugh about.

"Twenty bucks says I win," Gil boldly declared.

"Make it a hundred. I need to buy a few toys for Surry when I get back to make up for leaving her with my landlord," Betty poked her index finger into Gil's chest to make her point. *Hmm. He's well built too!*

"You're on!" Gil sounded sure of himself, but his body language said otherwise.

Fifty-Eight

Rogue Control

JOSÉ HAD BEEN THE BEGINNING of an expansion into South America. This was really a consolidation of the World Order Cabal's influence. The northern section of South America and several small banana republics had been experimented with, but nothing really seemed to click. Brazil was to be different. Families of up and comers were selected, their children educated for positions of power; their desire to manipulate the fate of their countrymen would be the Cabal's lever. A benevolent dictator could control a country for forty years. This was enough time to entrench the mechanisms of true power: corruption, greed, pride, lust, and envy in the next generation.

Instead, somehow an idealist had been created, one who rebelled against his parents and training. An arranged marriage was delayed at José's request, and then some upstart from America was getting her claws into the property of others. She was a trifle, not worth messing with, merely collateral damage if she got in the way. José was the real prize and the future of the Brazilian contingency. His father, Juan, had prepared a platform of power, land, cattle, and local politicians as the foundation for José's ascendancy to the central bank of Brazil. With their man at the helm of the Banco Central do Brasil, the World Order would be able to control the flow of money out of South America. Their three percent inflation tax seemed minuscule on the surface but, over time, it was massive. These people worked on a scale of centuries, not years, or even decades. They had a plan that was far larger than any individual, though each individual in the World Order wielded immense power while they were on this earth.

José had been chosen. He had been groomed. He resisted. He died. Life, liberty, and property rights are meaningless on a thousand year scale. Patience was all that was required. Every country, every politician, every leader would find a moment in their lives that required outside assistance. This group was waiting and willing to help for a price. The United States was no exception.

President Edward Wassel, 44th president of the United States of America, had been bought and paid for. His election had been arranged; in fact, his opponent was also bought and paid for. The World Order did not care which man or woman gained control of the White House. The Cabal had control of the selection process. Wassel was to deliver the Federal Reserve to the World Order. Most staunch nationalists would cringe at giving control of the U.S. monetary supply to foreign nationals. However, Wassel was neither an idealist nor a nationalist, unless you count Edward Wassel's desire to be the most powerful politician in America as a national interest. Press releases floated by Wassel's campaign indicated otherwise, that taking the Federal Reserve to the next level would align the interests of the United States with The European Union leading to a more stable economy. Complete control of the money supply meant complete control of the country. For forty years, complete control had eluded these patient men, the Cabal. The final piece of the puzzle was being arranged as they had planned for fifty years. Check and mate; however, Wassel died before he could deliver.

The presidential ticket of Wassel-Mathers was lagging in the polls and thanks to the last minute revelation that Mathers had a love child with a former staff member caused Robert "Bob" Merryweather to be inserted as last minute replacement for vice president. He was a placeholder and he knew it. Those in power knew it. His job was catchy sound bites and meaningless propaganda. He was an economist, not a lawyer, or a politician. He brought gravitas to the ticket on economic issues and a patina of morality that Mathers obviously lacked. The voters looked at Wassel and saw a career politician. In Merryweather, they saw a man with convictions whose only desire was to make every American better off.

Bob Merryweather found himself in the peculiar situation of being the most powerful politician in the world by default when President Edward Wassel died of a massive heart attack on December 17th, 2001, just eleven months after being inaugurated. Presidential briefings revealed far more than he was used to, including information that confirmed his long held but never uttered beliefs about who truly controlled the money supply of the United States of America and the rest of the world.

Bob Merryweather was not meant to be in a position to do anything about these beliefs, but he was not going to let the opportunity pass him by. He was approached by a shadowy figure, Tom Howell Sr., who knew far more about President Merryweather than was public knowledge. Tom Howell Sr. offered a lever of power: a secret spy group named Control. He told President Merryweather of a mothballed organization ready to be unwrapped and unleashed. An organization was waiting for the right moment to exert its power on the likes of the World Order Cabal. At eighty-six years of age, Tom Howell Sr. was too old to take the reins again; he only needed to designate a trusted leader to grab hold of the lever, someone of unshakeable integrity.

Colonel Getner and Bob Merryweather were distant family and President Merryweather knew he could trust the colonel with a secret mission. Remove the powerful families from controlling the central banks of not only the United States, but throughout the world. Colonel Getner would be trained, promoted, and entrusted with the secret weapon Tom Howell Sr. had at his disposal.

This newly reborn, ultra secret organization was referred to only as Control. The World Order Cabal now had a nemesis they could not track or see—Control. Funding was already arranged and beyond the purview of congress with several lucrative medical patents assigned to a labyrinth of front companies. International offices gave an excellent platform for gathering intelligence in the form of business records and contacts. The organizations did not even know their true mission. They only knew their individual mandates: intelligence gathering, clandestine operations, logistics, and personnel. Knowledge was compartmentalized into cells, just like a revolutionary force. Originally, Tom Howell Sr. took orders from Allen Dulles that were meant to accomplish goals beyond the abilities of the newly formed CIA; usually the chain of command at the CIA was too compromised for the delicate missions Control was entrusted with. This arrangement continued for eight years after Dulles retired until his death in 1969. Howell Sr. continued working on his own without direction until his retirement in 1978; however, his successor had proved inadequate, eventually leading to the mothballing of Control over the blown up Chinese freighter incident off the Horn of Africa. Now, the chain of command was once again direct to the president, but still without any congressional oversight. Getner was now the head of Control, handpicked by Howell Sr. and President Merryweather. Freeing the world from enslavement to the banks controlled by the ultra wealthy leaders of the World Order Cabal was Getner's mission. President Merryweather had silently declared, his proclamation to end the domination of the Federal Reserve and its siblings around the world by the power hungry Cabal. He would pay for this temerity with his life.

The "accidental" assassination of JFK by Oswald had not been in the plan, but Lyndon B. Johnson was just as manageable as any other man, he too had his weaknesses. Once again, the Cabal arranged an assassination attempt, this time for Merryweather. He was being warned that his was to be a one-term presidency but once again, the unthinkable happened: the assassin succeeded. Merryweather may have moved suddenly or maybe the wind was just a little too strong that day. It did not matter.

The United States was in mourning for the second time in three years and a new leader was anointed. Why did this matter? Because Merryweather had been the only politician who knew about Control. Tom Howell Jr. and General Getner were suddenly without a leader and no way to explain their previous directives to the new president, former vice president, Jared Spangler. Spangler had become Speaker of the House when Wassel was elected president. The existence of an organization, self funded and beyond the control of congress, whose only mission was to stop the World Order from finally controlling the USA, was beyond his understanding. Spangler's motto might as well be "Destroy what you don't understand."

Merryweather had known too much. He understood the power of the World Order and their ultimate desires, which is why he had authorized Getner and Tom Howell Jr. to set Control on its course of destroying the World Order. Together with Control they were rogues, responsible to no one but themselves. No governance meant complete power over their destiny, but it also meant no one to protect them from their mistakes.

Fifty-Nine

Into the Swamp

THE *WUMP...WUMP...WUMP* of the machinery would be maddening if Betty had to stay here much longer. *Even with these earplugs the noise is deafening! The floor shakes with every slam of the presses. How do these people stand this work environment?* The huge metal presses standing forty feet high were producing stamped steel parts from flat sheets. The workers wrangled the large sheets of saw tooth edged metal with into the presses with their rag wrapped hands. Shredded gloves were used beyond their normal lifespan to save money. This worked fine until a piece of the cloth snagged in the jagged metal, slowing the movement of a worker's hand. The press operator might not see a co-worker struggling to remove a gloved hand or maybe they were just on autopilot. Modern presses require both operators to simultaneously press large buttons out of reach from the massive pressure required to instantly mold the metal; this factory was not modern. In Panama, safety was important, but so was making enough money to survive another day.

Lorenzo Marin owned Multiservicios Marin del Mar S.A., a piece-work shop and the cover for Betty's trip to catch up with Dr. Salizar in Panama. Señor Lorenzo wanted to spend more time in America to get contracts from U.S. businesses for metal parts, but was having a difficult time getting his visa issues straightened out. Betty believed it would be simple enough to get a few strings pulled but was not going to let her bill or her talent appear to be smaller than they had to be. This was the old factory. Lorenzo was making a huge production out of her visit, a tour designed to impress Betty of his importance.

"This facility makes excellent profits but it is getting old. The equipment breaks down occasionally which slows production." Lorenzo was pointing out piles of raw steel at one end of the process and stamped metal parts at the other end. "Tomorrow's tour of my new factory in Colon will demonstrate our increased production per square foot and you will see how clean it is there." They were scheduled to visit his modern factory on the Atlantic side of Panama in Colon after a train ride tour along the Panama Canal. "We will refurbish this facility after you clear up my visa issues." He needed to increase his business with the east coast of America to justify the expansion of the new factory. Betty was his key to unlocking the U.S. Government red tape.

"Very impressive Lorenzo, I can't wait to see your other factory—perhaps we should get going so we don't miss the train?"

Betty was here to follow up on a lead Control had for a Central American member of the World Order. Catching up to a certain Dr. Salizar in Panama was the real reason for the trip. This lead was a small time player in the big scheme of things, but he was the beginning of the story and could lead to the unraveling of the World Order's regional operation, if Betty did her job right. From everything Betty had learned the past year at Control, the group they were hunting would grow three heads for every head you cut off, like the Hydra of mythology. They needed to follow the heads to the torso to stop the heart of the beast instead.

The tour of Lorenzo's run down facility was behind schedule. The Panama Canal train would not wait for her and she needed to join back up with Gil. They needed to cozy up to Dr. Salizar on the ride to Colon before attempting to feel him out on his Cabal connections on the return boat tour the next day. She could not get Lorenzo to end the factory tour on time and the train was leaving in less than an hour.

"The train is a bore. Take my limousine!"

"Thank you, but I really do want to take train." Betty needed to be on the train with Gil for the next part of the mission. "It's my first time."

Dr. Gualtiero Salizar was an important target. He owned a global network of hospitals and was a world renowned transplant surgeon. Medical tourism may have been his bread and butter, but the Cabal paid handsomely for the use of his wide-ranging facilities to move money, people, and equipment around the world. Chemicals, tools, and even people could be moved without suspicion from one hospital to the next. If facial reconstruction was not an option, a criminal could be transported with bandages as the disguise. Dr. Salizar was going to be on the train and then on the cruise through the Panama Canal back to Ciudad de Panamá from Colon.

Control found out about the good doctor when he lamented his story to the bartender of the Tegucigalpa Marriott Hotel in Honduras. He was speaking Portuguese, so he figured he could vent and no one would know what he was saying as the locals all spoke Spanish. Fortunately for Control, the bartender was a polyglot and placed in the hotel bar for just this reason. Now, Betty needed to determine if the good doctor was a friendly source of information or an agent for the World Order Cabal. The Cabal did not know about Control yet, as far as Major Howell knew, but they were always testing and searching for opposition. Control's prodding of the Cabal via testing Dr. Salizar allegiances could expose the very existence of Control to the Cabal. If the Cabal poked back, they were going to discover a hornets' nest.

Gil was meeting up with Betty for the train ride to play her supposed paramour. This interaction was another way to get Dr. Salizar off guard. The happy couple could use any aspect of their relationship, medical tourism, work, or play, whatever it took to get the skinny on the man who might lead them deeper into the organization they were hunting. Yet, Betty needed to be done with Lorenzo and quick if she was going to make her train.

A disturbance on the work floor was her opening to make a break for it. One of the workers managed to leave his hand in the machinery just long enough to lose the tip of a finger. Embarrassed, Lorenzo could not get Betty out of there fast enough while he pretended to be concerned about his injured worker. Betty thought he was more concerned about the lost time cleaning up the mess while workers milled about giving condolences to the injured party instead of keeping up with production. Time was money to Lorenzo. Lorenzo made his apologies and would drive to Colon and meet up with Betty that evening at the new factory. For Betty, it was time to get out of there and on to her real job—Dr. Salizar, her first head of the Hydra.

SIXTY

TRAIN FOR TOMORROW

GIL WAS IMPATIENTLY WAITING for Betty at the train depot. This was not an act. He knew she would not be late on purpose, but it was not like he could leave on this trip without her. He did not know Portuguese and while he could play the jilted lover or create a new story for the mission, it just was not going to work well. He had no real angle on starting the conversation with Dr. Salizar.

"The train will be leaving in five minutes, has your wife arrived?" asked the conductor rhetorically.

Gil was distracted by the conductor calling Betty his wife, perhaps it was a slip or misunderstanding. It could even be a translation issue. Gil rolled with it. "My fiancée should be here any minute...can you hold the train if necessary?"

Gil pulled out a roll of one hundred dollar bills. He did not want to flash cash to attract attention; he merely wanted to convey to the conductor that money was no issue to hold the train. Gil peeled off a crisp one hundred dollar bill and pressed it into the conductor's hand. The conductor stood there holding the bill as if there was doubt to his ability to grant Gil's wish with such a mediocre sample of the large roll. Gil peeled another off and tore it in half.

"You'll get the other half when she arrives," replied an annoyed Gil.

The conductor snatched the partial bill and ran off to the front of the train to stall the engineer. Gil smiled to himself. *He'll hand the torn bill to the engineer, offering him the other half if he waits for the order to leave. Everyone has their price. Sometimes they just need a little incentive.*

Ten minutes later, as the passengers began grumbling and looking at their watches, the conductor came back over to Gil shrugging his shoulders and pointing at his own watch. Gil peeled another hundred off the roll, not bothering to tear this one. He wanted the conductor's complete confidence in Gil's ability to make things right.

A cab came roaring up as Gil was handing the note over. With the brakes screaming in pain, the tires left a black scar across the driveway as the cab screeched to a halt, the grill nearly brushing the kneecaps of both men. Gil snatched the hundred dollar note back and handed the conductor the torn piece he was missing. With a glare that could melt ice in the Antarctic, the conductor expressed the universal language of don't screw me because it's a long train ride. Gil gave him the entire crisp bill that had been snatched back as well. A smile glowed from the conductor as if he had never had a cross word with his longtime friend, the American.

Gil and Betty scurried on board. The luggage had already been loaded.

"Darling, what kept you?" cooed Gil with a sharp edge in his voice.

A lovers' spat was not in the script, but it seemed like a good way to deflect the attention now focused on the reunited couple's entrance. Not a good way to conduct a clandestine operation, but to not have a scene now could actually cause the other passengers to stare longer, pondering why the delay and why the couple were so unconcerned about the delay. Gil made a show of giving his fiancée a good fight and Betty jumped right in.

"Well, if you hadn't left me behind or if your directions were worth a damn, I'd have made the train on time!" Betty sternly gave back as good as she got.

"Whoa, now, the directions came from the concierge at the hotel and you were the one who insisted on going to the gift shop on your own. Don't throw me under the bus!" stammered Gil as he tried to keep up with Betty's banter.

"Bus! Ha! That's a good one. This is just like the bus tour of Cleveland, you know. You bailed on me then too!" Betty thought she was going overboard here, but was going with the flow of fake emotion fueled by her pent up desire for Gil.

"Now wait a moment, Cleveland? Really? You're going to bring up Cleveland?" Gil elbowed Betty to make sure she knew it was time to make up. The shtick was wearing pretty thin.

The lovers' quarrel also gave them the chance to have a public display of affection as they forgave each other: Gil for being impatient and Betty for having had to buy that last trinket before leaving Panama City. Most of the passengers became embarrassed for watching and turned away. Dr. Salizar, however, apparently enjoyed a good soap opera and stared openly. Now they had Dr. Salizar's attention.

Betty and Gil headed to the bar car for drinks and a little post argument nestling. It really felt like being a double agent. Betty was supposed to be staying away from Gil, the ladies' man. She had resisted the repeated temptations of this hunk of a man, chiseled out of marble. Now she was supposed to be in love with him as part of her cover. This is why Howell had originally planned on Slim being her partner for this job. *Gil sure is dangerously handsome,* thought Betty. *This is so much better than Slim. He was just dangerous!*

Dr. Salizar joined the crowd for cocktails and began to mingle. He intended to get to know some of his fellow travelers. One never knew when or where a new client could be found for the medical tourism business. It could even be one of the current crop of itinerant cultural ticket punchers on this train, the type who had to go see the top one hundred tourist destinations in the world. The tourists on this excursion were the target market for Salizar: affluent, connected, and frugal. Common procedures like cataract removal or even complex surgeries such as a heart transplant were cost effective in second or third world countries. A first class hospital could be staffed at half the cost. Raw materials such as organs were easy to come by, whereas, a similar procedure in the United States might cost five or ten times as much. He began busily chatting up his fellow passengers.

Half way through the train ride, they arrived at the Gamboa and Chagres River Bridge. The fabulous Gamboa Rainforest Resort was to the northeast of the bridge. To the west was a freighter on the canal heading south to the Pacific. Betty and Gil had finally made contact with Dr. Salizar by buying a drink for him at the bar while they got their own refill. Their goal was to grease the wheels for the next day's boat ride, to become intimates in twenty-four hours. Liquor is quicker and Dr. Salizar was a scotch man. He did not often get good scotch, so when someone else was buying he was drinking.

"It has to do with my wife," he explained to his new best friends Betty and Gil. "She won't allow liquor in our home and she quizzes me about my travels to see if I have been buying booze at the hotels or bars along the way. If someone else is buying I can truthfully say I haven't bought a drink!"

"How clever!" agreed Betty and Gil.

They were enjoying the spectacle of the passing freighter when a thin, natty dressed man in a blue suit sat down behind Dr. Salizar. This immediately caught Betty's attention. The man had been watching Dr. Salizar from a distance for most of the train ride in the bar car. His thin hollowed out faced had a sinister scar across his left cheek, jagged as if a wound had healed poorly due to infection. He had the look of a mercenary. His face was familiar—but different. *Why do I recognize this guy? I've never seen a scar like this before, yet something is bothering me.* Betty refocused on the good doctor who was going on and on about his wife.

"She insists on hen-pecking me under the guise of deep love and caring, however, her henpecking only drives me away. These excursions to the hospitals in my network, hobnobbing with potential clients, sightseeing, and access to liquor provide freedom from her harping. She hates to travel, so all the more reason to go on these trips!" groused Dr. Salizar.

Just as the doctor threw his arms up in an exaggeration of his wife's way of dressing him down the "thin man" stabbed a needle into Salizar's neck causing a grim look on the doctor's face. Less than ten seconds later, Dr. Salizar collapsed into the table clutching his chest with panic written on his face. Screams from the watchers and flying drinks from the collapsing figure of Dr. Salizar created enough confusion in the bar car for the thin man to make his escape out the back.

Betty and Gil were momentarily trapped by the onward crush of people seeking to simultaneously flee and come to the aid of the doctor. Betty climbed out of the booth and ran across several tabletops toward the back of the train, giving a bit of a show with her skirt. She was not going to let the thin man get away without a little questioning. She had spent a considerable amount of time setting this mission up; the opportunity was not to be lost.

The thin man had managed to get back to the last train car full of freight. Packages destined for Colon and points farther east. There was nowhere else to go on the train. He turned to see Betty following him into the train's baggage car. Still wielding the syringe filled with what appeared to be enough for a second lethal dose, the thin man kept Betty at bay. She was not carrying a gun at the moment due to the urgency of her journey from Lorenzo's factory to the train. Besides, she was just as deadly at close range with her hands.

The thin man jabbed the needle at Betty to keep her away. This was a weapon she could respect. The thin man had a long reach, longer than Betty's. She went low in her jujitsu stance, crouching on her left leg and swung out her right to knock the killer down. She caught enough of his left leg to knock him off balance, but because he could grab the storage racks on either side of the train, he stayed upright. A stabbing swing with the syringe kept Betty at bay once again. He backed to the rear of the baggage car, unlocking the rear door with his left hand, and climbed out onto the back of the train. He slammed the door shut, keeping the barrier long enough between himself and Betty to climb atop the roof of the train. Betty followed. He swept down with the syringe keeping Betty from reaching the top. She backed down off the ladder, grabbed the fire ax attached to the inside rear wall and returned, swinging it with abandon at the thin man's outstretched arm. She connected just enough to knock the syringe out of his hand onto the roadbed below, bouncing harmlessly off the rail and into the ballast rock. The train was now on an angle as it ascended the Chagres River Bridge. The thin man's hand was bleeding profusely and he had a worried look on his face for a moment until it appeared he had made up his mind. Walking to the middle of the car he peered over the edge of the train as Betty steadied herself at the top of the ladder.

"Who are you and why did you kill Dr. Salizar?" Betty shouted over the noise of the train.

"He deserved to die," yelled the killer with an eastern European accent. His now obviously Slavic face, gray eyes, broad nose, and pale skin became contorted with rage. "He killed my family. He tried to kill me. He would have killed you."

"You remind me of someone, do you know someone named Michel?"

The thin man sneered at Betty. Before she could make a move to capture the killer, he ran to the opposite side of the rail car and leaped off the train toward the water below. His right foot caught the bridge as he nearly cleared the edge causing his body to tumble out of control. He slammed flat onto the water. His body floating face down on the surface was a sure indicator of his death.

†

Hours later in Colon, Betty and Gil were joined in a remote warehouse by several other Control agents. They had collected the body of the assailant and were going over the forensics. The corpse bore the scars of several operations including the removal of a kidney. A dragon tattoo was crawling up his right arm on the outside of the bicep. The left eye was artificial, possibly related to the nasty scar on his left cheek that ran to his lower eyelid. His lungs were scarred not so much with tar from smoking as from coal dust. McFluffy would trace the particulate matter to its origins, but that would have to wait until tomorrow and a fast plane to Control's headquarters. His clothes were tailor made from Milan based on the labels. He was very well dressed for a man with only two hundred balboas in his pocket, the local Panamanian currency, and two thousand Venezuelan bolivares. The Panamanian balboas were equal to dollars and the Venezuelan bolivares were worth about a quarter each. Seven hundred dollars was enough to get by on for a week or so, but he did not have any credit cards or other obvious sources for ready cash. He could have stashed luggage in a hotel or memorized a numbered account. Feelers would be placed for any unclaimed luggage or unusual transfers to the local banks.

The small amount of mud remaining on his shoes was scrapped off for further analysis and the clothing sealed in airtight packages to check for pollen and plant spores. These would be frozen for the trip back to preserve the evidence. With today's science, there are excellent ways to trace the comings and goings of a world traveler. The suit had not been cleaned in some time, so there was hope for a good amount of evidence even with the water compromising and perhaps introducing new trace material. Fortunately, they had samples to compare to, so they could eliminate the obvious.

Was he really Yuri Vasilyev? Was his passport genuine. DNA tests would determine the truth. The body was going on ice for now.

"Betty, what do you make of this?" asked Howell from the remote secure encrypted link.

"He said the doctor had killed his family and tried to kill him. From the missing kidney, I have to believe there will be some evidence in Dr. Salizar's medical network."

"That makes sense. What of the other items?" pushed Howell.

"The syringe and poison. Nothing special about the needle but the Venezuelan bolivares may point to a source—it's a long shot. Based on the speed of Salizar's death I sure want to know what it was. The syringe was recovered and McFluffy should be able to determine its contents. We need that double checked, though, as you know from our 'Slim' chances in the past of finding the source."

Howell understood Betty's code for the McFluffy situation. Slim had implicated McFluffy as a traitor only a month before. Howell had not come to a conclusion on this possible tip or misdirection as of yet. However, McFluffy was being watched carefully. Betty wanted Howell to be reminded of this without directly outing McFluffy in front of the others.

There was a lot to do in a short time. The canal cruise was canceled. Betty called Lorenzo with apologies; their meeting would have to be postponed. Betty and Gil boarded a private jet for their flight back home to Control; the flight would only take three hours at near Mach 1 speeds. By the time they arrived back at Control it would be five a.m.

SixTY-ONE

FLY BY NIGHT

A FLIGHT ATTENDANT SERVED DRINKS to the veteran operatives as the Gulfstream G650 climbed to forty-five thousand feet and began cruising near the speed of sound at 850 mph. Just as Betty was relaxing with her vodka tonic with a slice of lime the plane veered sharply to the left, causing Betty to sink into her seat at three G's and her barely touched drink to spill onto the cabin floor.

"What the hell!" Gil had fallen asleep shortly after takeoff and barely acknowledged the sudden maneuver.

"This is the captain speaking," a deep bass voice, calmer than Betty expected, announced. "Apparently we aren't the only unregistered flight out tonight over the Bermuda Triangle. Evasive action has been taken and we will arrive on time. Please enjoy the rest of your flight."

The flight attendant shrugged her shoulders and gave a wry look as if this happens all the time.

"Holy shit! You got to be kidding me!" Betty picked up and handed the now empty cup back for a refill.

Inside a nearly identical G650 headed in the opposite direction, a similar calmness by the crew was contrasted by the displeasure of the chief passenger. "Max! What the hell just happened?" yelled a pissed off Ernesto Montoya.

"Unidentified flight. Just like us," replied Ernesto's top man.

"One of ours?" inquired the master of financial manipulations, one eyebrow slightly raised. Ernesto had managed to survive in his current capacity by being suspicious of everyone and everything. "We were the only ones coming this way from the meeting—or are we being followed?"

"No. The signature is faked," D'mitri was reading from a report on his screen from the navigator, "and they did not attempt to contact us just as we ignored them."

"What does that mean?" an irritated boss wanted to go back to sleep but his staff was making it difficult with meaningless information.

"We don't know who they are and they don't know who we are. Our people would recognize our faked signature and properly avoid our airspace." D'mitri calmly explained in the plainest language he knew.

"Why didn't we avoid them sooner, Max!" demanded the bleary eyed tyrant.

"D'mitri, my real name is D'mitri" started the man called Max.

"I can't keep you Eastern Europeans straight. You are all like the first man, Max."

"Very well," with a resigned expression, the servant continued, "please understand that we are flying at almost one thousand miles per hour and the plane we passed was going the same speed in the other direction."

"So, why are you telling me this? I want to know what time it is, not how a watch is made!"

"Yes, sir." D'mitri, the man now known as Max took a deep breath to steady himself. "At the speeds we are flying combined with our need to be less visible, we can only see one minute ahead by radar. They are probably flying the same way."

"So, why does that matter?"

"The pilots had only a few seconds to decide what to do and then they had to move quickly to miss each other."

"This is an expensive plane. Why such a short time?" Ernesto rubbed his eyes, regretting it as soon as he started to wake up.

"Planes on normal flight paths, we see them much farther away." Max took pains to slow his speech down, his accent was minimal, but he did not want any misunderstandings. "This was unusual, like our intruders I told you about yesterday, at the compound three weeks ago."

"Listen, now that I'm awake, tell me again. I want to be clear about the dangers." Ernesto threw off his blanket and took the pillow from behind his head.

"They plan to breech our perimeter again and will attempt to interrogate you while looking for documents that can be used to unravel your methods." Max sounded nervous.

"What are you hiding from me!" demanded the prince of money laundering.

"We don't know how they are going to get in. We just know from the girlfriend—the informant, that they intend to stick their noses in our business." Max was starting to get defensive.

"What do you plan on doing about this?" quizzed Montoya.

"Our people will be ready for the unlikely; reinforcements will be at our backup site in case we need them. Everything will look normal to the invading operatives." Max shrugged his shoulders, "We take care of you as always or I lose my life and my family dies. Do you really think I don't have this handled?" An unusual level of anger rose from the distress Max obviously felt at the remote possibility of failing.

"Have you found a replacement for that damn Yuri? Goddamn it, why was he allowed to kill the doctor?" barked Ernesto.

Max hesitated for a moment. "His twin brother, Michel, will be with us in two days. He is more than capable to replace Yuri as our intelligence officer."

"Very well. Do not allow my sleep to be further disturbed." Ernesto repositioned his pillow and blanket for the remaining hour of flight time as Max dimmed the cabin lights and momentarily reconsidered his career path.

†

Betty yawned as she took the fresh vodka tonic. "I'm awake now, but tired as hell. Gil?"

Gil responded by snorting briefly in between heroic snores.

You don't look nearly as heroic or handsome with that drool on your chin, thought Betty. *Thank God, I didn't let my hormones get the better of me!*

Gil snorted again, wiped the drool off his chin with eyes half open, his grizzled beard scratching at the fabric of his sleeve, he gave Betty a knowing smile. "You know, you're not a bad operator, for a gal."

This time Betty's drink spilled on purpose. "Oh, I'm sorry, how clumsy of me!"

"What the hell? What is wrong with you?" Gil swatted the ice cubes off his lap and grabbed the blanket folded over the headrest in front of him. Mumbling he said, "Women! Can't even take a compliment," before turning away and going back to sleep.

"Chauvinist!" *I'm no feminist, but Jesus! What does a girl have to do to get a little respect! Breathe deep. Slow my heart rate down. I'm tired, Gil was half asleep. I can't let this come between us—we are a team.*

A communications link light blinked green three times before going red to alert Betty that a secure call was coming in. Before she could take a quick look in a mirror, Howell was facing her on the video link.

"I hope you have been resting on this flight. Margaret has left you a message that you have to be in court at nine am."

"But I need to clean up!" protested Betty.

"You'll just have enough time to get to your place, shower and change. I'll have a driver waiting for you." Howell looked off to his left, which made it appear he was looking at Gil. "You two getting along OK?"

"Peachy." Betty faked a grin. Whatever anger she harbored with Gil was now transferred to her boss. *Jesus, Howell, how come Gil always gets to rest after a mission and I have to keep going!*

"You don't have anything scheduled for the rest of the week until the briefing on your next foray into Ernesto's compound. Take some time off and rest."

Howell sounds like he actually is concerned about me. "Will do. Surry and I have some playtime to catch up on."

"How is it working out with Grace watching Surry?" Howell inquired.

"Oh, OK, I guess. I'll just be glad when I see my girl, even if it is for a few minutes before rushing off to work." Betty thought briefly about the time Tom had been in charge of Surry and the loft was trashed. *She could have been your girl too. Your loss!*

"OK, just be sure you get some rest. The next mission is going to be intense."

"I'll be ready." Betty disconnected the link just as Howell looked like he had one more comment or question. *It can wait until the briefing; he'll call back if it's important.* Betty was asleep and dreaming moments after leaning her seat back. Her last thoughts echoed in her head, *So little time to rest. So much to....*

Endnote

A LLEN DULLES SERVED EIGHT YEARS as the head of the Central Intelligence Agency (CIA) from 1953 to 1961. His involvement in the creation of the early U.S. spy agencies, before the creation of the CIA, gave him an insight into the strengths and weaknesses of a clandestine organization. Dulles was tasked with uncovering the deep, dark secrets of our enemies and in the process learned how to keep secrets from foe and friend alike. During the waning of WWII, Allen Dulles became aware that the Office of Strategic Services (OSS) would be reborn as the CIA. It also became clear to Dulles that the existing structure of the OSS was compromised by foreign spies and double agents, specifically the "Dogwood chain" of informants in occupied Europe. Alfred Schwarz, a Czechoslovakian engineer and businessman, was given the codename "Dogwood" by Lanny Macfarland, head of the OSS in Istanbul. Dogwood, in turn, hired or induced other agents to transport sensitive information out of the Axis powers. Eventually, the chain of agents was discovered by the Nazis. They began sending disinformation intended to cause misallocation of assets by the Allies. In 1944, the "Dogwood chain" was too unreliable and dangerous to leave in place; it was shut down and abandoned.

As the station chief at Bern, Switzerland, Dulles was instrumental in gathering information on the Nazis that was crucial to ending WWII. Information flowing through Dulles was deemed reliable and of high quality which led to an increase in his stature in the intelligence community. After WWII, he was part of the leadership team who created the CIA. Despite these key rolls, Dulles did not trust the new CIA infrastructure completely and looked to alternatives outside the normal channels to maintain control over the flow of information and the execution of orders in other countries. Dulles created a black on black ops program beyond the control of the United States Government.

In 1945, Nazis fleeing through Dulles's area of responsibility allowed him to confiscate ten million U.S. dollars worth of Nazi gold, a large quantity of forged Bank of England notes, and the printing equipment used to produce the counterfeits from Operation Bernhard. Counterfeits considered the finest forgeries ever produced and nearly impossible to detect. Operation Bernhard had been the brainchild of an SS officer with the aim of destabilizing the British economy by flooding the country with millions of forged bank notes. Agents began using the notes to pay for expenses abroad when the original plan of dropping them from Luftwaffe airplanes over Britain became unworkable. U.S. bank notes were forged by Operation Bernhard, but never circulated. These hundred dollar bills were just as perfect as the Bank of England notes and completely unknown to the U.S. Treasury.

Dulles, determined to prevent another "Dogwood" subversion of the United States spy network, ordered his young protégée to take the gold bullion, counterfeit bank notes, and the printing presses back to the United States. The confiscated Nazi loot was used to start a completely independent spy agency known as Control. Only Allen Dulles and his protégée knew of the creation of this spy agency. Control was beyond the reach of the U.S. Government oversight and self-funded by the Nazi gold and printing presses. With an endless supply of counterfeit U.S. bank notes at his disposal, the protégée was able to continue operations long after exhausting the gold and Bank of England notes. By 1957, the Bank of England began withdrawing all compromised banknotes and replacing them with new colored notes, so Control began printing U.S. hundred dollar bills exclusively, eventually producing one billion dollars worth of forged U.S. bank notes from 1945 to 1963. This fortune was used to build the hidden bunker, buy weapons and information, fund spying operations; whatever was needed, there was always enough money to pay Control's bills.

Because the Federal Reserve added twenty-five billion dollars to the monetary supply during the same period, Control effectively taxed the dollar two percent by printing their mostly undetected forgeries. The one hundred dollar bill was retooled slightly in 1950. The obverse side, commonly called the face or front, was modified making the forgeries out of date. Control was able to locate and induce the original Jewish prisoner of war forgers to make the appropriate modifications. When the dollar was no longer redeemable in silver in 1963 and the forgers unavailable for an update, Control began its decline and belt tightening. Heroin and cocaine became the means to launder the last of the counterfeit hundred dollar bills and the revenue source that maintained Control until its partial mothballing in 1978.

During Control's heyday, whenever a task was too sensitive for the CIA to handle, Dulles contacted his protégée through secret protocols. Control's mission was to be invisible while accomplishing mission goals. Better for the mission to be abandoned than for Control to become a known entity. The success of Control gave Dulles an uncanny ability to accomplish missions without CIA assets. Having Control off the books and at his beck and call boosted his standing in the intelligence community. This led to his ascension to the post of Director of Central Intelligence. Control remained his trump card throughout his tenure at the CIA and beyond.

After leaving the CIA in 1961, Dulles maintained his secret connection to Control until his death in 1969. When he died, only one man, his protégée, knew the secrets of Control. For nine more years, this man silently solved the thorniest issues facing the United States without the knowledge of his government. His power shielded by the dark cloak of secrecy.

As hard times and shrinking resources hit Control, the organization shrank. With the retirement of the protégée in 1978, new sources of income and supervision were required. Medical patents were procured from military research departments and a new corporation formed to market the devices throughout the world. These new offices became the field stations for Control; the visible network shielding the invisible spy agency, yet funneling information back to the master of Control. During the 1980's and early 1990's, a new menace appeared on the horizon of the United States. Ignored by the powers of the CIA, NSA, and such, this new threat was actually an old threat. A Cabal of the ultra wealthy, no longer fearing the unseen hand that had thwarted their missions during the cold war, regained their sense of urgency to conquer the world's monetary systems and thus worldwide supremacy. Their manipulations were invisible to the mainstream politicians unsophisticated in the dark art of economic control; meanwhile, even the more sophisticated rulers blinded themselves to this threat in exchange for power.

> "Let me issue and control a nation's money and I care not
> who writes the laws."

-Mayer Amschel Rothschild (b.1744 – d.1812)

Conspiracy theorists claim the Rothschild family controls half the world via proxy, rising from simple beginnings only two hundred and twenty years ago. An estimate of their wealth is one hundred trillion dollars as of the year two thousand. This is only an estimate because their wealth is hidden in vaults, works of art, and intangible assets such as power. If they do control the money supply they have unlimited wealth and the power to tax invisibly. If they need a billion dollars today to make a move in the market for the price of gold or oil, a few numbers are entered into the ledger of the controlling entity of the local currency (the Federal Reserve in the United States) and a billion dollars are created in an instant. The people of a country pay for this tax by having dollars, dinars, euros, or pounds that are instantly worth a little less. The money supply in the United States is ten trillion dollars and a one billion dollar tax is one hundredth of one cent on every dollar. Taxation at this level causes three and a half percent inflation annually. Apply that to the rest of the world and the people running the central banks are making one and a half billion dollars every day just by being in control of the money supply.

Robert "Bob" Merryweather was President Wassel's last minute selection for vice president of the United States for the 2000 election cycle. Merryweather was a placeholder. He knew it. Those in power knew it. His job was to spout sound bites and exude knowledge. Merryweather was an economist, not a lawyer or politician. He brought gravitas to the ticket on economic issues and laser white teeth.

When President Edward Wassel died of a massive heart attack on December 17th, 2001, just eleven months after being inaugurated, Bob Merryweather became the most powerful politician in the world by mistake. Presidential briefings revealed information that confirmed his long held beliefs that the Federal Reserve was under the control of foreign nationals. Bob Merryweather was not supposed to be in a position to do anything about this, but he was not going to let the opportunity pass him by. He found the means when a very well connected man made him aware of a mothballed, invisible spy agency that could be put at his disposal. A new leader would have to be selected to run the agency for President Merryweather. A man he would trust with his life.

President Merryweather believed he could trust Colonel Getner, his second cousin once removed, with a secret mission: end the Cabal's control of the central banks of the world. If word leaked out about this secret mission, Colonel Getner and President Merryweather's lives were on a short timer. This reborn, ultra secret organization was referred to only as Control. Funding was already arranged and beyond the purview of congress with several lucrative medical patents assigned to front companies. International offices gathered intelligence in the form of business records and contacts. The business side of the organization did not even know its true mission. Knowledge was compartmentalized into cells, just like a revolutionary force. The chain of command was direct to the president without political oversight. Getner was Control. Freeing the world from enslavement to the banks controlled by the ultra wealthy families of the World Order Cabal was Getner's mission. President Merryweather had declared silently his own proclamation to end the Cabal's control of the Federal Reserve and its siblings around the world. He would pay for this temerity with his life.

ACKNOWLEDGMENTS

I OWE A DEEP debt of gratitude to Carrie Martin. Without her support I would have accepted less than my best as good enough. Also, Meghan E. Dee, who persistently pushed for the swamp to be drained so the reader might better see what I see.

On a daily basis, Chris Ameling provided broad support for my writing that sustained me through the darkest times. Without her unyielding care, forward momentum for Betty's improvement would have ground to a resounding halt. Every time I thought a chapter was complete, she would find the obvious flaws before I could subject my editor, Meghan, to the torrid grammar, oversights, and obvious goofs.

Special thanks to Mary K. Hoefer for inspiring me to write and encouraging my Walter Mitty ways; I owe you a billion thanks. Nicky Dahm for being supportive and helping edit the original novella, Smoking Kills, which this book is based on. Beth Ann Bitner for making me laugh and appreciating my writing. Pat and Luciana McCool for correcting my Portuguese and Spanish. Any remaining errors are mine alone. Bob Saar—you spoke the truth and I hope this is what you meant. To my Dad, you helped make this novel happen and your gold star is on its way. Last but not least: Julie Smith for demanding more Betty every day.

Though they are gone, every day my grandparents Phil and Edna, John and Ruvie, and great aunt Mary give me strength and conviction that what I am doing matters. That what I am creating has meaning beyond the moment. That you would want to read what they helped me put on the page.

Please read on for an excerpt from A. J. Mahler's next thriller

POWER

THE BETTY CHRONICLES

Vol II

Available from White Bradford Publishing

ONE

LOST

July 14, 2009 — The crack of dawn

THE RISING SUN GLINTED off the peaks as Betty bobbed in the open sea off the Venezuelan coast. Three hours treading in the seventy-seven-degree water without a floatation device and with a gunshot wound in the meat of her left calf meant she did not have much longer to live. Betty began evaluating her options. *If a shark doesn't get me, hypothermia will.* Icy-cold tendrils bore deeper into her body, their pull winning out over her desire to live. *Everything I've fought for is lost. Why am I hanging on, anyway? Gil is either dead or dying back at Ernesto's . . . Howell is a lost cause . . . my parents and brothers are vulnerable . . . even Jil has turned on me! Why not let the ocean take me to the bottom?* Betty began to slip under the waves, but she was not ready to give up just yet. The thought of her dog in a crate or adopted by some unloving slacker pulled her back up. Spitting out the ocean and gasping for air, she mumbled at the waves, "Who will take care of Surry?"

†

July 14, 2009 — Four hours earlier atop Monte Ávila

Nine-millimeter rounds fired by the guards punctured the wing fabric, making it look like black Swiss cheese, as she took off from the mountain trail on the tandem glider, one bullet ripping through her boot and lodging in the meat of her calf. Gil's final act of driving the truck off the trail jerked the glider past the cool night air surrounding the mountain. The force generated enough speed to glide away and reach the warmer air of a fading updraft, which might give her the necessary altitude for the trip over the Ávila mountain range. Betty released the clove hitch knot of her umbilical cord to Gil as the truck plunged off the precipice; she banked right enough to see the truck lights cart wheeling into the dense vegetation of the *Parque Nacional El Ávila* before the ubiquitous clouds surrounding the higher range of the rain forest obscured her view of the wreck. The flashlights of the pursuing guards pierced the night air while their Spanish commands wafted up to her prying ears. Not knowing if Gil made it out of the tangle of metal and underbrush added to her burden, swelling her heart with pain to match the rawness of the wound in her calf.

The updraft from the mountain fought against the fabric, gripping then slipping around the garish pattern of holes. The rising warm air embraced Betty, grabbing her glider, dragging the battered craft higher. Blood dripped from her left boot. Her tears faded out of sight, evaporating before hitting the Venezuelan ground below. The tears were for Gil, for her past, for what could have been but never would be. The ache in her heart pounded long after the adrenaline of the fight had worn off.

She did not make it to the rendezvous coordinates—four miles out into the Atlantic, where Bud's water-taxi service was waiting for her and Gil. Her landing was off by at least two miles and thirty seconds of thrashing terror as she unbuckled, dove deep, and surfaced beyond the grasp of the glider. *It carried me to the safety of the ocean; it's willing to carry me to the bottom if I let it have its way.* She jabbed her SOG knife blade into the fabric, cutting a strip two and a half feet long by four inches wide, which she then clenched in her teeth. *Before you get away*, Betty thought, *I need one more thing from you.* The lack of oxygen pressed against her chest, but she resisted the urge to surface by letting out a tiny bit of air. Betty slid herself along the aluminum superstructure of the glider until her hand hit the object of her desire. She cut the last full bottle of compressed gas from its perch and surfaced. She had used the other seven to generate enough lift to make it over the Ávila pass. Waving goodbye, the tip of the right wing was the last to go under; the ripstop fabric had done its job despite the pockmark holes riddling its surface. She stored the bottle in the front of her spy suit. *I'll need this if a shark picks up the scent of my blood.* Betty went under the water long enough to put away the knife and tie a compression bandage on her calf. *Have to slow down the bleeding.* She clawed her way back toward the air, shredding the surface with her hands; her lungs aching from the mounting physical drain and the coldest water in the Caribbean Sea. The fatigue from the loss of blood clung to her, a spider's silk wound as tight as a cocoon.

The mission was a failure and a trap—Ernesto Montoya had been expecting them and Betty was captured while questioning him. *Gil! You saved me again, but you can't save yourself.* Betty wanted to hold on to the hope that Gil had escaped, but it was slipping away like the glider. *Holding on to you isn't going to save me, Gil. Please prove me wrong.*

Two hours before her takeoff, Gil had located Betty, and in a daring shootout they escaped through the snare he had set up earlier to entrap Ernesto's henchmen. The C-4 explosives ripped the guards to shreds as they advanced; bullets finished what survived the explosive charges. Gil took a grazing shot to his right shoulder in the shootout, but they both escaped relatively unscathed. Ernesto fled in his Bell 206B3 four-passenger helicopter while his remaining men hunted the hunters.

Thinking back on the escape of her quarry, Betty composed a rhyme: *Rattus Rattus fleas and all / escaped before the fall / run, Ernesto, run / I kill you with my gun.* She was poetically delirious.

The waves called to her; their invitation to accept her fate grew louder. The purpose of revenge and worrying over Gil's fate gave her pause. If she would just let go, her family would be safe. If she let go, the pain in her calf would subside. The ocean was her morphine. It would make the pain go away, and it was calling to her, telling her she should not care anymore.

The waves lapped her face as she slipped slowly under again. The cold, salty water entered her mouth. She could hear a voice faintly calling to her. *Is that Gil?*

"Betty, get your shit together!" The voice both mocked and ordered her. "Since when did you give in this easy?"

Betty jerked her arms down, forcing herself to keep treading water, spitting the salty ocean back at itself. *It's not time yet.* One of the guard's bullets had smashed her beacon light during takeoff. *If the beacon flashes but no one sees it, does it still flash?* Hypothermia's firm grip was beginning to sap her critical thinking skills, but she tried to analyze the situation just the same. Betty knew the glider had landed downwind and at least two miles short of the designated landing point; her shattered radio, ruined in the poolside fight, prevented her from contacting the rescue team waiting off the Venezuelan coast. Scanning the horizon from the crest of a wave proved once again that there was nothing out here but water. *Just a vast rippling. Wait.*

She had marked her landing site with the same fluorescent green dye used by downed pilots, but it had dissipated in the rough waters. As a wave drove her higher, she could see something against the contrast of the next wave. *No!* What was left of the fluorescent green dye was being disturbed by something. A vertical fin surfaced and sliced the ocean into a wake of dye. *A great white shark's fin. Shit!*

☦

Devon Miller, a new contract agent and veteran of the Navy SEALs, was waiting for Betty's signal for naught. He continuously scanned the horizon from the crow's nest with his night vision goggles, searching for the smear of fluorescent dye that should be spreading from the landing site. The rendezvous time had come and gone with no contact.

Captain Hargreave, the owner of this barely seaworthy fishing boat, kept barking at Miller that it was time to go. He clicked his mic and shrilled, "We agreed!" It was more of a shriek of terror setting in than a bark. The window of time he had agreed to had passed. Too bad for the people he was to pick up, but Hargreave was not going to risk waiting off the coast of Venezuela for the sun to rise. He turned the wheel sharply and gunned the twin engines to half speed on a northeastern heading. His excursionist and troublemaker would ignore him no longer.

Miller did not particularly care for the ship's captain or his tub, both of which were at Miller's disposal and would go where he directed no matter what the captain's opinion. Bud, Miller's contact at Control, had arranged the transportation to pick up the agents in the water. Why they were in the ocean to be picked up was not his concern. His mission was to pick up two people in the water four miles off the coast of Venezuela and deliver them to a safe house in Barranquilla, Colombia. He placed the red dot projected by the laser sight of his pistol on the map in front of the captain. When he had Hargreave's attention, he raised the dot to the man's forehead.

The old salt cut the engines back to quarter power and returned to the search pattern. With Miller's back to him, Hargreave shook his fist while uttering curses. With renewed focus on the mission and his lips clenching a freshly lit cigarette, the oaths turned to grave mutterings.

Miller would have preferred a speedboat, but the day before when he arrived at the slip reserved for this mission, Captain Hargreave was aboard the Colombian-flagged Bueno Pesquero and giving the correct sign and countersign. *Bud, you bastard, I hope you have a damn good reason for changing us to this tin cup.* They had been making a half-mile-radius circle around the coordinates for the better part of an hour. *This isn't working, time to widen our scope.* Miller made a wide circling motion with his arm while commanding Hargreave via the intercom, "Wider! Damn you, wider!"

The throaty hum of the trawler's engine drowned out the profane response of the captain as Miller peered into the inky distance of the night. The GPS signal was not active. No flares had been seen. The green fluorescent dye remained invisible. He began to play what-if. *What if it was me? What if I didn't make a clean escape and damage to my glider kept me from making the distance?* He made a decision. "Hargreave, you bastard child of a squid, head southeast and stay three miles off the coast."

Hargreave screamed back, "Closer? Are you out of your bloody mind?"

"You're damn right," *Yes, I am out of my fucking mind for being out here with you as my partner in your rust trap of an excuse for a boat.* "And you'll do as I say or by God you won't see your reward or the sun rise!"

Hargreave made an abrupt turn hard to starboard in the hopes of launching his nemesis from the crow's nest, but to no avail. His continuous muttering about the changing conditions of his employment went unheard over the now-roaring engine. A few more hours of abuse and he would get what he had negotiated for, a new boat with modern electronics—assuming the Venezuelan Navy was sleeping. The hard bargain he had driven with his contact, Bud, did not seem so rich in the poor light of the predawn sea.

†

The shark fin came closer and Betty felt the passing mass disturb the water. As she rechecked her bandage with hands numb from hypothermia, she rolled forward, and the cool water hitting her mouth triggered the mammalian reflex, making her gasp as she came up. The feeling in her foot seemed gone. Was it the ripstop fabric cinched too tight, or the chill in her bones brought on by her exertion and the extended exposure? Since she could not really feel her other leg, it was hard to say. She would have to loosen the bandage eventually or risk losing her leg. *Four hours. That's how long I have before I need to loosen it. But if I loosen it, the shark will find me for sure.* She thought about her options, of which there were not any. *They're too far out to spot me.* Prior to landing, Betty had strapped the emergency flare gun to her good leg. *My only hope is for the boat to circle out a little wider. A little closer than they should to the coast.* There had been a second flare gun on the side Gil would have occupied, along with four more cartridges. *I have one flare to shoot. I might need it to fend off that shark. If I wait until I see the boat, it might be too late. If I shoot it now, there might not be anyone to see it and I'm shark bait. Fuck me!*

Gauging how much longer she could hold on, Betty made her choice. Just before the night vanished, its murky cape scraping the waves as the rising sun cast it farther west, Betty launched her one and only flare. It was her last hope of rescue, but it would also tell the Venezuelans where to look. *Fucking Howell! Why didn't you plan for this?* It was a race to see who would get her first: the shark, Ernesto, or her rescue party.

ABOUT THE AUTHOR

A. J. Mahler lives in the Athens of the Midwest, also known as Iowa City. On nice days you might find him writing or editing on the Ped Mall or perhaps in a local coffee shop. Give him three nouns and he will tell you a story.

CPSIA information can be obtained at www.ICGtesting.com
Printed in the USA
LVOW06s0810091015

457585LV00002B/2/P